Witches' I
Book 3 of Dark

By BR Kingsolver

Cover art by Heather Hamilton-Senter

http://www.bookcoverartistry.com/

Copyright 2018

~~~

License Notes

~ ~ ~

Get updates on new book releases, promotions, contests and giveaways! Sign up for my newsletter.

Other books by BR Kingsolver

The Dark Streets Series
Gods and Demons
Dragon's Egg
Witches' Brew

The Chameleon Assassin Series
Chameleon Assassin
Chameleon Uncovered
Chameleon's Challenge
Chameleon's Death Dance

The Telepathic Clans Saga
The Succubus Gift
Succubus Unleashed
Broken Dolls
Succubus Rising
Succubus Ascendant

Other books
I'll Sing for my Dinner
Trust

Short Stories in Anthologies

Here, Kitty
Bellator

BRKingsolver.com
Facebook
Twitter

Table of Contents

Witches' Brew

Chapter 1

Sitting in my office surrounded by a mountain of paperwork, I dutifully tried to read and understand my tax return. It wasn't something I wanted to do, but Kathy, my accountant, insisted it was something I had to get done by Friday, on the pain of 'or else.' Considering that Kathy was a foot shorter than I was, and probably couldn't lift my sword with a crane, I wasn't sure what 'or else' might have been, but I wasn't in a hurry to find out.

It was a bright spring day, the sun was shining, and the Fairies had ventured forth from their winter hibernation. Their chatter and singing made a nice backdrop as they cast a happy mood on the day.

I was almost finished with the tax return and my list of questions for Kathy when the Fairies went crazy, and not in a good way, the noise outside escalating to an ear-piercing level. My first thought was that the neighbor's Labrador retriever had managed to broach my wards again. I thought the animal had learned its lesson. The last time I'd seen it, it looked like a pin cushion covered with Fairy spears, galloping home with its tail between its legs.

A fancy black car pulled into the nursery, and two men in black suits got out. The Fairies attacked in mass. I watched with interest. They hated most predators, especially dogs and cats—except for my friend Isabella—but they usually either liked or ignored people. The two fellows were persistent, however, dodging Fairy spears and bursting into my office. They smelled like dogs. I watched silently as

1

they ignored me while pulling little six-inch spears out of their clothing and various parts of their anatomy. The longer they ignored me, the more my irritation increased, and the more my estimation of their intelligence decreased. Being rude to an Elf was a classic way of committing suicide, but they did have my curious attention.

Finally, one of them finished wiping blood off his face and hands with his handkerchief and said, "You got some nasty little friends out there. Be a shame if someone sprayed them with pesticide, ya know?" He had a bit of a West Virginia twang to his voice.

"Whatever you want, Harold Vance should know better than to send you here," I said. "Tell him to call me." Vance was the alpha of the largest Werewolf pack on the east coast, and the major crime boss in the Washington, D.C., area. He was a landscaping customer of mine, even after we had a little run-in the previous summer.

"We ain't with Vance," the thug said. "He's on his way out. So, if you want to do business safely, you'll be dealing with the Savage River pack from now on."

They were both young, but my estimation of their intelligence fell even further. Age can impart wisdom, but in my experience, sheer stupidity was incurable.

"And why do you think my business needs protection?" I asked.

He sneered at me and made a show of looking out the window. "You got a lot of money tied up in vehicles and machinery. Greenhouses are kinda fragile, ya know? And a fire would do a lot of damage to all those trees. Even if you got insurance, you'd be out of business for a while. A little preventive insurance would probably be a good idea, ya know?"

I stood. I was at least six inches taller than he was,

and as I towered over him, I thought his eyes might pop out of his head. I took two steps to round the desk and entangled my fingers in his hair. Another two steps, dragging him along, brought us to the door. He missed the doorway, and his face slammed against the wall. Blood gushed from his nose.

His buddy reached under his coat, but he was too slow. I grabbed him by the throat with my other hand and squeezed as I lifted him off the floor.

I carried them outside onto the porch. The second Were clawed at my forearm, his face turning a deep red. It irritated me, so I cracked their heads together, then carried them down the steps to their car.

"Tell your alpha that if any of you puppies ever show up around here again, I'll hang your heads on my gateposts. And I'll blame him for anything that happens here, even if you're not involved." I hoped their alpha was brighter than they were. Elves don't threaten, they promise.

The second guy was turning rather purple by the time I released him, and he slumped to the ground, gasping raggedly for air.

I slammed the first guy's face into the windshield hard enough to crack both the windshield and his face. Then I let go of him, and he fell in a heap. His face was a real mess, and I was so angry it was hard to resist the urge to kill them both. I stared down at him, trying to get my temper under control. Then I decided, what the hell, and kicked him. If felt so good that I kicked him again.

I walked over to the second idiot and kicked him just for practice.

"Now," I announced, "I'm going back into my office for a box of matches. If you're still here when I get back, I'm going to light this car on fire and then call the police." I leaned down close to the guy I had just kicked and said, "Do I make myself clear?"

Of course, I didn't need matches to start a fire, but I took my time sauntering back to the office and straightening my papers. I heard the Fairies launch another assault, and then a couple of minutes later the Weres' car started, and they drove away. Instead of the matches, I grabbed a bottle of spelled wolfsbane extract, went outside, and sprinkled it across the nursery entrance between the gateposts while chanting a spell. When I was finished, I sketched a rune on both gateposts, then said the Word to invoke the spell.

I wasn't worried by the thugs' threats. My wards would protect the nursery and the Fairies from anything the idiot Weres might try. But before, I hadn't blocked them from driving through the front gate when it was open. That taken care of, I made myself a calming cup of herbal tisane and returned to the damned tax return.

I'd been away almost six months, and although my landscaping business didn't need me in the winter, everything went into overdrive once the trees started budding. Planting, hiring, evaluating existing clients' needs, and working with new clients—were all of sudden importance. Of course, the parts of the business I liked—such as working with the plants and planning gardens—came with the baggage of owning the business and having to deal with that side of it.

The world had changed a bit while I was in Europe with Cassiel, but I hadn't noticed because I'd been so busy. We spent the winter traveling around, and then attended my cousin's hand-fasting in

Ireland. I had flown back to the States from there, but Cassiel ran into visa hassles. So strange. As a realm walker, he could cross to another dimension anytime he wanted to, but Earth's governments thought lines drawn on a map were so sacred that they wouldn't let him cross that imaginary boundary.

I told him he should have put 'Heaven' as his place of birth on the visa application instead of 'Alfheim.'

When he finally got it straightened out, I drove out to the airport to pick him up.

On our way back to Georgetown, we passed a mall advertising a new store—Witches' World. I smiled and pointed it out to Cass.

I cooked dinner at home for him that evening, with candles and the good china. I had even sewn a sexy new dress for the occasion. I couldn't believe how much I missed him, and it had only been a couple of weeks.

Cassiel attempted several times to call his sister, who lived in DC. She, like him, was a Paladin and a realm walker. Her phone message indicated that she was indeed in another realm. He let me listen to it once. *This is Naleema. I'm on an out-of-this-world vacation. Leave a message, and I'll ring you up when I return.* She had a beautiful voice.

Since he didn't have another option for a place to stay, I happily told him he could stay with me as long as he liked. I spent a couple of days showing him the museums and the sights around Washington, then I turned him loose on the city when I returned to work on Monday morning.

One evening, I saw a commercial for the Witches World on television, advertising potions, charms, herbs, alchemical and ritual devices and apparatus.

5

Cass looked it up on the internet—he didn't have the problems with computers that I had. It turned out that a group called the Sunrise Coven had leased a defunct bookstore and opened the business.

The following day, I insisted on going to check it out. The mall had been on the decline for some time, and the coven had moved into a space abandoned when a nationwide book chain went bankrupt. On first impression, I was extremely disappointed. It looked like a Halloween store, full of costumes for kids' parties, and souvenir schlock for tourists and delusional wannabe witches. However, some of their goods were legitimate, although overpriced. I could feel the magic emanating from some of the charms and potions, and the simple fact of the store's existence and the number of people in the store were telling. Seeing magical items sold openly shook my world a little.

"Do these love potions have a money-back guarantee?" I asked one of the shop girls, a young witch of limited power.

She laughed. "Oh, no." She pointed to a sign that said, "All sales final. No refunds. Results may vary, depending on many factors."

"That isn't very encouraging," Cass said.

The girl shook her head. "A love potion only serves as an attractant. If the person is interested, it will sharpen their interest. If it really made anyone fall in love with someone, that would be a compulsion spell, and only black magic delves into that sort of thing. We only deal in white magic."

"I've never seen a store quite like this," I said.

She preened. "We're opening another store in Alexandria next month, and the coven elders plan on having ten stores open by the end of the year."

"I'm surprised there would be such a market," Cass said.

"Oh, yes, witchcraft is all the rage. I worked for a store up in Baltimore called Magical Secrets, but when I joined the Sunrise Coven, I moved down here. This is much larger."

"What do you think?" Cassiel asked as we left.

"I want to see the store in Baltimore." So, we drove north to Baltimore.

Magical Secrets occupied an old rowhouse facing the Inner Harbor in a popular area with lots of bars, restaurants, art galleries, and boutiques. The first floor had potions, tinctures, extracts, teas, spells, charms, and other prepared goods. I was impressed with the selection. No love potions or other fake come-ons. On the second floor, we found supplies and apparatus for spells and alchemy.

I grew a number of specialty crops in my greenhouses. My training as an alchemist allowed me to turn such crops and other items into extracts, potions, and poultices that had value to a certain clientele. I had supplied witches within a day's drive of Washington with such goods for thirty years.

"I might have found another customer for some of what I grow," I told Cassiel as I surveyed their selection of healing herbs.

The rowhouse had three stories, so I started toward the last stairway. As I put my foot on the bottom step, I felt a veil part, and I realized that someone without magic would never see the stairs. The magical bazaars in Dublin and some other cities had an entrance similarly hidden.

The top floor had far more exotic ingredients for sale, such as mandrake root, wolfsbane, nightshade, dried insects, snake venom, and other-realm plants and animal parts. There was also a selection of minerals, such as malachite dust, silver powder, pyrite, and hematite. I could see why this section was protected. They had enough toxic ingredients to poison the whole city.

The sales ladies on the first two floors hadn't paid us much attention, but the witch on the third floor was different. I judged her to be between fifty and seventy, with streaks of gray in her long black hair. She was still pretty, but she would have been beautiful when she was young. Her dark eyes narrowed as they followed us around the room. She absolutely reeked of power, one of the strongest witches I'd ever encountered.

"What is your interest?" she asked after a while.

"I'm an alchemist and apothecary," I answered. "I see why you have this room shielded."

"You don't approve." Her tone made it a statement, not a question.

"I neither approve nor disapprove," I said. "It's not my place. I use a lot of these ingredients." I motioned toward the mandrake root. "They are usually more difficult to acquire." And although the shop's prices were high, when you figured in airfare to Europe or Asia, I usually paid more.

"Kellana Rogirsdottir?" she asked.

I turned in surprise. "Have we met before?"

A hint of a smile curved her lips. "No, but the TV newscasters said the Dragon woman lived in DC. I don't imagine there are too many green-haired elves in this area."

I shook my head. I was seriously considering dyeing my hair.

"You know," I told Cass after we left the store, "I

8

never wanted to be famous, and it's a pain in the ass sometimes."

He chuckled. "Stop rescuing the world, and you won't have that problem. Don't worry, your fifteen minutes of fame will soon fade away."

We watched a movie on TV that night, one of those that runs an hour and twenty minutes but with the commercials takes three hours. Twenty minutes of movie followed by twenty minutes of commercials until I was about ready to scream. Then, a commercial came on that sounded at first like an online dating service.

Tired of being lonely? Being afraid? Living in the shadows? You don't have to be alone anymore. There is strength in numbers and acceptance from those like you. Call 202-555-1234. The Raven Coven welcomes witches and wizards, no matter your gift, no matter your strength. You don't have to live alone in the shadows anymore. 202-555-1234. Find out what acceptance and the power of a coven feel like.

"Did you see that?" I asked turning to Cassiel.

"Mmm-hmmm," he replied. He had his nose buried in a book.

"That commercial."

"Huh? Sorry, Kel, I wasn't paying attention."

"It was a recruitment commercial for a witches' coven."

"Hmmm. Wonder if they're for real." He still didn't act like he was paying attention.

The movie came back on. Cass set the book in his lap and paid attention to the TV again. I had a feeling the female star interested him more than the plot. I waited until the next commercial break, and when he started to pick up his book again, I snatched it away.

9

"No. I want you to pay attention to that commercial when it comes on again."

But it didn't. Not during that commercial break, nor the others following it.

It wasn't the first strange commercial I had seen since returning from Europe. The third anniversary of the Beltane that changed the world was approaching, and Earth was beginning to settle into a new normal.

The following morning at breakfast, I turned on the TV to get the day's weather forecast. Instead, I saw a young blonde woman with a microphone breathlessly talking about a murder. She was at the scene where the body had been found in a wooded area on the west side of the Potomac.

Something in her voice caught my attention. She seemed really rattled. As I listened, I noted that she said the police didn't want information on the cause of death disclosed. Over the previous three years, I had noticed a difference in the language used when reporting on a normal murder as opposed to one with a paranormal cause. I understood that. A drug dealer getting shot was something Humans understood. They were less matter-of-fact about a person who was torn apart by a demon.

The reality of magic, paranormal beings, and creatures from other realms was starting to take hold. Humans might not have liked their new world, but they were past denial. Demons materializing on main street and eating your next-door neighbor tended to get people's attention.

Chapter 2

The Washington Cherry Blossom Festival brought thousands of tourists into town each year, but it also always spurred some of the locals to plant their own trees. I considered it the kickoff event of the summer landscaping season.

A long flat-bed truck packed with young Yoshino cherry trees about six feet tall sat in my nursery. The driver leaned against his truck and drank coffee while he watched Ed Gillespie, Jamie Cowan, Cassiel, and me unload the truck. Ed was my foreman, and Jamie was the other year-round employee who worked in the yard. Once we set the trees on the ground, Fred and Kate, the Gnomes who lived at the nursery, watered them and checked for disease and insects.

After the fourth or fifth tree I hauled off the truck, I found myself fantasizing about levitation spells. Unfortunately, that wasn't something I knew how to do, and Cassiel's magic lay in other areas.

Even though the temperature was barely sixty degrees Fahrenheit, Cassiel took his shirt off. His body heat was wonderful in bed at night, but his propensity to shed his shirt in public was embarrassing. Embarrassing for me, since I tended to pant and drool. I was also afraid that Jamie, who kept tripping and running into things, was going to get hurt if she didn't start paying attention to something besides Cass.

We had unloaded half of the two hundred trees when Karen Wen-li and David Torbert of the FBI's Paranormal Crime Unit drove into the yard. Karen was around thirty years old, tiny, not more than five feet tall, thin, with long, straight black hair. She came from a line of Asian witches. Torbert was close to six feet, muscular, and probably close to two hundred pounds, with a broad nose, dark brown skin, and black curly hair. He had no magic but was sensitive to it. I liked him because he "got" my sense of humor.

"Did we catch you at a bad time?" Torbert called.

I ignored him, directing my gaze at Wen-li. "Can you do a levitation spell?"

At first, she didn't hear me, staring at Cassiel with her mouth hanging open. I stepped in front of her and said, "Focus, girl. Can you do a levitation spell?"

She laughed and shook her head. "Sorry. Who is that?"

"Cassiel. He followed me home from Europe."

"I need to get out more," she muttered.

Turning to Torbert, I said, "Yes, it's a bad time, unless you're in a volunteering mood and need some exercise."

He sized up the trees, and to my surprise, took off his suitcoat and tie, and tossed them across the seat of his car. Rolling up his sleeves, he said, "I probably owe you a bigger favor than this, but we'll call this a down payment." We all stared at him as he climbed the steps onto the truck, picked up a tree, and carried it to sit beside the others we had unloaded. I looked at his arms and chest, deciding he was in pretty good shape.

"Well, I'm not going to argue with an officer of the law," I said, and climbed up to grab another tree. With his help, we got the rest of the trees unloaded, I signed the invoice the trucker handed me, and he drove away.

I led everyone to the cottage next to the office building, where I pulled a large jug of lemonade out of the fridge and set it and some glasses on the table. Before I sat down, I handed Cassiel his shirt and gave him a look. He grinned and winked at me but put it on. Angels were even more arrogant than Elves. Cass was half of each, and he was very aware of the effect he had on women. I couldn't blame them. He had that effect on me, too.

"Okay, what is so outrageously important that you're willing to do manual labor to bribe me to talk to you?" I asked Torbert.

He cast glances at Ed and Jamie.

"Agent Torbert, once upon a time, I worried about the world finding out that I'm an Elf. Unfortunately, those days are gone. My employees understand that I don't dye my hair. So, unless it's something secret that they shouldn't hear, or if them listening might put them in danger, you can speak freely in front of them."

Ed simply shrugged. Having worked for me for more than ten years, he knew I wasn't Human long before the veils ripped. Jamie, on the other hand, sat up a little straighter and showed every sign of paying attention. Since she and Ed lived together, she probably knew more about me than Torbert did.

"In that case," Torbert said, "it's about these magic shops that are springing up all over the place. The FDA—the Food and Drug Administration—is very worried about what the shops are selling, and they came to us. We don't know if what they're selling is safe, or how to tell whether it is or not."

Karen said, "Some of the potions...well, we can't even figure out what's in them. For instance," she pulled a small bottle out of her pocket, "the label says arnica, but when we analyzed it, that's only part of the contents. And the potion is far stronger than an arnica extract would be." Karen was a witch, but not an alchemist. Her talents lay in other areas.

I took it from her and could feel the magic it contained. "That's because the potion is spelled," I said. "An arnica extract or distillation would be much weaker. Any herbalist can mix herbs and alcohol to extract the essential oils. It takes special equipment to do a distillation. But the potions an alchemist or apothecary mixes are then spelled, and so the potion contains magic. I don't think your science can detect that."

"So, how do we differentiate good spells from bad, and tell if the ingredients are good, or if the charms and potions do what the seller says they will?" Karen asked.

"Hire some witches," I said. "You hire scientists in other areas, so acknowledge the new reality." I looked at the bottle in my hand. "You're right to be worried. Charlatans could be peddling poisons or spells that do things other than what is claimed, and you'd never know it. I saw love potions for sale, and there is no such thing."

Jamie looked disappointed. I winked at her and she blushed.

"Well, that's what we wanted to talk to you about," Torbert said. "There are a number of Congressmen, and Congressional committees, that are considering the issue. They think they need to pass laws on what witches can do, and what they can sell. We need to provide them with some expertise, or God knows what they'll come up with."

Karen leaned forward. "Kellana, every crazy in the country, both for and against witchcraft, is clamoring to grab those senators' and representatives' attention. We need someone who knows what they're talking about to provide knowledgeable and objective information."

I squirmed uncomfortably in my chair and shot a glance at Ed. He knew a lot more than I did about Earth's and the United States' political systems.

"I have a business to run," I said. "All that crap last summer came close to ruining me, and now you want me to take time out and spend it with your politicians? All I want to do is mow lawns and water flowers."

Karen started to say something, but I held up my hand between us.

"Hang on," I said. "First, you tell me that no matter what I do or say, I'm going to have some sort of crazy upset at me. Do you understand that being crazy doesn't stop someone from controlling powerful magic? And you want me to make myself a target?"

"So, the FBI has a Paranormal Crimes Unit," Ed said. "Does that mean the FDA is going to have a Paranormal Drugs Unit?"

"I don't know," Torbert said. "Kellana is probably the most knowledgeable resource on other realms we have, so I wanted to get her opinion and hope she can help us out."

"I'm an expert? Should I be charging for my consultations?" I laughed. "Cassiel or Miika are far better sources about other realms."

"Send me an invoice," Torbert said. "I haven't seen or heard from Miika in at least seven months."

Torbert and Wen-li had introduced me to Miika ap th'Tenir, a half-Elven mage from my realm of Midgard. I hadn't heard from him either. He called me one night at the end of the previous summer, said he was going out of town, and had to cancel our fourth

15

date. Just when I was starting to feel romantic.

But Torbert's tone was so grim that it stopped me cold. Not knowing what to say, I got up from the table and poured myself some more lemonade.

"Speaking of beings from other realms," I said when I returned to my seat, "I had a visit yesterday from a couple of Werewolves who said they were from the Savage River pack. Told me that Harold Vance was going down and I should buy some insurance from them."

"Protection?" Torbert asked, his brow furrowed. "You should have called us."

Karen laughed. "Where did you bury the bodies?"

I gave her a wink and a grin in thanks for breaking the heavy atmosphere. "I showed them out, and I'll be surprised if they come back. But there's a Werewolf barrier across the entrance now, to go along with the ones I had already laid for Vampires and demons. And I gave the Fairies leave to kill them if they showed up again."

Torbert snorted a laugh. "Kill them? With those little spears? Or do the Fairies have some kind of magic we don't know about?"

I shook my head. "In the wild, when they have to protect themselves from beasts far larger than they are, they poison those spears. That's part of the reason I grow so much monkshood here."

My visitors' eyes grew larger as the ramifications of that sank in. Monkshood, also called wolfsbane, was full of aconite alkaloids, and was one of the most toxic plants on Earth.

"Well," Torbert said, "the prospect of a Werewolf gang war goes right along with the rest of the madness we're seeing. We truly have a witches' brew of difficult and dangerous situations."

Karen said, "Besides your Werewolf conflict, it seems something similar is going on with three large covens. They have come out very publicly, jockeying for members, territory, and power."

"Human covens?" I asked.

She nodded.

"I don't know how knowledge of other realms is going to help you with that. You probably know a lot more about Human witchcraft than I do."

Torbert shifted in his chair, looking uncomfortable. "What in the hell is the difference between a mage and a witch? You seem to make a distinction, but it's all magic, isn't it?"

"Not really," I answered. "The difference between mages and witches is sometimes considered a difference in strength, but that's not true. It's a qualitative difference. Mages—also called wizards, sorcerers, or conjurers—pull their magic from the upper realms—the realms of the gods and archdemons. How much magic they can pull depends on their skill level and innate ability to hold magic, what we call power. Learning and practice can expand how much power they can wield."

I took a deep breath and a sip of lemonade. "Witches, on the other hand, pull their magic from the world around us. They can't access the upper realms. Witches tend to have an affinity for one kind of magic or another. For instance, I'm an earth witch, sometimes also called a hearth witch, kitchen witch, or hedge witch. I have an affinity for the earth, plants, and animals. I have a secondary affinity for water. Karen, on the other hand, has a very strong affinity for air. That's what she builds her illusions with. Others may have an affinity for fire or energy."

Karen shot a glance at Torbert, then said, "Then there's the problem of Ivy City."

That didn't surprise me. Ivy City was an old industrial area near the Bay, and the area still had its run-down rough spots. Because old warehouses were cheap, a number of nightclubs had opened in the area. Many of those nightclubs were run by non-Humans— Vampires, demons, and shapeshifters, mostly. But the majority of the clientele was Human.

"The owner of *Sensual Labyrinth* seems to be taking over the entire district," Karen said. "She's buying up property, renovating it, and it looks like she has plans to turn the area into some sort of a paranormal theme park."

"She?" I asked, shaking my head. "That place is ruled by a greater demon. Maybe a pair of them. Who is this *she*?"

"I think she's a succubus," Torbert said.

"Ah. Blonde? Looks like Jayne Mansfield?"

He looked at me in surprise. "Yeah, that's the one. You know who Jayne Mansfield is?"

"I do have a television. Movies and TV is how I learned English. The succubus isn't the owner; she just fronts *Sensual Labyrinth*. The real power there would scare people to death if he revealed himself. Literally. You think those demons who eat people on the street are scary? They're cuddly little baby kittens in comparison."

"We're also hearing rumors about maybe half a dozen mages in the area. One or two may be Human, but the rest are from other realms," Karen said.

"They act like cults," Torbert said. "They're attracting followers, buying large mansions and land, and, well, sort of acting like feudal lords. Some have

18

had conflicts with local and state authorities. They defy our laws, and unfortunately, our laws don't provide very clear guidance on what to do about them."

"Remember when I told you that paranormals didn't respect your laws?" I asked. "All of these beings, who are not Human, come from places with different societal systems, different types of governments, completely different belief systems, completely different ways of thinking. While some of the paranormals, such as me, are related to Humans, many are completely different biological beings. And they think so differently than you do, that they're unfathomable. You need to start from that point in trying to make sense of what you're seeing."

We sat in silence drinking our lemonade while I let that sink in.

"More lemonade?" I asked, rising from the table. I refilled all our glasses but didn't sit down. Leaning against the kitchen counter, I said, "They probably don't understand your laws. Elvish doesn't even have words to express the concept of representative democracy. If I tried to explain your system of government to my mother, I'd have to describe it as a cross between a village council and mob rule. If you want to see what you describe on a large scale, go visit one of the Alfenholms. Elves have lived in a feudal society for at least a hundred thousand years. We're the ones who introduced it to Earth."

"Who in Congress is leading all this?" Ed asked.

"Representative Sarah Faire on the House side," Torbert said, "and Senator Richard Bowman in the Senate. Unfortunately, they don't get along and have some very different ideas about what needs to be done."

He pulled a small stack of papers out of his briefcase and laid it on the table. "Read this over and let me know if you're interested. It's a contract for consulting services from the PCU. I'm not asking you to donate your time, Kellana. We'll pay you the same hourly rate as you charge for landscaping design work."

Karen grinned. "I looked up your rate on your website."

"I have a website?" I asked Ed. I couldn't even touch a computer without it burning out, so that revelation was a shock.

"Yep. Jamie and Kathy and I put it together last winter."

"So, if you're interested in making some side money, Representative Faire would like to meet with you," Torbert said. "Just account for your time and send me an invoice at the end of every month."

Chapter 3

Representative Sarah Faire's home was a large, white four-story townhouse in Georgetown, sitting behind a high wall with wrought-iron spikes on top. Based on what I knew about real estate in the area, the house was probably worth several million dollars. Ed told me that many members of Congress had local homes in addition to homes in their districts, but Faire's house seemed excessive since her legal residence was less than a dozen miles away in Virginia.

I had to press a button on an intercom at the gate, but it buzzed and opened almost immediately. Cass and I exchanged a look as we entered, then we climbed a dozen steep steps. A servant opened the front door as we approached and conducted us into a large opulent parlor. It was like walking into a museum, or a European great house, with cast-plaster crown molding, painted silk wallpaper above mahogany wainscoting, and thick Persian rugs on the floor, complimented by heavy, upholstered wood furniture. The décor was old fashioned by twenty-first century Earth standards, as though the house hadn't been updated since it was built. If the whole house was that well-kept, I needed to up my estimate by at least another million.

But something about the servant and the feel of the house bothered me, and I couldn't figure out what it was.

Sarah Faire solved the mystery. A pale, dark-haired woman of medium height, dressed in a loose blouse and harem pants walked into the room. Earthen legends of Vampires had a number of facts wrong, but they were long-lived, and they gained in power with age. The house probably felt comfortable to her rather than anachronistic.

"Please," she said, probably noticing my reaction, "don't be afraid. I don't feed on magic users."

That was a wise choice. Vampires were drawn to me like flies to honey—"sweet blood" they called me. The blood of the higher races gave them a high, but also a nasty hangover. If a Vampire indulged regularly, their health deteriorated, and our blood would eventually kill them.

Faire offered us chairs, and the Human servant came back with tea and cookies on a silver tray. Taking a closer look at him, I judged him to be in his sixties, tall and thin, with the typical pale complexion of a Vampire's blood whore. I tried to be subtle about scanning the tray and casting a purification spell, but nothing reacted. No poison or drugs.

The Vampire waited until we relaxed a bit before she spoke again. Leaning forward with her hands clasped before her, she said, "The world has changed in the past three years. Drastically changed. As a newcomer to this realm, I'm not sure you understand what a shock it has been for Humans to confront the idea that paranormals are real. They have always known about us, of course, but as stories and myths. Very few of them actually encountered any paranormal prior to that disastrous Beltane."

Cassiel shrugged. "I know things are a bit unsettled, but I expect they'll calm down. Humans and paranormals exist together in many realms."

"The upheaval has only begun," Faire said. "The veils are shredded. Much of what is happening has been kept from the public. There seems to be a permanent rift between Transvyl and Earth in

Canada, and one from Were to a farm north of Oxford in England. China is a complete mess. A rift opened from Daemon to an area north of Shanghai. The communist government panicked, and in its ineffable wisdom, dropped a nuclear bomb on the rift."

"*Danu merde*," I breathed.

"Yes, what was a small rift is now a major breach between Earth and both Daemon and Hel. U.S. intelligence says that Shanghai is a full-scale war zone, and the Humans are losing. We have managed to suppress that news, but once word of that gets out, you can expect a much stronger reaction from the Humans in this country. What happened here in Washington is a minor kerfuffle in comparison."

"Your intelligence may not know of it," Cassiel said softly, "but there is a rupture between a portal in Kazakhstan and one in Sweden. It created an open route between Earth, Asgard, and Heaven." Portals were the standard method of travel between the realms, operated by mages with specialized magic. "The Angels have been unsuccessful in closing it, and they're having a hissy fit. Another breach in Heaven has created an open route between Olympus, Gehenna, and Earth. You might notice that Earth and Heaven are becoming nexus points for connections between the realms."

The Vampire Congresswoman leaned back in her chair. "There are six billion Humans on this planet and only a million Vampires, maybe ten or twenty million people with enough witch blood to manifest any power, about the same number of shifters, and a handful of Elves. We have survived because we lived in the shadows. But if Humans decide paranormals as a whole are a threat, and they mobilize their militaries against us, we don't stand a chance."

"But Vampires *are* a threat to Humans," I said. "You can't dismiss what Claudiu Dalca was doing." Dalca owned the nightclub *Fang*. When the world turned upside down on Beltane, the PCU discovered he was kidnapping Humans and selling them across the veils to Transvyl as food.

Cassiel shook his head. "What is it you want from us?"

"I've never been to Alfheim, of course," Faire said, "but I understand that you have many races that coexist there. I want to find a solution, so we can do that here."

I snorted. I didn't need to tell her I had only been to Alfheim twice as a tourist. Midgard was similar enough. "There are several races, but with an almost constant state of hostilities between them. Alfheim is no more peaceful than Earth. Even Heaven has its conflicts, and the Angels allow no one else to live there."

"I don't see what we have to offer," Cassiel said. "What is it you want from us?"

Faire leaned forward and focused on me. "Director Torbert tells me that while you're from another realm, you've been here a long time. Is that true?"

"A little over seventy years," I said. "Yes, I know what it's like to live in the shadows."

"And you're a witch? You have contacts within the Human witch community?"

I nodded.

"I need a consultant—an expert—to provide insight and factual information on the paranormal and magical communities. Vampires and shifters are different from the other paranormals in this realm,

24

wouldn't you agree?"

"Yes, but the majority of the witches and mages on Earth were born here."

Faire smiled, but her eyes were hard. "As was I. My first husband and I built this house in 1923. My family has lived in this realm for over five hundred years. We are not all like Dalca."

She turned and called out, "George, would you come in, please?"

The servant who had attended us earlier came in.

"I was born in 1888," Faire said. "George and I are about the same age. We've been together for a hundred years. The relationship is not one-sided."

George bowed. "I have been very lucky. I have lived beyond everyone I knew growing up but have been loved and comfortable the entire time. Not too many beings of any race and time can say that." He turned to Faire. "Will that be all?"

She nodded, and he left.

"I don't understand how you expect Humans to accept beings who prey on them," I said. "Are you going to extend civil rights to demons? I think that an open portal from Transvyl to Earth is a particularly scary thing, considering the way your people breed and the food and population pressures Transvyl has traditionally experienced."

"You do know your history, don't you?"

"I went to school. Elves have always conducted commerce with other realms."

"Then you know that when Elves last lived openly in this realm, they enslaved the Human population. We aren't the only predators. And if some sort of legal framework to protect all sentient beings isn't put into place, all paranormals, including Elves, Human mages, and witches, are at risk. I truly believe a backlash is coming."

"So, you want to grant paranormals equal rights with Humans," I said. Faire nodded. "The problem," I continued, "is there is already an immigration issue in this country. If you create a refuge for paranormals in the U.S., they'll flood in here from all over the world. How are you going to deal with that? Visas? Citizenship? This realm doesn't even allow Humans to live anywhere they want."

I had entered the U.S. as a refugee and gone through the hassle of becoming a naturalized citizen. I couldn't imagine the U.S. government dealing with hordes of paranormals crossing the borders.

Faire followed us to the door when we left. Picking up a thick envelope from a table in the foyer, she handed it to me. "A sign of good faith. I look forward to hearing from you soon. We do not have the luxury of time."

I looked in the envelope as we descended her front steps and discovered it was stuffed full of hundred-dollar bills. I showed it to Cass, who raised an eyebrow.

"What do you think?" he asked me.

I shook my head. "I have a hard time justifying making it easier for evil to settle in this realm."

Cass stopped and turned to me. "Evil is everywhere. Kellana, the cosmic struggle is not between good and evil. There are good Werewolves and evil ones, good Elves and evil ones. The battle is between order and chaos, and at the moment, chaos threatens more than it has in millennia. You may not like Sarah Faire, but she is striving to bring some order to this realm. If she can make even a small difference in restoring balance, I will support her."

I searched his face. Not only was I deeply in love with him, but he had proven himself to be brave, kind, and the sweetest man I had ever known.

"That's what the Paladins do?" I asked.

"Yes, we support order."

I nodded. "Well, I can't say I'm comfortable with the world as it is. I grew up in an extremely ordered world, and I miss it. I miss the order in my life before the veils shredded. I'll call Torbert in the morning and tell him I'll help."

Cass opened the gate and held it for me. I stepped through and found six Werewolves, four of them shifted, and the other two in Human form. One was the guy I'd half-strangled at the nursery, and he held a pistol pointed at me.

"Well, what have we here?" Cassiel said from behind me.

The Were knew how fast I was, so I froze, debating whether the slight motion of sketching a rune might startle or scare him into pulling the trigger.

"You should be very careful of who you associate with," the other Were in Human form said.

"If it were up to me, I wouldn't associate with you guys at all," I responded, "but I keep running into you. What do you want?"

"Just mind your own business," the Were said. "Don't get involved with that Vampire bitch, or you'll regret it."

I sighed. "You're very rude. Why do you and your buddies think it's okay to be rude to strangers?"

Lightning flashed past my shoulder and hit the Were's pistol. I drew my sword from my bag and stepped away from Cassiel to give myself room. One of the wolves launched himself toward me, a mouth full of teeth leading the way. I cut him down in mid-air. One of his buddies partially dodged my backswing, and I cut him across the shoulder. He screamed and rolled away.

Cassiel was barely competent with a blade, although his quickness and reach gave him an advantage over a Human. But Vampires and Werewolves weren't Human, so I had given him a paintball gun when we first arrived in the States. He didn't bother to draw his short sword but pulled out the gun and shot the Were in Human form in the face. Vampirebane and wolfsbane had similarities but were most effective when used against the beings the potions were designed for. On the other hand, no matter what race you were, vampirebane burned like crazy if you got it in your eyes.

The other Weres backed away. I rushed over to the guy who had held the gun and grabbed him by the throat. Lifting him off his feet, my face less than six inches from his, I said, "You are the luckiest son of a bitch in the world, but third time's a charm. Your luck has run out. If I ever lay eyes on you again, you won't survive. Understand?"

I have rarely seen a person as terrified. He tried to say something, so I loosened my grasp. As he slid to the ground, he rasped out, "Yes."

Looking around, I saw the Weres were hemmed in by a dozen Vampires standing between them and escape.

"Are these vermin giving you a hard time, Mistress Rogirsdottir?" one of the Vamps asked.

Glancing over my shoulder, I saw Sarah Faire standing on her front porch, silhouetted by light from the doorway behind her. She walked down the steps and stopped inside her gate.

"They suggested that I'm associating with the wrong people," I said. "Have you been mean to them or something?"

She looked at the dead Were, still in his shifted form in death, and chuckled. "Not as mean as you have."

"Savage River pack," I said. "Mean anything to you?"

Faire showed her fangs. "Richard Bowman."

"The senator?"

Nodding, she said, "Yes." Raising her voice, she called, "Tell Bowman that Georgetown and Ms. Rogirsdottir are off limits. There won't be any survivors if there are any further incidents. Peter, let them go, but make sure they take their refuse with them."

We watched the wolves shift, then gather their dead companion and carry him and their wounded away.

"I was told that you and Bowman were working together on the paranormal legislation," Cassiel said.

"We're both working on paranormal legislation," Faire said, "but we have major differences in our goals. Don't trust him."

"He hasn't given me any reason to do so," I said.

Cass and I walked the few blocks home, from the super-rich section of Georgetown to my snooty upper-middle class section. A couple of Vampires shadowed us the whole way, but I didn't feel threatened.

Chapter 4

The following morning, Ed and I read through the contract Torbert had left. Ed had a degree in history and was attending law school when he came to work for me one summer. He discovered that he preferred landscaping and never finished his university education. But he was still a news junky, and I could always count on him to explain Human governmental and societal issues I didn't understand.

I did strike out the clauses that required me to testify to Congressional committees. After Ed explained what that entailed, I had zero interest. I signed the contract, then called Torbert and said he could come pick up his copy.

I was finishing the last of the paperwork that my staff insisted I read and sign when I heard the Fairies go crazy. I started to get upset, but then I realized the Fairies' sounds weren't those of angry war cries, but rather cheers of celebration. I looked out the window and saw a pickup truck pull in and park. The nursery didn't do any retail business, but sometimes clients, or prospective clients, dropped by.

I stood up and went to the door, opening it just as a short Mayan woman, black hair braided down to her butt, bounced out of the pickup.

"Isabella!" I leaped down the steps and rushed toward her. She was dressed in blue jeans, cowboy boots, and a red flannel shirt; her dark eyes sparkled above high cheekbones, and white teeth showed bright in her round, brown face. The Fairies swirled around her truck and circled her head, landing on her shoulders, pulling on her hair and her clothes, chattering at her. She probably couldn't understand them, but she laughed, and they laughed with her.

"They call you Mama Cat," I told her, "and they bid you welcome!"

"*Buenas dias! Como estas?*" She held out her arms as though to hug me, then pulled them back. "Sorry. I forgot that Elves don't hug."

Elves do hug, but primarily when we're planning on getting very intimate.

Smiling at her, I reached out and clasped her arms just below the elbows. She hesitantly clasped mine the same way.

"This is what Elves do," I said. "It creates a circle, and we exchange our energies." I chuckled. "It also makes it difficult to stab someone in the back, which is one of the two reasons we would hug someone. It's good to see you. What are you doing in DC?"

Isabella Cortez was a professor at the University of Colorado, and it was the middle of a semester.

"I'm on sabbatical. I tried to contact you, but you were out of the country."

"How long are you here for?" I asked.

"That's a long story. Can I take you to lunch? I'm famished."

I gave my office a guilty glance, then said to hell with it. "Sure, sounds like a great idea. What are you in the mood for?"

We walked over to Georgetown. On the way, Isabella said, "George Washington University offered me a job, and I took it," she said. "I'm moving to DC and need to find a place to live."

"That's great! But I thought you liked Colorado. All that open space in the mountains."

"I do, but I've been there for twenty years, and people are starting to notice that I haven't aged. I was thinking about moving to South America, then all you paranormals invaded, and I figure I can take care of the suspicious glances by simply relocating. I've been studying Werewolves in the Rockies and the Southwest, and this will give me a chance to compare those groups to urban shapeshifters."

A cop walked by, and I did a double take. "Isabella, did you see that? He was carrying a paintball gun."

She turned to look, then laughed. "Yeah, your idea caught on. The government signed a contract with the Colorado Elves to manufacture demonbane. They're building a factory in Utah."

We found a table in a pub, and after we ordered, she said, "Okay, tell me how you managed to end up on TV again."

Of course, a Dragon landing in the middle of a major city caused a stir, and TV cameras had caught me returning the Dragon's eggs. So, for the second time in a year, I incurred some unwanted fame. While we ate, I told her about the Elves in Ireland and Iceland, and about the hunt throughout Europe for the Dragon's egg.

"So, what happened to the hunky Nephilim?" she asked.

"All of that, and all you're interested in is a man?"

"Mmm-hmmm. Sounds delicious."

I gave her my best exasperated expression, and she stared back, a patient and expectant look on her face.

When I decided I wasn't going to wait her out, I said, "He's staying at my place."

A smile lit up her face. "Oh, good. I was hoping to meet him." Then she pursed her mouth and looked thoughtful. "I guess I need to find a hotel or something."

Shaking my head, I said, "No, your room is available. You do know that a house in the DC area will be expensive."

Her smile broadened. "Oh? I thought you were allergic to romance."

"Only to romance with the wrong man."

We walked back to the nursery, grabbed a couple of Isabella's bags, and left her truck there under the watchful eyes of the Fairies. Between them and the wards I had set around the property, I knew it would be safe.

"New car?" Isabella asked as we got in my car. Demons had destroyed my car the previous summer.

"Money from the Icelandic Elves," I replied. "I didn't expect any payment from them, but I wasn't about to turn it down. I'm still fighting with the insurance company about my old car. 'Destroyed by demons' evidently isn't one of their normal coverage categories."

We stopped by a couple of markets, then drove to my home in Georgetown. It was early enough that most people were still at work, so I was able to find a place to park close to the house.

I carried the groceries to the kitchen, and Isabella headed for the stairs. Suddenly, I heard a startled, "What the hell?"

Turning to look, I saw Isabella and Bess standing ten feet apart, eyeing each other.

"Isabella, this is Bess. Bess, this is Isabella. She's a demigod jaguar shapeshifter."

Bess looked Isabella up and down, sniffed disdainfully, then walked past her toward me. She stopped in front of me—the top of her round head even with my knees—looked at the bags I carried, and asked, "What is that?" in her high, squeaky voice.

"A duck, some vegetables and fruit, and some steaks for Isabella," I said.

"Put it in the cold box," Bess said. "The menu for tonight is already set." She brushed past me and preceded me into the kitchen.

I put the groceries away, then went back to where Isabella stood staring at the kitchen door.

"What was that?" Isabella asked.

"Bess. She's a Brownie. She moved in last winter when I was in Europe. She decided the house had been unfairly abandoned and needed someone to care for it."

"She lives here?"

I nodded. "She lives in the pantry."

"How do a Brownie and a kitchen witch get along in the same space?"

"We're still negotiating." I grabbed one of her bags. "Come on, let's see if Cassiel is here."

"Can't you evict her?" Isabella asked as we climbed the stairs.

I gasped, horrified. "Evict a Brownie? That would be a lifetime's worth of bad luck. I'd be lucky if the house was still standing in a year." I shook my head. "You don't evict a Brownie. I'm just glad she's decided not to evict me. They can make your life hell if they decide you're bad for their house."

I had no idea how old Bess was, or where she had been before she found my house. She might be irascible at times, but the house was spotless, I hadn't washed a dish since I came back from Europe, and she worked for food.

Of course, every crumb of food I had left in the house was gone when I arrived. I made a note to ask my elderly neighbors if their house had magically started cleaning itself. And if their grocery bill had gone up.

We deposited Isabella's bags in my guest room and then went looking for Cassiel. We found him in my tiny backyard, sitting at the table reading a book. Carolyn, the woman who left me the house when she died, had a great library, and Cass spent a huge amount of his time reading.

"Hey," I said, "put the book away. We have a guest. Meet my friend Isabella."

He looked up and smiled, then stood, rising to his full six-and-a-half feet. He looked big sitting down, but a lot bigger when standing, with his broad chest and shoulders that supported the musculature for his wings. Golden hair spilled over his shoulders and his pale blue eyes—the irises almost white, with deep blue darts and a dark blue ring around the outside—always drew the attention of people when they first met him.

"Gods," Isabella breathed, "he's beautiful."

"Yeah," I muttered under my breath. "I never get tired of looking at him."

"This is the cat shifter?" Cassiel asked.

"Jaguar," I said. "Do you know what a jaguar is?"

"They have spots, right?"

Isabella laughed. "Yeah, I have spots."

I went back into the house and popped the tops on three beers. Bess floated in front of the stove, stirring something in a pot. We were still a couple of hours away from dinner, but it already smelled wonderful. I decided that it was a good day.

That night, Isabella, Cass and I discussed the PCU agents' visit and our meeting with Sarah Faire.

"It's been interesting watching the reaction and the changes now that magic and paranormals are out in the open," Isabella said.

"Just a spectator sport for you?" I asked with a laugh.

"In a lot of ways. Remember, I was born during a period when mage-kings ruled and there was more traffic between the realms. In a few hundred years, the veils will heal, and there will be another bunch of changes."

Cassiel chuckled, but then his expression grew serious again. "The issues your friend Torbert is worried about are common throughout the realms, especially now that the veils have breached."

He didn't say anything else. He seemed to stare off into space, and the silence grew until I said, "This is the sort of thing the Paladins try to hold down, isn't it?"

Turning his face toward me, he said, "Yes, it is. We believe there's a natural balance in the universe, but unless order is maintained, the tendency is to devolve into chaos. We try to give order a helping hand where we can."

Cass took a deep breath. "All too often, mages try to take advantage, building a following and expanding their power, much as Mondranar was trying to do in this realm. If left unchecked, they tend to squabble with each other rather than cooperate."

"Mage wars," I said.

"Yes, not a pleasant prospect. Take a look at China. The demons destabilized the country, and mage-lords took advantage. Now, instead of a single

36

country, it's devolved into about two dozen entities. Some are ruled by non-magical Human warlords, but more than half have become either autocracies or oligarchies ruled by mages, not all of whom are Human."

I told Isabella I would help her find a house as soon as I plowed through the small mountain of contracts and other business paperwork my staff handed me on my return from Europe.

I managed to clear most of my paperwork, then went into work early the following morning, and was ready to go with Isabella when she stopped by the nursery at ten o'clock.

"We'll take my car," I said. "That way you can look around. Where to first?"

She had a list she had made from the internet, and a client of mine who was a witch and a realtor had given me the lockbox codes.

Isabella gave me an address in northwest Georgetown, and we headed there first. When we arrived, it was easy to see that the townhouse for sale had seen better days. Definitely a fixer-upper.

"They want a million and a half for this?" Isabella asked, obviously appalled.

I laughed. "Welcome to Georgetown. Find a good contractor, spend a couple hundred thousand, and it could be nice."

"If they want that much money for this dump, how much is your place worth?"

"Add another million. If I hadn't inherited it, along with a small trust fund to maintain it, I wouldn't be able to afford the property taxes, let alone a mortgage. Carolyn's grandfather built the place, and it was handed down through the family. I planned to move back to the cottage at the nursery when she died, but she surprised me."

"That cottage would be a definite step down."

"Oh, it's not bad. I lived there for twenty years before Carolyn invited me to live with her. It's a lot more spacious now than when I first built it. Originally, it was one room with no electricity, heat, or air conditioning. I used magelights and witchfire to cook and heat the place. After a few years, I added the bedroom, and then the parlor later."

We looked at a couple of more houses, working our way northwest parallel to the Potomac. All of the places were in the millions. Isabella obviously had more money than I had thought, but it was none of my business.

"Is there a reason we're following the river?" I asked. The east side of the river was mostly parkland along the old Chesapeake and Ohio Canal. I often went there to get away from people and feel like I was away from civilization.

She shrugged. "I thought maybe living close to the river, I might be able to escape civilization occasionally."

"Good thinking."

We left the District and crossed into Maryland. The next house she directed me to was odd. Nestled in trees away from major roads, it had originally been a small cottage. Someone had renovated it and added a two-story square tower. It still wasn't very large, with two bedrooms and one bath. But inside, it seemed light and spacious, with lots of windows, and it sat on a very large lot. From the bedroom on the second floor, we could see the forest, the canal, and the river less than half a mile away.

"Oh, this is perfect," Isabella said. "All this yard, and space to run close at hand. It's only six hundred thousand. Call your friend. Tell her I want to buy it."

"You're sure? Traffic in the mornings going to work is going to be a killer," I said, feeling weak in the knees. I had literally never considered buying a house. I had paid a third of that to buy the land for the nursery decades before.

She laughed. "I'm not going to drive. I'll shift and run down by the river. It's what—twelve, fifteen miles? Piece of cake. I can probably catch breakfast on the way." She pointed at a fat squirrel perched on the branch of a tree next to the house.

I called the realtor, and she agreed to meet Isabella at the house the following day.

"Do you want to test that commute before you commit to the house?" I asked.

She gave me a puzzled look.

"We can leave the car here, run over to GW, then take the bus back to the nursery, get your truck, and retrieve my car."

She turned and looked out at the forest along the river, then said, "Sure. If you're up for it, let's go."

We had to cross a major road, but it only took us five minutes to slip into the forest. Isabella shifted, and we took off. She fell into a ground-eating lope, and the pace was comfortable for me. We ran along the old canal towpath.

It was a warm March day, the trees were budding, and the wildlife was out enjoying its first extended taste of spring. Along with the birds, squirrels and rabbits, we surprised a small herd of five deer bedded down for the day. Isabella watched them run off, almost vibrating with excitement.

At times, the forested area between the road and the water narrowed significantly, and a couple of times Isabella had to shift back to her Human form due to us encountering people. Farther south, we ran into some marshy areas, and she handled the terrain on four feet better than I did on two.

Isabella suddenly stopped. I slowed and saw the big cat look around and up, then shift to her Human form. I walked back toward her.

"What's the matter?" I asked.

She pointed. "Fairies," she said, a trace of wonder in her voice.

"Yeah. Fairies, Pixies, Nymphs, and Sylphs hang out around here. Probably a few less savory other-realm creatures, such as boggarts and Werewolves hunting rabbits. They were out and about up by the house as well, but you were too busy sniffing after the rabbits and squirrels to notice."

Isabella shook her head. "Fae don't smell like prey. You're right, I didn't notice them. Boggarts and Werewolves?"

"Yeah, that's about the worst of it. I haven't seen any kelpies or hellhounds." A fairy lit on my shoulder and spoke into my ear. "Yes," I told him, "that's Mama Cat."

He let out a squeal and flitted away. Almost immediately, he came back with a couple of dozen friends. They flew about Isabella, looking at her, touching her. One hovered directly in front of her face, studying her. All the while, they were laughing and calling to each other.

"Come on, Miss Celebrity," I said. "Shift and let's get going. I'm getting hungry."

"What language are they speaking?" Isabella asked.

"Low Elvish. It's kind of the *lingua franca* throughout the realms. Almost everyone speaks it, from Fairies to demons to Angels. To my knowledge, only Humans, Vampires and Weres don't use it, but those races don't produce any realm walkers."

"Can you teach me?"

"Yeah, sure. You understand spoken language in your cat form, right?" She nodded. "I can start giving you the basics on our way to lunch. Now, shift, and let's go."

So, as we trotted, I told her basic words and phrases, and outlined the structure of the language. High Elvish was the formal language of the Elves, Aesir, and Angels. Low Elvish and its many dialects were spoken more by the common people. The farther one traveled from Alfheim, Asgard, and Heaven, the more the language diverged, but it was usually still understandable.

The run took us about forty-five minutes, and Isabella had to shift to her Human form for the last mile. I told her I wasn't about to walk through Georgetown with a jaguar unless she was on a leash. Secretly, I didn't think that would work, but the idea offended her enough that she changed.

We ate lunch, then caught the bus to the nursery, and she drove me to retrieve my car.

"You know, that's a lot of money," I told her. "You could stay with me."

She smiled. "Thanks for the offer, but you and your honey deserve some privacy, and I prefer my own space. As for the money, that's about what I sold my cabin in Colorado for, so I'm not worried about it." She leaned forward and whispered, "I don't worry

41

about money. I know where the Mayans hid their gold from the Spaniards. I'm the one who hid it." She winked at me.

Chapter 5

Every other weekend I normally took a drive out in the country. The first weekend of the month I went south, and the third weekend I went north. I enjoyed getting out of the city, smelling country air and feeling nature. Sometimes I wondered if there was something wrong with me. Surely, living in the middle of a big city was unnatural for an Elf.

The Cherry Blossom festival was starting, and a horde of tourists descended on Washington. Cassiel and Isabella wanted to go and see, so I wished them well. They declared me boring and went off to play tourist on the National Mall.

"Some of us have to work. Say hello to the demons," I told them with a cheery smile. For some reason—maybe tourists tasted better than the locals— the National Mall had an extremely high number of demon attacks. One witch I knew attributed it to all the evil embedded in the Capitol building.

I drove out of Washington toward West Virginia, the back of my van loaded with trade goods. The nursery had extensive greenhouses, and I grew a number of specialty crops. I mixed a wide variety of potions, elixirs, and poultices that I sold. And because I had such a complete laboratory, I also mixed various concoctions for other witches.

My first stop was with an old friend who owned a shop near Harper's Ferry, West Virginia. Linda portrayed herself as an herbalist and a spiritual healer. She was also one of the most powerful Human witches that I knew. I brought her herbs and flowers, and she traded me wild plants and fungi she gathered in the West Virginia hills.

I also mixed a number of healing potions for her, both Elven recipes and some that she gave me. I wasn't a healer, and some of the recipes she gave me didn't respond to my magic. That wasn't a problem, as I would extract and mix the ingredients, then take them to her to spell.

I had three cases of small potion bottles for an elixir that deadened pain, harmlessly sedated a patient, and promoted healing. At least, it would do all that as soon as Linda worked her magic on the stuff. As it was when I drove it out of Washington, a person could drink an ocean of it while bathing in it and feel no effects at all.

I pulled up in front of Linda's shop and carried the cases of potion inside. She had a customer, so I set the cases down by the door, silently waved at her, and went outside for the rest of her order.

After the customer left, Linda came around the counter and swept me into a hug. "Kellana, it's so good to see you!"

I always felt awkward with huggers. For one thing, Elves only hugged when they were intent on getting very intimate. The second thing was simply the physical awkwardness. I was six-feet-six, and Linda was five-feet-two. When she hugged me, her face was right in my chest, and all I could see was the top of her brown head.

She locked the front door and put a 'closed' sign on it. I carried the unspelled potions down to her basement and placed them on top of a small black pentagram painted on the floor. Linda poured a circle of Kosher salt around them, stepped inside the circle, and closed it.

It was interesting to watch a magic user from a different discipline work. Whereas I would have drawn a rune in the air above the potion bottles and invoked it with a Word, Linda lit candles at the cardinal points, chanted in a language that sounded like Latin, ignited something pink in a brazier, then chanted some more. It seemed like a lot of work to me, but I couldn't argue with her results.

When she finished, she broke the containment circle by scuffing the salt with her foot and lifted one of the cases. I leaped forward.

"Here, let me take that for you." I plucked the case holding four hundred bottles of potion out of her arms. I had visions of her tripping on the stairs. "Where do you want it?"

I deposited the case in an upstairs closet, then went back and retrieved my two cases and took them out to the van. I would keep half of the case and sell the other bottles. The arrangement worked well for both Linda and me.

Linda brewed some tea and placed cookies she had baked on the table. She was what people tended to describe as an "earth mother", a hippie in her mid-fifties. Carolyn had introduced me to Linda and her mother thirty years earlier. She traced her family back to England during the Inquisition, their immigration to America during England's civil war and Cromwell's witch hunts.

"I need some advice," I said, and told her about the PCU, Sarah Faire, and the FDA contract.

"It's a trap," she said. "It sounds as though Faire and Bowman want legal rights and residency for Vampires and Werewolves crossing the veils, but most witches are Human, or at least part Human, and we've been here forever. The FDA just wants to control what we do and put us out of business."

"I don't understand. How can they put us out of

business?"

"By regulating our products. Kellana, it takes years, sometimes decades, and millions and millions of dollars to get a new drug through FDA's certification process. Even then, the drugs can only be prescribed by doctors." She pointed to the cases of bottles and charms I had brought. "I sell that antibiotic potion you brew for twelve dollars a bottle, which contains twelve daily doses. Some antibiotics the drug companies sell cost twelve bucks a pill, and a prescription involves four pills a day for ten to fourteen days. Your potion is far more effective. Think of all those lost profits by the drug companies, and all that power lost by the FDA. I'll bet that they plan to outlaw all magical cures because they don't understand them and can't control them."

She stood and retrieved a package of herbs from a display on the counter. "The second I have to list the ingredients, this will be illegal. Hell, the cops here would put me in jail if they knew what was in it."

The package was labeled VHH and contained valerian, hops, and hemp—marijuana. I sold it as a tranquilizer and a sleeping aid. The last element of mixing the herbs was a light spell that bound the properties of the herbs together.

"But I saw some real crap being sold in a store called Witches World in Bethesda," I said. "Not really harmful in itself, but harmful if you took it instead of a truly effective medicine or instead of seeing a healer. And some of it could be harmful if you took too much. Not to mention charms that had no magic at all. A complete rip off."

Linda shook her head. "Yeah, I know. I drove down there and checked it out when it first opened. Kellana, the answer is for witches to police ourselves.

46

Good luck getting that cleared with the government or getting witches to actually work together."

"That reminds me," I said. "The PCU told me that there are three covens competing with each other, and not playing very nice. There's also a wolf pack trying to move in and take over territory claimed by the pack in DC. Do you know anything about any of that?"

She scowled. "Oh, yeah. One of the covens is here in West Virginia, and I've been pressured to join. You're likely to hear the same thing from the rest of your clients. The covens aren't very kind to independents. The core circle in the so-called Bluegrass Coven thinks they're the Goddess's answer to all the ills of the world. Then there's the Raven coven, and the Sunrise Coven. I think they're closer to cults than true covens, and I think some of them are dabbling in the dark arts."

I felt a sinking feeling in my stomach. "Blood magic?"

"Worse. A young man came to me a couple of weeks ago. I was friends with his mother and I'd known him his entire life. He told me of a ceremony where a circle cut the heart out of a living man and the participants ate it."

"*Danu merde*. What were they trying to do, call a demon?"

"No, calling on the gods of chaos and binding themselves to enhance their power."

"Where was this?"

"Somewhere in Northern Virginia, on the banks of the Potomac. The circle leader said she wanted to draw on the power of running water to enhance the spell."

Perverting the pure, clean power of running

water. It made me want to vomit.

"The day after he came to see me, he killed himself," Linda said.

I continued my route, visiting five more witches I had done business with for years. Two of the women told me they would like to buy my goods, but they had joined a coven—one the Bluegrass Coven, one the Raven coven. Both said they could only sell coven-approved items, and both encouraged me to join their covens. It was pretty weird to hear almost exactly the same words from women who professed to be rivals.

The other three women reported being recruited, and one said she felt "pressured" to join the Raven coven. She also told me the Ravens were opening a superstore in Baltimore called Raven's Roost Magical Supplies, and predicted the store I had visited, Magical Secrets, would soon be out of business.

When I got home, I joined Isabella and Cassiel on the back patio. Isabella poured me a glass of wine, and I told her about the sacrificial ritual. The Mayans and later the Aztecs and Incas practiced Human sacrifice, so I wanted her take on the story Linda shared with me.

"Yes," she said, "we practiced Human sacrifice to the bat god Camazotz, an Archdemon in your terminology. It wasn't to embrace chaos, though. We did it to propitiate Camazotz so that he would allow the rains and good harvests. We did it in the interests of order. It doesn't sound as though your witches are interested in order."

"Chaos serves those magicians who are interested in personal power," Cassiel said. "That sort of ritual is common in many realms."

"Could one or more of these covens be using such rituals to bind their members to them?" I asked.

"Oh, hell yes," Cassiel said, and Isabella nodded vigorously.

"Think about that young man who killed himself," Isabella said. "Now think of all those who didn't, who will partake in the next ritual. They're digging themselves in deeper and deeper. It's standard cult brainwashing and reads like the script for every rogue Werewolf pack I have ever studied. Start off with a small outrage, and gradually build until Human sacrifice doesn't seem like such a big deal."

"A coven with hundreds of members is every bit as dangerous as a mage-led cult," Cassiel continued. "Individually, a witch may not have a mage's power, but a complete circle of thirteen witches can wield considerable power. Now think about a circle made up of thirteen circles. You can blast holes in reality with that much concentrated power."

I met Karen at FDA headquarters for my meeting with the administrator in charge of the new and strange magical phenomena. For some reason, I didn't expect the security checkpoint at the FDA headquarters. The guards called my contact there, and she came out to greet Karen and me.

"Miss Rogirsdottir? I'm Susan Davis," she said, extending her hand for me to shake it. She was in her early fifties, with short light brown hair, a navy dress and pumps, conservative jewelry and makeup. "What seems to be the problem?"

I gestured to the box I had brought. "They want to know what's in the bottles. They want me to open them. But, Ms. Davis, they really don't. They also want

49

to search my bag, and that's not going to happen. They don't look in my bag when I visit the Justice Department."

She pursed her lips, then asked, "What's the problem with opening the bottles?"

I shrugged. "Some of the potions are volatile. I brought these for your scientists to evaluate, but that should be done in controlled conditions."

Karen stepped forward and showed her credentials. "I'll vouch for her. If you remember, Director Torbert said she should be treated as one of our agents."

Davis nodded. She spoke with the guards for a couple of minutes, then one of them made a phone call. Eventually, Karen and I signed in, and Davis countersigned for both of us. A guard gave me a little visitor badge to clip to my lapel, then I picked up my box and followed Davis to an elevator.

"I reserved a meeting room," Davis said. "Would it be better to meet in one of our labs?"

"Yes, that would be better. One with a sealed glove box," I said.

We ended up in a different building. A man in a white coat and another man in a dark suit greeted us—Doctor Giles and Doctor Foreman. I set my box on a round table, and we all took a seat.

They all stared at me. I had made an effort that morning to dress formally. Formally for an Elf, that is—just as I would dress to meet the Queen. My hair was done up in fanciful swirls with half-a-dozen braids threaded through it, held by jeweled combs, and showing my ears, adorned with dangling peridot earrings matching my necklace. My hairdo added at least four inches to my six-foot-six height. I wore a pale rose-colored translucent tunic with loose, billowing sleeves, and tight maroon leggings. That was probably why the guards were so suspicious. I looked far more exotic than their normal visitor.

"So, what do have we here?" Doctor Foreman, the man in the suit, asked.

"This is a selection of potions, salves, extracts, and distillations," I said. "The purpose of most of them is medicinal. A couple are simply to enhance well-being. I also brought some charms—spelled costume jewelry that a person might wear. Everything is labeled, and I have an ingredient list." I pointed to a small box in one corner of the larger box. "That box contains a selection of potions and charms I purchased at Witches World on my way over here. All of them are worthless, or nearly so. Some of the potions contain the same ingredients as potions I made, but they aren't spelled, so they don't really do what the store says they will."

"You're a witch," Davis said in a tone that made it a question.

Holding out my cupped hand, I kindled a flame that danced above my skin. Davis's eyes widened, and she reached out, barely touching the flame.

"Ouch! It's really fire!"

I urged it out of my hand, and made it dance about above the table, then extinguished it.

"Have you ever witnessed real magic before?" I asked. They all shook their heads.

"You're not Human," Foreman blurted out.

"No, I'm not. I'm an Elf, from the realm of Midgard. I'm also a naturalized American citizen, and I've lived in this country for more than sixty years."

Foreman opened his mouth again, then closed it. To Human eyes, I looked to be mid-twenties at most.

51

With my flat chest, many thought I was even younger. I couldn't count the number of basketball and volleyball coaches who had tried to recruit me to their university.

Karen leaned forward. "Ms. Rogirsdottir was instrumental in neutralizing those who destroyed Arlington last summer, and in helping us restore order. The PCU has no doubts about her loyalty, or her veracity."

I fought to maintain a straight face. I didn't feel much loyalty to any government, even the Queen of Alfheim.

"Ms. Davis," I said, "the only way you're going to be able to evaluate these potions is to hire some witches. I think if you put the potions in a spectrometer, you won't be able to tell much of anything, but I've never done it. To my knowledge, no electronic or mechanical device has ever detected magic."

"Can we evaluate them by their effects?" Giles asked.

I pulled a small bottle out of the box. "This is a healing potion. Give it to someone with a major injury and it will keep them from bleeding to death and accelerate their healing process, but it won't reset a bone or remove their appendix." I picked up another one. "This will kill a tumor if it hasn't grown too much. Give too much of it and you'll kill the patient. But it isn't a cure for metastatic cancer." I shrugged. "Magic works better than a lot of your medicine, but much of what I make is used to supplement what a magical healer does."

"Can your healers cure cancer?" Giles asked, eagerly leaning forward.

"I don't know. I never heard of the disease until I

came to Earth, but I'm not a trained healer. This particular potion is from a Human witch that I know."

"So, Elves don't get cancer?" Foreman asked.

"My understanding is that many, if not most, cancers are due to environmental toxins," I said. All of the Humans nodded. "We don't have the industrial pollution in Elven realms that you have here. We don't use chemicals on our food. I suppose we'll know in a few hundred years whether the Elves who have moved here get some of your diseases."

"You own a nursery, is that right?" Davis asked.

"Yes, but not a retail nursery. I mostly grow plants for my landscaping business and for my own and my employees' consumption."

"So, how do you control insects? Magic?"

I grinned at her. "Fairies, mostly, and a couple of Gnomes."

They stared at me.

"A colony of Pixies used to live in the park next door, and they're primarily insectivores. But a blood mage poisoned the park, and the Pixies had to move. Using the Little People has its advantages. They coexist with butterflies and bees, whereas pesticides kill the pollinators. You can come by sometime and see how it works."

The way they stared at me made me think that they didn't really believe what I said. I left the potions and charms with them and agreed to stop by a week later. When we left the building and walked to our cars, Karen burst out laughing.

"Did you see the looks on their faces when you said you used Fairies for insect control?"

"Yeah, that was pretty funny."

"By the way," she said, "you look absolutely

fabulous. Where did you get those clothes?"

"I made them. I make all my clothes."

"You're kidding."

"Have you ever tried to find clothes for a woman my height? Besides, I'm a hearth witch. When I first came to this country, I worked as a seamstress and a chef. I also cleaned hotel rooms, which wasn't much fun. But I don't think I've ever worn anything that either I or my mother didn't make." I thought for a moment. "Well, an aunt gave me a cloak one winter solstice, and a shawl another time. I mean, the silk for this tunic was expensive, but it only took me a couple of evenings to sew it, and do you know how much it would cost in a store?"

When we got to the visitors' parking lot, I said, "I don't think they're going to ask me back more than a couple of times. There's really nothing for them to do. Do you think they'll actually hire any witches?"

"No, probably not," Karen said, "and that's sad."

Chapter 6

Congresswoman Sarah Faire called me and asked if I could come to see her.

"Yes, but not to the Capitol or any place that has security screening in place."

I heard a chuckle. "I'll buy lunch," she said. "Meet me at Eastern Market at eleven-thirty."

It was the first time a Vampire ever invited me to lunch. Usually they just jumped out of the bushes and tried to bite me without going through the formalities. Eastern Market wasn't a restaurant, but they did have a number of vendors who sold prepared foods, along with fruits and vegetables. There was also a butcher shop.

Vampires were normally nocturnal, and definitely light-sensitive and sun-averse, but they didn't turn to ash in a sunbeam or anything like that. I had been to Transvyl, and although it was cloudy and gloomy there, Vampires did go outside in the daytime.

Faire wore a broad-brimmed hat, sunglasses, and long sleeves—and she was standing in the shade as she waited for me outside the market.

She bought me a fruit salad and herself a Styrofoam cup of blood from the butcher. We strolled outside and sat at a table in the shade. Faire watched me through her eyelashes as she sipped her lunch through a straw. I dug into my salad and waited for her to tell me why she wanted to meet.

"I'm kind of disappointed you took your hair down," she finally said.

"What?" I was so surprised I stabbed myself in the lip with my fork.

"That incredible hairdo you did for the FDA."

"How did you know about that?"

She smirked. "Security footage. I have my contacts."

Yeah, she probably did. Humans evidently weren't able to identify a Vampire or a Werewolf unless the paranormal was getting ready to tear their throats out.

"It was a pain in the ass," I said. "I don't know why I bothered."

"Trying to impress them?"

I shrugged. "Yeah, and trying to look non-Human. I hoped that if I was exotic enough, they would take what I had to say more seriously."

Faire shook her head. "And they didn't? I'm not surprised. My source says that they locked up all the stuff you took them and scheduled a series of meetings to argue about what to do with it."

"And that's what you're going to do with anyone foolish enough to testify in front of your committees," I said.

Her eyes narrowed, and all traces of humor faded from her expression. "Yes, that often happens, but things are devolving. We can't continue without some sort of framework to incorporate paranormals into society."

"Paranormals like you and me, you mean. People who look like Humans."

"Well, I don't think we're going to convince demons to abide by our laws, or settle down and start farming," she said.

"What about Fairies, or Gnomes, or Brownies? Kirin and Kitsune? Selkies and Dryads? Do you really think that giving Pixies the right to vote will be embraced by the Christian churches?" I shook my

56

head. "What you want is protection for your own people, so that you can prosecute me if I kill a Vampire who's trying to feed on me."

I had been thinking about the new normal and wasn't sure what all the different factions were trying to achieve. Although she tried to mask it, for a few seconds her face twisted, letting me know that whatever else our meeting might accomplish, I certainly had succeeded in making Sarah Faire angry. Oh, well.

"Ms. Faire, in every realm I know of with more than one sentient species, they tend to fight with each other. Vampires always hide in the shadows because of their unfortunate tendency to prey on any animal with iron-based blood, even those who are sentient. If your people would stop trying to feed on Humans, you probably wouldn't have a problem."

"So, you won't help me," Faire said.

"I didn't say that. I'm all for restoring order, but you need to think globally, not just about the problems Vampires have now that Humans know you're real. There have been real witch hunts, both here and in other countries, and a lot of the people persecuted or killed weren't witches. I would strongly recommend bolstering the PCU with more witches, some Vampires and Werewolves, and other paranormals. You have to control the paranormals as well as protect them. Until Humans believe everyone is subject to the same laws, I don't have much faith in any laws your Congress dictates."

She regarded me with a stern, unyielding face, then it suddenly collapsed. "Oh, hell," she said, shaking her head, "that makes so much damned sense I don't even want to argue with you. Yes, Vampires in this realm are used to policing our own. But if we're going to ask for cooperation from the government, I guess we're going to have to cooperate with them."

I thanked Representative Faire for lunch and walked to the Metro station. In the middle of the day, I wasn't paying as much attention as I would have been at night, so it was a surprise when I realized two men and a woman were blocking my path. I changed direction to walk around them, but they moved so that they were still in front of me.

Three witches, and their faces didn't show friendly, welcoming expressions. I sketched a rune and spoke the Word to invoke a personal-protection spell.

If I was confronted by Vampires or Werewolves, I could draw my sword and deal with them. At most, I might get arrested for cruelty to animals. That was exactly the scenario which Sarah Faire feared.

But the witches were Human, and stabbing them would definitely be murder under the law. I couldn't even plead self-defense, since magic legally didn't exist. I was protected by my shield from a bullet or a knife, and possibly against a fireball, but if they dropped a piano on me, like a cartoon coyote on a roadrunner, I probably wouldn't fare very well.

And since I wasn't a particularly strong witch, one of them might be strong enough to get through my shield. Chances were that all three together could.

"You should be careful who you associate with," the woman said.

"I've been hearing that a lot lately. Is there something I can do for you, or did you stop me just to give me some friendly advice?"

The man on my right said, "A lone witch is

vulnerable. Without a coven to protect you, it would be a good idea to keep your head down. Collaborating with the FDA and that Vampire bitch could be bad for your health."

"And your business," the woman said.

They had West Virginia accents. I sighed. "And what coven would you suggest I join?"

Her laugh was rather ugly. "You could try the Raven coven. They might accept alien monsters."

"I see. Well, I'll certainly take that under consideration. Is there anything else?"

The man on my left suddenly moved toward me, his hand trying to grab me. I reached out with my magic and touched a bush growing next to the sidewalk. The branches nearest us shot out, growing two feet in an instant, and tripped him. His face hit the sidewalk hard.

Drawing my sword from my bag, I leaped forward, sweeping low toward the other two witches' legs. The woman stumbled back, and the man attempted to jump to his left but caught his foot and fell. I rushed past them, and only my speed allowed me to elude the two Werewolves who leaped at me from where they were hiding.

I had taken half-a-dozen steps when a fireball hit my shield. I kept going, knowing none of them, even the wolves, could run fast enough to catch me.

A ball of energy hit the wall of the Metro entrance as I ducked down the stairs. I didn't slow down, taking the steps five at a time and praying I didn't break an ankle.

Three different Metro lines ran through the Eastern Market station, and all would take me where I wanted to go. A train stood at the platform with its

59

doors open, and running full speed, I managed to jump on as the doors started to close.

On the way to the nursery, I thought about that close call and what I could do about it. Retrieving my car, I went home and found Isabella and Cassiel sitting out on the back patio. I told them about my meeting with Faire, and the encounter with the witches.

"I'll just have to go with you whenever you go out," Cass said when I finished.

"Yeah," Isabella said, "at least one of us, if not both."

While that made sense, I didn't consider it an acceptable answer to the situation. I went up to my lab and paged through my grimoire for an hour, then went back downstairs.

"Isabella, I need some hot peppers. The hotter the better."

She shrugged and smiled. "Okay. I like hot food, but I didn't know you did."

Cass snorted. "Elves cook some spicy stuff."

"Yeah," I said, "but I want the killer peppers. Habaneros at least, Scotch bonnets would be even better, ghost peppers if you can find them."

"Sure," Isabella said. "How much?"

"A couple of bushels. Can you also call around and see if you can find some low-cost lead crystal? Try some of the junk antique stores."

"What are you cooking up?" Cassiel asked.

"Have you ever heard of pepper spray?"

Isabella laughed. "I have, but how is that going to help against magic users?"

"I'm going to try mixing it with a potion that

nullifies magic. I've never mixed it, and don't know if it will work, but normally one needs to drop a personal protection spell to cast an offensive spell. If I can mix the capsaicin from the peppers with the potion and put it in paint balls, I should have something I can use against a witch. Demonbane would be lethal, and that's a problem. The cops tend to take a dim view of killing Humans. I don't know how wolfsbane would affect a Human, and vampirebane just gives Humans a light rash."

Cass chuckled. "Witchbane. I like it."

In the end, Isabella found habaneros, Scotch Bonnets, ghost peppers, and Thai peppers. It took me three days to extract the capsaicin—the chemical that made the peppers hot—and brew the potion.

We sat around the table outside sharing a bottle of wine along with fruit and cheese. Two large stainless-steel pots bubbled away in a corner, with a large fan blowing the smell of hot chilis and ethanol out of the yard. Luckily, my neighbors in that direction spent their winters in Arizona and hadn't made the migration back to Washington as yet.

"I guess I don't really understand magic," Isabella said. "From what I've seen, you're a fairly powerful witch. But I was really surprised at how afraid you were of that run-in with those witches the other day."

"Witchcraft is a very broad catchphrase," I said. "Power and particular talents are inherited. Study and practice and age define how proficient a witch becomes with what she or he is born with. Cass's father was a realm walker, and he inherited that. I could study a thousand years and never understand how he does it."

"So, your parents didn't have any offensive power?"

"My father isn't a witch, or a mage. He only has the innate magical abilities that all Elves have. My mother is an earth witch, alchemist, and healer. In spite of a hundred years of study, I'm a very weak healer. I am a strong alchemist and earth witch. I do well with plants, and I can clean this whole house in less than two hours." I chuckled. "It's kind of ironic that a witch with an affinity for cooking and domestic things has attracted a Brownie."

"Maybe she's a lazy Brownie and you're easy," Isabella said with a laugh. "But your mother couldn't do any of those fireballs or force beams, or lightning thingies?"

I laughed with her, then sketched a rune and spoke a Word. A ball of light appeared in my hand. "This is pure energy. I can throw it, and it will blast the hell out of anything it hits. But it's not very large, it takes me some time to cast it, and it drains me. If I could pull energy from a tree or a meadow, it would help replenish me. In the city, I might be able to generate three or four of them, but the time to do a new one would get longer and longer." I spoke another Word and let the spell's energy flow back into me.

"The lightning, the electrical energy I can wield, is much the same," Cass said. "I'm not very strong that way, though I've gained strength as I've grown older. But I pull the energy from a different source than Kellana does. I pull it from the upper realm, and from any kind of electrical field that's nearby. I can do a fireball, but I need fire close by to pull that energy from. But my magic is very different than Kellana's."

Isabella was silent, staring off into the distance, then poured herself another glass of wine. She raised an eyebrow at me. I nodded, and she topped off my glass and Cassiel's.

"I've seen you create fire," she said as she set the bottle down. "You do it seemingly effortlessly. How is that different than creating a fireball as a weapon?"

I shrugged. "Any Elf can light a candle. I've been able to do it since I was in my twenties. A fireball requires a lot more power than a simple open flame."

"Have you ever tried?" she asked.

"Oh, sure." I laughed. "I tried several times and produced a pathetic little thing that sputtered and died after about half a minute."

"Cassiel said he's gained in power with age. How long ago did you try a fireball?"

I thought, then said, "Probably about seventy-five years ago."

"Why don't you try again?"

"No!" Cass said, sitting bolt upright in his chair.

With a laugh, I said, "I don't think that would be a good idea with all these alcohol fumes in the air. But seriously, practicing that sort of thing should be done far from anything flammable."

Cass eased back in his seat. "It's usually a good idea to make sure you have good command of a fire-suppression spell before you start practicing with fireballs."

I nodded. "Just because someone can conjure a fireball, doesn't mean they can control it. That requires practice."

The next day, Cassiel ground into powder the leaded glass Isabella found at an antique store, and then I cast the final spells to fold the finished potion inside of paintballs made of thin, leaded glass. I loaded three paintball hoppers, kept one for myself, and gave one each to Isabella and Cassiel.

"Don't shoot anyone by accident," I told them.

63

"Even with a healer treating someone, it could potentially blind a person who gets it in their eyes. It's about five times the strength of the U.S. military's pepper spray formulation."

Chapter 7

Bess told me that some people tried to break into my house when Isabella, Cass, and I were all gone. Then the Fairies reported that Human strangers were watching the nursery. I called Karen Wen-li.

"I don't know what you can do about it," I told her, "but I know Dave always gets upset with me when I deal with threats myself. So, I figured I'd at least tell you."

"Let me come out and look around," Karen said.

Ed and I were in the midst of interviewing summer workers, so I said, "Can you make it after three this afternoon?"

"Sure. I'll see you then."

When Karen showed up, she had another woman with her, and when they got out of the car, I could feel she was a witch. I grabbed my bag and stepped out of my office to meet them.

"Kellana, this is Meagan Humphrey. She's been with the FBI for about ten years, and she just transferred to the PCU."

Humphrey appeared to be mid-to-late thirties, about ten years older than Karen, and a head taller. Slender, busty, with shoulder-length brown hair, blue eyes, and a pale complexion, she wore a powder-blue pants suit and a white blouse.

She stuck out her hand, and I shook it. "Ms. Rogirsdottir, I've heard a lot about you," she said.

I rolled my eyes. "I'm sure. Yes, I'm the homicidal Elf who attracts trouble like I'm fond of it."

They both laughed.

"That's not exactly what I've heard," she said.

"Well, that's what I feel like at the moment." I told them about the confrontation at the Metro station.

"An alien monster?" Karen laughed.

"Well, you have to admit, I do fit the description. I am an alien from another realm, and with green hair to boot."

"But...you're beautiful!" Meagan blurted.

It always made me uncomfortable when people said that, since I wasn't really sure what it meant. Humans said that about lots of women who looked very different from each other, and I had never been able to figure out what the translation was in Elvish. The closest I could get was a virtual synonym of 'elegant', which in Elvish was normally applied to noble ladies.

"That's the worst kind, don't you know?" I chuckled. "The Fae have a bad reputation of swapping changelings, seducing men into fairyland, spoiling milk, and other nefarious deeds."

Karen laughed, then asked, "Can you show me the people who are watching you?"

I called to a Fairy who was flying by and spoke to her. She flew off, and I started walking to the nursery entrance. Wen-li and Humphrey followed me. We went through the gate and followed the fence line toward the large oak tree growing at the corner of my property.

"Karen," I said as we walked, "you know I don't hold back if I have to defend myself or my people, but this is the first time I've really had problems with Humans. And these witches are Human. I don't want to go to jail for killing one of these fools, but if they don't leave me alone, there's going to be blood."

Humphrey gave me a long side glance but didn't

say anything.

A couple of dozen Fairies flew past us and stopped at the corner, circling around and crying out. I cast a dispel-glamour spell and revealed a man sitting in the shade with his back against the fencepost.

"The Fairies can see through glamours?" Humphrey asked.

"Yes, they always see what's really there," I answered. "There aren't a lot of spells that affect them."

Karen increased her pace and moved in front of me. I hung back and watched as Humphrey joined her. Both pulled out their identification cards and held them up.

"I'm Special Agent Wen-li with the FBI. May I ask what you're doing?"

He leaped to his feet, surprise showing on his face. "I'm just sitting here," he said.

"According to the lady who owns this place," Karen motioned to me, "you've been here watching her for several days now. So, what are you doing?"

"Nothing. Just enjoying the day."

The Fairies didn't believe him and began jeering and calling him a liar.

"There isn't any law that says I can't be here," the man protested. "This is a public right of way."

Humphrey gave him a smile that wasn't very friendly. "Have you ever heard of stalking laws?"

One of the Fairies landed on my shoulder and whispered in my ear. Looking around, I saw several people walking in our direction. Slipping my hand inside my bag, I wrapped my fingers around my paintball gun. A glance back at the nursery entrance showed Cassiel and Isabella standing there watching.

Turning back to where Wen-li and Humphrey were questioning the man by the tree, I saw several more people approach from that direction. A quick count gave me a total of twelve people, in an area where any pedestrian other than an occasional neighbor walking his or her dog was a curiosity. Half of them were witches, the other half were Werewolves. I was willing to bet they all came from West Virginia.

"These people giving you a hard time, Harry?" one of the men called.

Humphrey turned and flashed her ID. "This isn't any of your business," she said. "Just move along."

"Harry's not doing anyone any harm," another man said. "You can't just go around harassing people."

"I said, move along," Humphrey replied.

One of the men, almost as tall as I was and very fat, moved forward, crowding Humphrey and obviously trying to intimidate her. "You're awfully pushy for a little broad. Maybe you should move along yourself and mind your own business."

Humphrey gave him a cold smile and gestured with her hand. The man's feet flew out from under him, and he crashed hard to the ground. All the people around jerked in surprise.

A woman started forward, an angry scowl on her face. "You stupid bitch! What did you do to him?"

At the same time, the man Karen was talking to pushed past her, almost knocking her off balance, and headed toward Humphrey. Karen stuck out her foot and tripped him. He went down on his hands and knees.

I pulled out my paintball gun and fired twice at the ground directly in front of the people nearest me. One of the men stepped forward into the mist rising from a shattered paintball, then cried out and recoiled. I hadn't expected to find such willing volunteers to test my new potion.

A couple of the Weres started to shift. I didn't worry about them, since they had their backs to Isabella. It would take them a minute or two to complete their shift, but my friend could shift into her jaguar shape instantly. The roar of a large cat rattled the neighborhood and confirmed my faith in her. Every Were, whether they had shifted or not, turned to face her direction.

I turned back toward the witches and Weres coming from the other direction, but I shouldn't have worried. Karen had her pistol out, though no one was threatening her. A fantastical green, red, and gold snake-dragon thing about ten feet tall loomed between her and the gang confronting her. It was an illusion, and a damned good one. In addition, the Fairy contingent had increased to about forty or fifty, and they were industriously launching their spears at the intruders.

I fired three paintballs past Karen, through the snake thing, and they popped on the ground at our aggressors' feet. Again, the result was quite gratifying. Those with any sense backed off, a couple of fools stood there and stared at the remains of the paint balls until the mist reached their faces.

Checking in the other direction, I saw a large spotted cat racing toward us. Two wolves faced her, and another Were was in the process of shifting. When Isabella got close, one wolf got smart, tucked his tail between his legs, and took off in the other direction.

"Don't kill them," I screamed.

Isabella batted the nearest wolf without slowing

down. He flew through the air and landed rolling on the street. Above her, my golden-winged honey swooped down, clubbed two witches in the head with his fists, and rose back up into the sky. I had to stop and stare in appreciation of how glorious he was.

The sound of Meagan Humphrey's voice brought me back to earth. She was talking into her cell phone. Karen had one foot on the head of the prone man who had been watching my place from the tree, and she was in the process of snapping handcuffs on his wrists.

Karen glanced up at me. "I don't have enough handcuffs for this crowd. You wouldn't happen to have anything that will work, would you?"

I whistled, and a cloud of Fairies swirled around my head. I promised chocolate and sent them off to bring zip ties from the nursery.

Cassiel swooped down and circled us. "Do you want the ones who ran?" he shouted.

"I want all of them," Humphrey shouted back from where she crouched over the fat man, putting her handcuffs on him.

"Hold up your paintball gun," Cass yelled to me.

I held the gun up as high as I could reach. He flew over me and snatched it from my grasp, then banked and headed toward the American University campus next door.

"He's an Angel?" Karen squeaked, awe on her face.

"A Nephilim," I answered. "Half-Angel, half-Elf."

"I need to get one of them," she said, watching him fly away.

"If you like girls, he has a sister," I said.

"Nope. I want one just like that."

70

Sirens sounded in the distance, coming closer. I looked around. Isabella had a Were penned on the ground and was growling into her face. The wolf was peeing all over herself. Humphrey was gathering several wolves and witches into a tight group and ordering them to sit on the ground. Several of them were alternatively gasping, crying, screaming, and moaning, rubbing at their eyes and skin. The wolf in the street was trying to get up, but one of his front legs wasn't cooperating.

The Fairies returned with the zip ties, and the PCU agents proceeded to complete the confinement of their prisoners just before the first cops arrived. Out of the corner of my eye, I saw Isabella shift to her Human form. I also noticed that some of the Fairies with the zip ties didn't stop, continuing in the direction Cassiel had flown. They liked him a lot because he went flying with them.

Karen went to talk with the cops, holding her identification out in front of her. Across the street, I could see the nasty old lady who lived there watching us through her window and talking on her phone. I sighed, anticipating another rant from her about me disturbing the neighborhood.

I called a couple of Fairies to me, then gave them some instructions. They flitted off in the direction of the nursery.

While Karen and Meagan talked with the police, two PCU SUVs and a van pulled up. Dave Torbert and several other agents got out and joined the conversation. A couple of the agents wandered over to where the witches and wolves sat on the ground.

"Looks like quite a party," one of the agents said.

"Just another fun-filled Tuesday afternoon at Fairyland Nursery," I replied. "We try to make sure our neighbors don't get bored."

After a while, Dave Torbert approached me, a sour look on his face.

"Aren't you proud of me?" I asked. "I called the authorities and didn't kill anyone."

He shook his head, and I could tell he was struggling to keep from smiling.

I leaned close. "I can make some lemonade or coffee, if you wish, but for me, I'm going to have a shot of *agavirna* when this is all over."

His eyes narrowed, and he looked around. "I have a feeling I might need a shot myself when I hear this story."

Looking past him, I saw Ed pulling a wagon filled with water buckets toward us. He carefully skirted the captives and handed me a bottle with a hand-lettered label on it. "This the right one?"

I gave him a smile. "Yes, thanks, Ed. Come, let me show you how to mix this."

Walking over to the wagon, I put about three drops in each bucket, then used a stick I found under the oak to stir them. "Wait three minutes, okay? The potion is already spelled, so you don't need any magic."

After three minutes, I said, "Grab a bucket." I took one myself, walked over to one of the prisoners who was in witchbane agony, and said sharply, "Look at me." The woman turned her face up, valiantly trying to open her eyes, and I poured the bucket over her. She sighed, fell over, and went to sleep.

I caught Ed's eyes and nodded toward one of the affected men. Ed repeated what I had done.

We treated three more casualties, while Torbert and his agents watched us. When we finished, Torbert asked, "What did you do to them?"

"I know how you feel about bodies, so I mixed up some special pepper spray for my paintball guns." I nodded toward the buckets. "That was the antidote. I think they suffered enough, and Goddess only knows how one of your doctors would have tried to treat them."

Cassiel returned a few minutes later and led the PCU agents to two witches and a Werewolf he had captured. The PCU brought them back, and I treated them for the witchbane, then the PCU and the cops loaded up all their prisoners and carted them away. Of the twelve I had counted at the onset of the confrontation, only two managed to escape. I led my friends and three of the PCU agents to my cottage inside the nursery.

In the kitchen, I put on a pot of coffee, pulled a jug of lemonade out of the fridge, and then turned to the job of distributing chocolate to all the Fairies who had helped. I did that under the glowering gaze of their queen, who wasn't happy with me getting all her subjects drunk in the middle of the day. But in the end, she didn't turn down the piece I offered her, so I didn't feel guilty at all.

"So, that gets them drunk?" Karen asked. "Does it hurt them at all?"

I shrugged. "Probably isn't very healthy, but I've never seen any lingering effects. I don't give them very much, and I don't do it very often."

Opening a cabinet, I pulled out a bottle of green liquid and sat glasses in front of everyone. Karen's eyes grew very wide, and Isabella laughed at her. I poured about three fingers in each glass, then raised mine. "Praise to the Goddess," I said, and drank about half of my serving.

Karen barely sipped hers. Torbert and Ed took about the same amount I did, while Cassiel, Meagan Humphrey, and Isabella drained theirs. Meagan's eyes popped open very wide, and she gasped.

Karen laughed at her. "I probably should have warned you about *agavirna*."

I topped off everyone's glasses, then pulled larger glasses off the shelf and placed them on the table with the jug of lemonade.

"There will be coffee in a few minutes," I said as I sat down. "Goddess, what a day. You PCU agents really know how to throw a party."

That got a laugh from everyone.

Karen gave Dave a quick briefing on what had happened. When she finished, Ed said, "You know, you probably should give me one of those paintball guns. What would we do if they come back and you're not here?"

That sobered me. As unstable as the veils between realms were, a rift could occur anywhere at any time. My wards wouldn't stop a demon from crossing the veils inside the nursery. Even an Imp crossing at night could cause a disastrous amount of damage before the Fairies could drive it off.

"Yeah, I can do that. I should ask Maurine if she's comfortable using one." Maurine was my office manager and the person who was on the premises most of the time.

"Jamie grew up hunting with her father," Ed said.

I nodded. Jamie was solid, with a calmness about her personality. I wouldn't worry about her shooting the wrong person.

"Do you know what that mess was all about?" Torbert asked me.

"It seems I've gotten on the wrong side of the state of West Virginia," I said. "The Bluegrass Coven and the Savage River pack appear to be allies, and they're making a play to oust the Chesapeake pack and the Sunrise Coven for control of DC. I don't know how I got pulled into this. I haven't spoken to Harold Vance in months, and I don't even know a member of the Sunrise Coven."

He shook his head, then asked, "How did your meeting with Sarah Faire go?"

"Meetings. I've met with her twice. Dave, she isn't interested in controlling paranormals, she's mainly interested in gaining legal protection for her bloodsuckers so that honest, Goddess-worshiping Elves can't defend themselves properly. You do know that Senator Bowman is a Werewolf, don't you?"

Torbert nodded.

"Well, he's the alpha of the Savage River pack, and from what I can determine, he and Faire don't get along. Isabella took a look at the legislation they've each proposed, and they don't seem to be aimed at the same things."

"No, they aren't," Torbert said. "Bowman's bill makes it a crime to assault or kill any paranormal, but also prevents FDA or any governmental body from exercising oversight or control of magical potions or charms. Faire's bill doesn't mention magic at all. It gives what she calls 'refugees' from other realms immediate residency and equal protection under our laws. That would also benefit the Weres, of course."

"And turn the U.S. into a haven for paranormals from all over the world," I said. "Does her bill prevent those refugees from draining people's blood? And depending on how Bowman defines paranormals, that bill could make it illegal to kill a demon. Let me know

75

if you figure out another way to stop one, but I don't think throwing one in jail is going to do the trick."

That evening when we got home, Cass asked, "What's the matter? You've been unusually silent since we left the nursery."

"Oh, it's nothing. I've just been thinking about something that new PCU agent, Meagan, said. She called me beautiful."

"And what's wrong with that? You are beautiful," he said.

"You're sweet, but you know that's not true. I'm just a plain farmgirl, not some noble lady. Now, I know that Humans barely know the difference between an Elf and a Troll, but I don't want people thinking I'm pretending to be something I'm not. I'd be mortified if a high-born lady heard someone say that. I mean, all you have to do is look at me to know my great-grandfather was a Wood Elf. I've got green hair."

I got up from my chair, and he rose at the same time. He took me in his arms and kissed me. Then he stared into my eyes. We were the same height, so it was easy to look into each other's eyes.

"Kellana, you are beautiful. You may be a farmgirl, but there is nothing plain about you. You'd be considered beautiful in Alfheim or Heaven. Plenty of the nobility have green hair, or brown, or even black. You're just being silly." He kissed me again.

"But, what does it mean? I don't even understand what people mean when they say that." I gave him a quick kiss, then put a hand between us and gently pushed him away. "You are the sweetest man, even if you are delusional," I said, and started to turn away.

"Where are you going?"

"To get a snack. I'm hungry."

"So am I."

The next thing I knew, he swept me off my feet and started to carry me across the room.

"Hey, wait. The kitchen's the other direction."

"That's not what I'm hungry for," he said, leaning forward to kiss me as he started up the stairs.

I didn't get my snack, and Bess scolded us for being late to dinner, but by that time I didn't care.

Chapter 8

An assault on my wards awoke me in the middle of the night.

"Cass, wake up." He came awake almost immediately. "Someone's outside, testing the wards. Can you go up to the roof and see what's going on?"

He jumped out of bed and headed for the door.

"Cass! At least put on some pants." It was three o'clock, but Humans had such strange ideas about nudity. The cops would probably arrest him instead of whoever was trying to break in.

He grabbed a pair of pants from the wardrobe and continued out the door. I quickly slipped on a tunic, grabbed my bag, and followed him.

"Isabella!" I pounded on her door. "Go downstairs and protect the doors!"

"Which one?" her voice came.

"Both of them! If anyone gets in, try to capture one alive."

I followed Cass up to the roof, where I found him fastening his trousers. His wings were already spread. "Some bloody witch is throwing fireballs at the house," he said.

Peering over the roof, I saw two shadowy figures hiding in the bushes of the house across the street. There was a flash of red light, and then a fireball streaked across the street toward my house. I followed its course and watched it splash against the invisible shield created by the wards. So far, the wards were holding.

I turned at a sound behind me, and saw Cass rise into the air. "Be careful," I called.

Taking my bow from my bag, I knocked an arrow, aimed, and at the next flash of light, loosed. The fireball again splashed harmlessly against my wards. Things were quiet for about a minute, then someone jumped from the bushes and ran down the street. My next arrow took the runner in the back of the leg, and he or she fell.

Casting about for any other movement, all I could see was Cass as he swept down the street and landed next to the wounded witch. He put his hand on the person's head, then turned back to look up at me. I heard sirens in the distance. A lot of sirens, coming from all directions.

Looking around, I noticed a number of very bright areas that stood out from the light glow of the city. And then I saw the smoke. Smoke from at least a dozen different spots. There were also four fires burning across the river in Virginia.

Not seeing any additional threats in the immediate area, I called to Cass, "Bring him along."

I saw him pick the person up, and then I ducked back inside and down the stairs.

"Isabella, call the PCU. We have a couple of customers for them."

I opened the front door, and Cass carried a man inside. He rushed through the sitting room to the downstairs bathroom and dumped the man in the tub.

I must have had a quizzical look on my face, because Cass said, "Easier to clean up the blood in here."

"Why is he unconscious?"

"I put him to sleep. Easier to deal with him. I also coagulated his wound. What about the other one?"

"I don't know. I assume he or she is dead. There

wasn't any movement or sound."

"I'll go check."

"Does anyone need an ambulance?" Isabella asked as she walked in, her hand over her phone. She looked down at the man in the tub. "Oh, I guess so." She walked back out and said into her phone, "Yes, I think an ambulance would be appropriate."

Cass came back a couple of minutes later. "I like to think my night vision is pretty good, but I had trouble figuring out where your target was until I was halfway across the street. Yes, she's dead. You're a helluva shot."

"Bitch was hurling fireballs at my house. She planned to cook us all."

First, a cute little powder-blue sports car showed up carrying Meagan Humphrey, then an ambulance, and finally, a black SUV arrived carrying a couple of additional PCU agents.

"I didn't mean to get anyone out of bed," I told Meagan. She was wearing jeans and hiking boots, and it was obvious she had combed her hair with her fingers.

"I live about a mile away," she said. "It's been a pretty busy night, so a lot of us are missing some sleep."

"A lot of fires?" I asked.

"Yeah. There's a whole mall on fire up in Rockville." That was where Witches World was located, which, to me, put some context on the situation.

"Where are the bodies?" she asked.

"The dead one is over here," I said, and led her to the dead witch in the bushes across the street. "She was throwing fireballs at my house."

Meagan crouched down and looked at the corpse very closely. I bent over and looked, too.

"Bluegrass Coven," I said. "She was one of the witches who hassled me at the Metro the other day."

"Where were you when you shot her?"

"I was standing on my roof when she was shot."

"You're a very good shot."

"Where I come from, everyone is a good shot."

She stood. "The report said there are two of them?"

The ambulance pulled up about that time, so I led her and the paramedics into the house.

"This one was lucky," Meagan said, peering into the bathroom as the paramedics began to examine my victim.

"Not really. We wanted to capture him alive. I thought you might be able to torture some information out of him."

She snorted, then got herself under control. "We don't torture prisoners in this country."

"More's the pity."

"It really doesn't work, you know. Any information you get that way is very suspicious."

I winked at her and smiled. "I know, but it's a lot more fun. Oh, hell, Meagan, I wouldn't torture anyone, but I sure as hell wouldn't let criminals out on bail so they can continue committing crimes. That's crazy."

She shrugged, then asked the paramedics. "Does he have any identification on him?"

One of them gestured to the pair of jeans they had cut off him. She searched through the pockets and pulled out a wallet. "Roy Williams, Franklin, West

81

Virginia."

"Bluegrass Coven comes from around there, as does the Savage River pack," I said. "He's a witch, not a Werewolf. It wouldn't surprise me if all these fires are homes and businesses of members of the Sunrise Coven."

"That's not something I want to hear," Meagan said, shaking her head. She took a deep breath. "Now that I think about it, though, I wouldn't be shocked. Do you have a night watchman at your nursery?"

"No, but I'm really not too worried about it. My wards are much stronger there, and Fred probably wouldn't be too happy about anyone trying to burn the place down."

"Fred?"

"The Gnome who lives there. Gnomes aren't aggressive, but I don't think he'd take kindly to someone trying to light the place on fire."

Gnomes swam through soil like fish did through water. When I first bought the land and built the rudimentary one-room cottage, a burglar tried to break in one night. When I got home, Fred asked me what I wanted to do with him. Knowing the man shouldn't be there, Fred had reached up from inside the earth, grabbed an ankle, and simply pulled the burglar underground. Not a lot of oxygen underground.

Fred wasn't angry or trying to be malicious. I'm not even sure he understood the burglar couldn't breathe dirt. I thanked Fred and told him to take the guy deeper. After that, I built a fence and cast a set of wards to prevent a repeat occurrence.

"Are you the mistress of a Fae colony?" Meagan asked. "Fairies, Gnomes, anything else?"

"Only Bess. She's the Brownie who lives here. There used to be a colony of Pixies living in the park next to the nursery, but a blood mage killed the park."

Meagan shook her head. "You don't happen to have a truth potion, do you?"

"I don't know. I can look in my grimoire."

She looked surprised, but said, "Sure."

We tromped up the stairs to my lab on the third floor.

"Wow. This is quite a setup."

"Carolyn, the woman I inherited the house from, was an alchemist, apothecary, healer, and a registered pharmacist." The lab had some traditional witchcraft apparatus, but a lot of modern equipment was mixed in as well.

"A mass spectrometer?" Meagan asked.

"Helps to figure out what someone's been poisoned with. I don't use it much."

One of the things about a magical grimoire was that it might contain a spell, but that didn't mean I could read it. If I didn't have the power, or the talent, or the needed predecessor skills to execute the spell, the grimoire wouldn't show it to me. No truth spell. I made a note to myself to ask Cassiel. He was a mage, and his magic was far different than mine. He might know one, or maybe the grimoire would reveal it to him. There wasn't any sense showing the book to Meagan, since it was written in Elvish.

I didn't get rid of all the strangers until the sun came up. I wanted to fall back into bed, but instead I got dressed and headed to work. As I started out the door, Bess stepped in front of me and handed me a pot with a lid.

"You need to eat. This will stay warm until you

take the lid off," she said in that funny voice of hers, then she floated off toward the kitchen. I didn't think she actually floated most of the time, but I never saw her feet beneath her long skirts, and she moved so smoothly and silently that it always looked as though she never touched the ground.

I drove over to the nursery, arriving shortly after Ed. I split the contents of the pot with him. Stewed apples, wheat porridge, thick bacon, and hard-boiled eggs. So much that even Cass couldn't have eaten it all.

Later, I was in the cottage making a pot of *dalesh* to keep myself awake when Dave Torbert showed up.

"Smells good," he said as he came in and sat down.

"*Dalesh*, it's an Elven drink. I can make a pot of coffee."

"No, had too much coffee. I would take some of your lemonade if you have some."

I poured him a glass, myself a mug of *dalesh*, and sat down. "Rough night?"

He took a long drink of the lemonade and nodded. "More than sixty fires throughout the metro area. A couple of magical battles when people, such as you, objected to being set on fire. That mall in Rockville burned, but Witches' World wasn't touched."

"They had wards in place," I said.

He nodded again. "So it seems. Kellana, there's a problem with that witch you killed. She's Human, and a U.S. citizen. I can't just brush it under the rug the way we usually do when a Vampire or a Werewolf is killed."

"Who told you I killed her?"

"Didn't you? Who else might have shot her with

an arrow?"

"There are a lot of people who know how to use a bow. They hunt deer around here with a bow. I hear it's very popular in West Virginia." I grinned at him. "Skill with a bow is even an Olympic sport."

He stared at me. I got the feeling he was exasperated, which was exactly what I intended. I wasn't stupid enough to admit I had killed the woman.

"Agent Torbert, that woman was trying to burn down my house with me inside. What if my neighbors' house had caught fire? They're elderly."

"That happened in a couple of places. A whole damned block of houses burned to the ground."

"I also saw your agents take a gun from her, and from the man with her. I thought that was illegal in DC. Now, if that's all you're here about, I have work to do."

With a sigh, he said, "No, that's not everything. I'd like you to go with Meagan and Karen to talk with the witches who were burned out, and especially the owners of Witches' World."

"Today?"

"Well, or tomorrow at the latest."

"Tomorrow then. Tell them to pick me up here at ten o'clock." That would give me time to get some sleep and maybe get some work done in the morning. "You know, I think the reason they're targeting me is because I'm working with you. I had that one run-in with the Werewolves, but there's no reason this witches' coven would be concerned with me."

"Except that you're an alien monster," Torbert said with a grin. Then he sobered. "Don't ever underestimate the power of prejudice and hate."

85

Chapter 9

The pictures on TV didn't truly convey the devastation at the mall—or the incongruity of the section that contained Witches' World looking pristine against the ruins. Or almost pristine. When I looked closer, I could see smoke stains on the outside walls. That gave me some insight into the wards protecting the store.

The area was cordoned off, crawling with people in various kinds of uniforms. A group of unhappy-looking men and women in street clothes stood near the Fire Marshal's car. When we walked by them, I could feel their magic.

Karen and Meagan spent some time talking to various officials, and after about half an hour, Karen turned and waved me over. A woman appearing to be in her sixties joined us, and Karen introduced her as Shawna Greene.

"We're going inside with one of the people from the owners' group and an investigator from the Fire Marshal's office," Karen said.

"Inside where?" I asked.

"The store that's still standing."

"Oh. I don't think there's anything to learn in there. Don't they want to know what started the fire?"

The investigator winked at me. "You and I will get along just fine. Everyone but you and me wants to know why that store didn't burn."

"Because it was protected by magic?" I ventured. With a shrug, I said, "Doesn't look like it helped much, though."

Greene gave me a sharp look. "What do you

mean?"

"I could be wrong."

As we approached, I could see how hot the fire had been. Steel trash dumpsters near the buildings had melted, as had a car left there overnight.

"That was the night watchman's car," the investigator said. "He got out alive."

Shawna, the witch who represented the owner group, chanted an incantation, then led us to the door. The front of the building showed no apparent damage but was coated with soot.

She opened the door, and smoke billowed out.

"Oh, no!" she shrieked.

Karen and Meagan turned to look at me.

"If the wards allow air to pass, then they might also allow smoke to pass. You have to be very careful about how you craft such protective spells to ensure they protect you completely," I said.

"The wards at your house and at the nursery allow air through," Karen said.

"Yes, but my wards are specifically constructed to only allow certain molecules to pass," I said. Just because you can perform magic doesn't mean your education should neglect science." I gestured toward the inside of the store. "Otherwise, you can end up with a mess like this. Far too many witches are in a hurry to show off their power when they should be studying the details and intricacies of their craft. I'm not a very strong witch, but I pay attention to details when I cast a spell." My mother, an alchemist and apothecary, had trained me. She drilled into me that when I was mixing stuff people planned to ingest, a screw up could kill someone.

We donned masks and ventured into the store. It

87

was immediately apparent that all the soft goods were ruined—clothing, furnishings, any unsealed foodstuffs. Rather than escaping unscathed, I estimated that at least half of what was in the store would end up in a landfill. The building itself would take months to renovate, but I doubted the Sunrise Coven would bother. They'd take the insurance money and open a store somewhere else.

"We're ruined," the Sunrise witch wailed.

"Don't you have insurance?" Meagan asked.

The look on the Greene's face twisted into something savage. "No, we don't! We warded it! Why would we waste money on insurance?"

I had to admit, it pissed me off every time I wrote a check to the insurance company, but I did it anyway. The policy didn't have a magic exclusion. I suddenly wondered how long it would be before insurance companies figured out the new reality. I'd need to pay attention to any changes in my policy.

While we accompanied the investigator through the ruins of the rest of the mall, Meagan asked me, "What do you figure? Fireballs?"

I shook my head. "I don't think so. I think they cast some sort of combustion spell."

"We think it started in several places," the investigator said.

"Could be," I said. "The thing is, the outer walls are concrete and block, the framework inside is steel. Concrete doesn't burn very well, even when subjected to magical fireballs. A combustion spell could set off anything inside that was flammable."

The investigator looked thoughtful. "I don't know anything about magic," he said, "but that makes sense. You can cast a spell on something you can't see?"

I nodded. "You would cast a spell to heat up an open space and anything combustible would catch when the temperatures got hot enough."

"And you could do that?"

"Me? No. I don't do fire on that scale. If I wanted to destroy the mall, I'd burst all the water pipes and flood the place. I'm not sure if their wards would have protected them against that, either."

We spent about an hour at the mall, then Meagan and Karen took me to visit the scene of a couple of homes that had burned. Both belonged to members of the Sunrise Coven. The witches living at both houses had escaped, though one woman was taken to the hospital for smoke inhalation. I shuddered looking at them, thinking about what might have happened to my house if my wards hadn't held.

Then we drove to a house in Kalorama Heights, one of the ritziest parts of DC. The house sat across from Rock Creek Park, and there wasn't much left of it except the stone walls. I had a couple of clients in the neighborhood, and knew the houses cost more millions than I could even dream of.

"At least four people died here," Meagan said. "We haven't found the bodies of the children yet. Our intelligence says that the family weren't members of the Sunrise Coven, but they were allied in some way. Personal friends of Shawna Greene and some others on the council."

We walked around the property. A small cottage in the back had also burned, but the detached garage was untouched.

"One body was found in the cottage, the other

three in the house," Meagan said. "They were burned so badly that we haven't identified them individually yet. A Stephan Rosenthal and his wife Gertrude, their two children, the housekeeper, and the gardener lived here."

"This one is odd," Karen said. "You can feel the residual traces of magic, but they also used an accelerant—probably gasoline. Also, three of the four bodies we found had their skulls crushed. It looks as though they were beaten to death before the fire."

I wandered over to the cottage. Like the house, it was built of stone, and while the outside walls still stood, the roof had collapsed, and the interior was ash.

"I don't smell any gasoline here," I said, "although I do at the main house."

"The body in the cottage wasn't beaten, either" Karen said.

Something bothered me—a faint magical residual—and I walked around the property trying to figure it out. I couldn't feel it in the back, but it grew stronger as I walked back around to the front. Passing the front of the house, the feeling started to diminish.

Sure enough, there was a strong feeling of living magic directly in front of the house, and it grew stronger as I walked toward the street. It didn't stop there, so I kept going, past the sidewalk on the other side and down into Rock Creek Park. By then I was sure I followed a trail.

The area was overgrown with trees and brush, with numerous fallen branches. I couldn't walk in a straight line, but I could tell when I deviated from the trail I followed. I came upon a drop off and slid down the embankment about four feet. The trail ended at that point. The tunnel's mouth was spelled, and a dispel-glamour spell didn't affect it at all. Magic radiated from the hole, but the fear was far stronger. I sketched a rune and said a Word. Nothing happened.

Karen had been following me, and she came up close. "What is it?" she whispered.

"I think I found the missing children. The trick is going to be overcoming their fear. One of them spins very strong illusions. I've cast two different spells and can't penetrate it."

She nodded and moved around me. "I'm Karen Wen-li of the FBI's Paranormal Crimes Unit," she announced. "We're investigating a fire across the street." While she talked, she moved her hands in an intricate pattern. A hole, large enough for a man to crawl into, revealed itself.

I whistled a low, warbling note and waited. A couple of minutes later, two Fairies flew up and hovered in front of my face. I explained what I wanted, and they whirled away and hung in front of the tunnel, peering inside and chattering to each other.

"I'm going to send my friends in to see if you're all right," I called. "They're just going to see if anyone is hurt and needs any help, so don't be afraid, and please don't hurt them." To the Fairies, in Low Elvish, I said, "See if there are any hurt children in there."

One of the Fairies flew into the tunnel, and the other one slowly followed. Karen gave me a look, and the expression on her face told me she was holding her breath just as I was. We waited.

It took about five minutes, but the male Fairy flew out and landed on my shoulder. Soon, the other Fairy emerged, flying slowly backward. It looked as though she was encouraging someone to follow her.

A head of brown hair poked out. Karen squatted

91

and held out her identification. "It's okay," she said. "We're here to protect you."

The girl turned her eyes toward me. "Hello," I said. "You've met my Fairy friends. Have you ever met an Elf before? I'm Kellana."

Her eyes widened, and her mouth fell open.

"I'm a good witch, sort of like Glenda in the Wizard of Oz," I said. "You're a witch, too, aren't you? You're very good with illusions." I pointed at Karen. "Karen's an illusion witch, too."

We waited.

"Is that really a Fairy?" Her voice was achingly young.

"Yes, honey, that's really a Fairy," Karen said. "Are you Elise? Is your brother with you?"

"Yes, ma'am." She glanced toward me, then said, "Are the bad people gone?"

"Yes, they're gone. The police are at your house, and Kellana and I came looking for you. Come on. I'll bet you're hungry and thirsty."

The girl crawled out of the hole, then turned and helped her little brother. I estimated she was about twelve, and he was eight or nine. When both were standing, Elise looked up at Karen and said, "Those people killed my parents. A woman beat my mother until..." her voice trailed off and her face screwed up as though she was going to cry, but she bit her lip and struggled to maintain her composure. She put an arm around her brother and pulled him close.

I stepped a few feet away and pulled out my phone. When Cassiel answered, I said, "I need your skills. I have two kids here who saw their parents murdered." I gave him the address. "We're in the woods across the street, down by the stream. I don't think the kids have seen their house yet."

"It's burned?" Cass asked.

"Yeah. Maybe you could bring a couple of blankets and some sandwiches or something to eat. They've been hiding in the park since night before last."

As I walked back, I reached in my bag and pulled out a water bottle, then handed it to Elise. She gave it to her brother. He took a long drink and handed it back for her to drink.

"What's your name?" I asked him.

"Robert."

"Do you like dried fruit? I have dried peaches and dried apples."

He nodded so hard I thought his head might fly off.

"Well, let's sit down here and let you kids eat something," I said. Karen gave me a puzzled look.

"I have a friend, a healer who's going to come and check you guys out. You've been out here a long time by yourselves."

If the children were impressed by the Fairies, they were completely awed by Cassiel winging in twenty minutes later. I wasn't going to try and explain the difference between an Angel and a Nephilim to a couple of kids, but it probably didn't matter. They just stared at him with their mouths open and their eyes popping out of their heads.

Cassiel opened a small backpack and pulled out a thermos of hot chocolate, carrots, grilled-cheese sandwiches, and a couple of apples. I detected Bess's hand in that. Cass was a sweetheart in many ways, but his kitchen skills weren't particularly notable.

While the kids gobbled their first real meal in more than twenty-four hours, Cass checked them out,

93

then put his hand on each of their heads in turn and cast a spell. When he did that, I saw their faces smooth out and their bodies relax. That's what I hoped he would do when I called him. As the daughter of a healer, I knew how important it was to deal with their mental and emotional trauma as early as possible.

Cass drew Karen and me aside. "I've treated their trauma. You know the pain of such events decreases with time. The spell hastens that process. It won't interfere with their memories, but it creates a distance from the events. You should be able to question them, if you need to."

Karen nodded. We went back and sat with the kids while they finished their meal. When they finished eating, I poured them some more hot chocolate.

"Can you tell me what happened?" Karen asked Elise.

It was an ugly story. Their mother answered the door and five people, a woman and four men, forced their way in. The woman hit Mrs. Rosenthal with a metal rod and knocked her down. The intruders threatened to kill her unless Mr. Rosenthal opened the vault, then they dragged him upstairs. While they were gone, the woman finished beating Mrs. Rosenthal to death. Elise and her brother witnessed that, hidden in a corner by an illusion spell the girl cast.

When the men came back downstairs, the group spent almost an hour hauling artworks out of the house and putting them in a van and an SUV. When they were finished, they spread gasoline throughout the house, tossed a fireball inside, and left.

"My grandparents built the tunnel a long time

ago," Elise said, "when they came here from Germany. When those people found Olga, our housekeeper, and killed her, too, I took Robert into the closet, and we went down into the tunnel."

"You seem to be pretty good with illusions," Karen said.

Elise preened a little. "I'm better than Mama, and she was all the way grown up."

"Do you suppose you could create an illusion of the people who broke into your house?"

Elise was very good. It took her about five minutes, and she could only hold the illusions of two people at a time, but we got a good look at the intruders. The look of hate on the woman's face as she beat Mrs. Rosenthal to death wasn't something I'd soon forget.

Karen called Meagan, who called someone to come and take the children away. After they were gone, she listened to Karen tell Elise's tale.

"Rosenthal was an art dealer," Meagan said, "as was his father. The family came here from Germany in the late thirties. We'll find out who the insurance company is and get a list of the art that was in the house. It sounds like this was a planned robbery rather than part of the war between the covens."

I wasn't ready to concede that. It sounded more like some of the Bluegrass Coven taking advantage of the chaos. Whether the coven leaders endorsed the robbery or not, the Rosenthals weren't the only people who died that night.

Chapter 10

It was kind of funny watching the news on TV as various government officials tried to explain all the fires. They could have used someone to help them keep their stories straight. One would think that as much practice as Humans had with lying, they would be better at it.

What wasn't funny was the Sunrise Coven's retaliation. Karen kept me informed as to the magical incidents the PCU investigated. A group of five young witches from the Bluegrass Coven were found in an alley near Tyson's Corner in Virginia, just across the river from DC. Three didn't have any detectable cause of death, the other two looked as though they exploded.

One of the Bluegrass council members was shot on the street one day. The following day, one of the Sunrise Coven members was shot through her kitchen window with a high-powered rifle. Dave and Meagan said what was happening reminded them of an old-fashioned gang war. That reminded me about the Werewolf territorial conflict. When I asked Karen about the Weres, she gave me a puzzled look.

"We haven't had any incidents with the wolves," she said. "With the covens blowing up, I haven't even thought about them."

I doubted the wolves were being passive. I mentioned the issue to Isabella.

"They're just being quiet about it," she said. "The shifters are even more used to living in the shadows than the witches are. I'd guess their battles are taking place in the shadows, probably at night, and they aren't calling hospitals or cops when they take casualties."

I remained wary, unable to shake off the feeling that the Savage River pack hadn't forgotten about me.

Isabella had a meeting with the realtor, and we loaded four red oak saplings in her truck, so I could begin constructing the wards to protect the property. I chose red oak because it was a fast-growing species and native to the area.

We met Ruth, the realtor and a witchy friend of mine, at the house. While she and Isabella sat down with contracts and other paperwork, I hauled the ten-foot trees to the corners of the property. It wasn't easy. I had to maneuver around bushes that needed trimming, fallen tree limbs, and assorted trash. The house was beautiful, but no one had maintained the yard in a long time.

For each tree, I marked off a point ten feet in from the corner of the lot, then sketched a rune and said a Word. Soil displaced, leaving a hole. I placed the tree in the hole, cut off the burlap holding the root ball, and then pushed the dirt back into the hole.

I had just finished planting the first tree and started toward the house to get a hose to water it in, when a large wolf rose from behind a bush. From the corners of my eyes, I could see movement of more wolves, and I was bare handed, other than the knife I used to cut off the root wrapping. I threw the knife and hit the wolf in its back leg.

My bag, made of Dragon skin by a mage and containing a pocket dimension that held as much as a large closet, sat on the ground a few feet behind me. I never went anywhere without it, and never worried it might be stolen. I had set a binding spell on the bag, and when I took it off, it tended to follow me around like a lost puppy.

Reaching out, I called the bag, and when it hit my hand, I reached into it to draw out the sword inside.

"Isabella!" I called as I tried to maneuver myself into a position where a tree or a bush could help protect my back. A wolf slipped behind me. I spun and swung at it, slicing it across the shoulder. With a cry of pain, it scampered away from me. Stepping toward an overgrown lilac bush, I whirled back to face the pack and was able to back into the bush.

It still wasn't a good position. A wolf feinted on my right, and as soon as I turned my head in that direction, it jumped back, and a wolf on my left dived in and snapped at me. They were too close for me to use a paintball gun without breathing the fumes myself, so I drew my athame with my left hand.

"Isabella!" I wasn't sure she could hear me.

In addition to the wounded wolf, I faced seven more. They circled and feinted, and occasionally, when they thought I was distracted enough, actually attacked. In less than five minutes, I and several of the wolves were bleeding from multiple wounds.

Isabella roared. The sound froze the wolves, and I took advantage, beheading the largest one. That brought the pack's attention back to me.

From the direction of the house, the sounds of the gods-own dog-and-cat fight erupted. Isabella against a Werewolf was bad news for the wolf. But a pack of them, using the same tactics they were using against me, might get lucky and take her down.

A wolf trying to grab my ankle brought me back to my own problems. I kicked it in the head, then stabbed a different wolf coming from another direction. Movement from the other side alerted me just in time. I raised the athame and the leaping wolf drove itself onto my blade. It crashed into me, knocking me down and snapping at my face even as the light of life faded in its eyes.

A sharp pain erupted in my leg, and then another in my sword arm as a wolf's teeth closed on me. In a panic, I struggled to move the dead wolf off me and free my athame.

Isabella's rough snarl sounded close, and then mortally wounded wolves screamed. The pressure on my leg ceased with a pain even sharper than before, and then the wolf biting my arm let go. It leaped away from me but died in the air as a sharp-clawed paw tore its throat out.

I finally managed to push the wolf away, then rolled and rose to my knees. My sword was gone, my right arm useless, but I held the athame ready to try and defend myself.

Beyond the blood-soaked jaguar, I saw Ruth holding a crystal the size of a golf ball in her hand. A beam of light shot out from it and fried a wolf that was trying to run away. The only wolves I could see were dead ones.

Everything went dark. The ground was hard when it hit me.

My bedroom ceiling greeted me when I awoke. The bed felt like mine, and it was very comforting.

Lifting my right arm took a bit of an effort because I felt weak and lethargic. White scars—new scars—on my forearm told me that the nightmare I vaguely remembered had really occurred. I moved my left leg, bending the knee and pulling it toward me. The calf felt stiff with an unnatural pulling in the muscle.

Lifting my head, I looked around the room and

discovered Cassiel, fast asleep, sitting in a chair near the bed. The door opened, and Bess floated in carrying a tray.

"I felt you wake," she said, bringing the tray to the bed. "Sit up."

I pushed myself into a sitting position.

"Put a pillow behind you."

I grabbed Cass's pillow and did as the little Brownie directed. She set the tray down on my lap. I saw a bowl of broth, a bowl of porridge, a large glass of fruit juice, and a cup of tea. Even using magic, it would have taken me a few minutes to prepare that food. I wondered how Bess knew to start preparing the food before I woke up.

"Do not spill," Bess said, then turned and floated out of the room. I glanced at Cass, who was still asleep.

I finished the broth and was working on the porridge when Cass woke up. He cracked an eye, and when he discovered I was awake, the other eye came open, and he sat up, then stood. Approaching the bed, he said, "How are you feeling?"

"Hungry, but Bess brought this. How long have I been out?"

"Three days. You were in pretty bad shape. Nothing life-threatening, but you lost a lot of blood."

I nodded and drank some more juice.

"The arm was broken?" I asked holding up my spoon.

"Yes, both bones. I don't know if you can use your sword left handed, but it will be some time before you get the strength back in that arm. You're also going to probably have a bit of a limp. I healed your leg, but I can't replace the chunk that wolf bit out of your calf.

100

You'll have to rebuild the muscle over time."

I took a deep breath. "Thank you. How's Isabella? She had blood all over her."

He shook his head. "Very little of it hers. I think your friend Ruth broke a fingernail. She was very upset about it, but I told her that was beyond my expertise. As for the Werewolves, twelve dead. Your PCU friends came and took the bodies."

"You called the PCU?"

"Isabella did. She said they provided waste-disposal services."

I almost snorted my juice at that. She had a low opinion of the PCU as a whole, though she liked Dave and Karen.

"She also told them to expect a lot more Werewolf bodies. I believe her final word on the subject was, 'You may be willing to put up with this kind of shit, but I am not.'"

"I didn't even get started casting the wards around her new house."

"Meagan from the PCU cast some, and Ruth cast a spell she said would warn of Werewolves. They said the spells would hold until you could do something more permanent. Ed went over to Isabella's and finished planting the trees. He also sent a crew over yesterday to clean up the property. Isabella tried to pay him, but he refused to bill her or take any money. Told her she could argue with you about it."

He gave me a dose of one of my potions, then took the tray back to the kitchen when I finished eating. While he was gone, I thought about the wolves. So far, I had been reactive to the threats from coven and pack. I really didn't want to get involved in the quarrels between the locals and their rivals from West

Virginia, but I seemed to get dragged in every time I turned around. So far, only one side seemed to consider me a target. Perhaps I should talk to their enemies and see if I could get some help.

Chapter 11

I spent a couple of more days lying around until I got bored, then I had Isabella drive me to work. By the end of the week, I felt stronger. But every time I stood and tried to walk, or tried to lift something heavier than a pencil, I was reminded of my wounds. Cass gave me some exercises to do, but it was slow going.

One day, I called the alpha of the Chesapeake Werewolf pack.

"Mr. Vance? This is Kellana Rogirsdottir. I'd like to meet with you concerning the Savage River pack."

Harold Vance and I weren't friends. The last time I saw him in person, I roughed him up and killed two of his pack members. To my surprise, he didn't cancel our contract to maintain the landscaping at his estate north of DC.

We agreed to meet for lunch at a restaurant in Bethesda the following day. Isabella and Cassiel accompanied me, and I assumed Vance would have a full complement of thugs guarding him. Vance controlled most of what the FBI called 'organized crime' in the Mid-Atlantic region—prostitution, loan sharking, extortion, drugs, guns, bribery, and anything else Vance felt might earn him a dollar. Being comprised of Werewolves, his organization dominated any Human gangs that operated in their space.

From what the PCU could tell me, the Savage River pack had happily lived in the West Virginia mountains for decades, if not longer. Rumors and myths of Werewolves in that area had circulated for centuries. But when the veils shredded, thousands of wolves, cats, and eagles had crossed into Earth's realm from the shifters' realm of Were. Several hundred new wolves joined the Savage River pack, the pack's leadership changed, and they moved into more urban environments. With a strong presence in Morgantown, Pittsburg, and Charleston, they had evidently decided to challenge Vance's pack in Washington.

Vance had told me he would make reservations, but I didn't expect him to reserve the whole damned restaurant. We walked in and found the place deserted, except for one table, and the Weres in Human form standing guard around the room. We sat down at the table with Vance and one other Were I didn't know. I introduced Isabella and Cassiel simply as friends of mine. From the expression on Vance's face, he didn't recognize either of them.

"We've already ordered," Vance said, motioning to the menus in front of us. "I'll take care of the check." I took one look at the prices, realized I would probably never eat there again, and ordered the lobster salad. Cass ordered a fish dish, and Isabella ordered a huge rare steak, which garnered a nod of approval from Vance and his crony.

"So, Miss Rogirsdottir, you said you wish to discuss the Savage River pack?" Vance asked.

I nodded. "For some reason, they've decided I'm an enemy of theirs, or maybe that you're a friend of mine. I really don't know, but they and their friends in the Bluegrass Coven have declared war on me."

"That's too bad," Vance said.

I waited, but he didn't say anything else.

"You don't seem too worried by another pack moving into your territory," I observed.

"A bunch of country hicks," Vance said with a hint of a snarl. "They don't know what they're doing. We'll take care of business, it's just a matter of time."

Vance's associate leaned forward with a puzzled expression. "What was that you said about the Bluegrass Coven?"

"The Bluegrass Coven and the Savage River pack have an alliance of some sort," I told them. "Didn't you know that?"

The two Weres exchanged a look that told me they hadn't known.

"You haven't seen any new drugs show up in your territory?" Cassiel asked. Their reaction told me that they had.

Cass smiled. "Spell-enhanced marijuana or other spelled drugs would be new and exciting. I've seen it in other realms. For the coven, having Werewolf enforcers keeps them from getting their hands too dirty."

"You heard about the fires a couple of weeks ago?" I asked. Everyone in the city knew about the fires. "That was the Bluegrass Coven launching a strike against the Sunrise Coven. They tried to burn my house. You own a lot of property. Think about it."

That hit home, but the reaction was far more extreme than I expected. Vance almost came out of his chair, hands on the table, and snarled, "How did they try to burn your house?"

Taken literally aback, I leaned as far back in my chair as I could. "Uh, a witch. She threw fireballs at it."

"Scummy bastards!"

Isabella, snarky smile on her face, leaned forward and said, "I take it that you had a fire or two?"

Vance visibly struggled to get his emotions under control, finally drinking half a glass of water. "Yes, a warehouse and a couple of other properties. We couldn't figure out how they started. The fire marshal finally declared it must have been faulty wiring. One building I'd believe faulty wiring, but three?" He shook himself like a dog. "No accelerants, no real reason for the fires."

"The fire marshal wasn't looking for magic," I said.

Vance's companion leaned forward. "You called this meeting. What do you think we can do for each other?"

"I'm sorry, I missed your name," I responded.

He chuckled. "Georgio Moretti. I work for Mr. Vance."

The waiter showed up with our meals, and the conversation was put aside for the moment. As our water was refilled—no one at the table was drinking alcohol—and the waiter sorted everything out, I thought about what I wanted, and what I was willing to trade Vance to get it.

"I need help with the Savage River Werewolves," I finally said after the waiter left. "I was ambushed by fifteen wolves, and I need help handling the numbers. In exchange, I can supply you with wolfsbane in a form you can handle, and I can cast wards over some of your assets that will prevent fires."

"And where does Bernard Conrad come into this?" Moretti asked.

I looked up from my salad in surprise. Conrad was leader of the most powerful Werecat pride in the Mid-Atlantic. "He doesn't, as far as I know. Why?"

Moretti nodded at Isabella and sniffed. "You have a cat with you."

She grinned at him and his face froze. "Yes, I am a

cat, Señor, but I'm not from Were. I'm a different kind of cat."

"The jaguar," Vance said quietly. I had shown up at Vance's home once with Isabella in her shifted form. Vance hadn't been home, but I knew he'd heard about our visit.

Isabella winked at him and returned her attention to her steak.

Moretti shifted his eyes toward Cassiel.

"He's my boyfriend," I said, and took a bite of my salad. Let them guess. None of the Weres in the room stood taller than Cass's chin—or mine, for that matter—but he was twice as wide as I was.

"How many wolves do you think you need?" Moretti asked.

"About thirty, around the clock." I watched Moretti's eyes widen, but Vance didn't react. "A few to patrol around my home and my business. The rest to play bodyguard when I'm out in the city. The witches and wolves from West Virginia are watching me, possibly intercepting my cell phone. They've ambushed me twice when I've gone out, and they shouldn't have known where I was going."

"When can you start?" Vance asked.

"I can fireproof your house this afternoon."

Vance nodded. "You've got a deal. But you take care of my wolves. Understood?"

I met his eyes. "Understood. They play straight with me, and I'll treat them as my own, and you know how I treat my own. Just make sure they know not to get in my line of fire."

"That's good enough for me," Vance said. He turned to Moretti. "Detail some people who have some sense. She won't put up with morons."

"Are you going to cast wards around his whole estate?" Isabella asked.

I laughed. "I don't know how to tell one pack from the other. No, we're just going to use that foul-smelling stuff I've been mixing the past couple of days on the house itself." I had prepared two fifty-gallon barrels of fire suppressant. The chemicals were easy to obtain, and there wasn't anything special about the mixture—until it was spelled.

We swung by my house to pick up supplies, then the three of us drove to Vance's estate in Silver Spring. Vance's place covered about two and a half acres, surrounded by a ten-foot brick wall. Forest covered about an acre, while the rest was mostly lawn and a paved area around a swimming pool.

We put the barrels onto low carts with wheels. A pump with two hoses attached went into each barrel. I gave a hose to each of my friends, then showed them how to apply the retardant. "Just shoot the liquid on the angles—inside and outside corners—and along the edges of the roof," I said. "No need to cover the walls."

We were about two-thirds done when I heard a shout of alarm. Turning toward the voice, I saw a bunch of Werewolves racing through the front gate and attacking the guards. Gunshots rang out.

"Heads up!" Cassiel shouted.

Looking up, I saw a fireball descending toward the house. I sketched a rune, raised my hand toward the flames, and spoke a Word. The fireball splashed against the invisible shield in the air.

"Cass, Isabella, back away from the house!" I called. If I could only protect half of the house, that was better than nothing. I sketched the rune for fire, then overlaid it with a protection rune, and overlaid that with a rune of binding. I spoke the Word to invoke the spell, and watched the walls of the house shimmer, sparkle, then gradually return to normal. I would need to cast the spell again on the parts of the house we hadn't covered, but the front of the house would repel any more fireballs.

When I turned, I saw a lot more wolves coming through the gate, but also some coming from the other side of the house. I knew there was a back gate through the wall. More fireballs arced over the wall, luckily aimed toward the part of the house I had protected.

Some of Vance's pack shifted, some stayed in Human form and fired guns. I pulled my paintball gun out of my bag and made sure it was loaded with sleepy gas and not wolfsbane. I didn't want to kill any of my new allies.

Unfortunately, the paintball gun was too heavy for my weakened right arm to hold steady enough to aim properly. Pulling my sword from my bag with my left hand, I staked it into the ground in front of me, so I'd have it handy, then used my left hand to steady the gun. The gun's range was about a hundred feet, and before the closest wolf came into range, I laid down a line of sleepy-gas paintballs in front of them.

Most of the charging wolves veered off, but three tried to run through the gas. That was a bad decision, and all three went down.

"I've heard about that pink stuff," Moretti said as he walked up beside me carrying a submachine gun. "You know it permanently stains leather."

"I'll keep that in mind," I said. The summer before, I dropped a couple of paintballs inside of a luxury Mercedes. Personally, I thought the black car looked good with a Pepto-Bismol pink interior. "I told you they've been following me."

"I never doubted you. Interesting timing on this attack, though."

A large jaguar bounded up on my other side. I could see several knots of wolves fighting in front of me, and more wolves coming through the front gate. Moretti fired a burst toward the gate, and a couple of wolves jerked and stumbled.

"Where's Cassiel?" I asked Isabella. She turned partway to face the house and held up one paw as though pointing up.

"He's around back?" I asked. The large cat nodded her head and swiveled back to face the wolves. "I set the spell on this side of the house," I told her. "I'm going around back to see if Cass needs any help."

Both the cat and the Werewolf with the submachinegun nodded without looking at me. I pulled my sword out of the ground and trotted around the house.

Two unfriendly wolves greeted me when I turned the second corner. Considering that I had been there working on the house for almost three hours, I assumed all of Vance's wolves knew I was on their side. That relieved me of any indecision, and I reacted to the closest wolf's snarl with a swinging sword. The wolf was slow.

The second wolf launched himself teeth first. I shrunk to my smaller size and watched him sail over me. He landed and whirled about, presenting his side. My sword slid through him, just behind his shoulder.

Thanking the Goddess and my father for his insistence on my sword training including both hands, I snuck around the next corner and looked down the long back of Vance's house.

I didn't see any more hostile wolves, but a fireball flew over the wall toward the house. Before I could do anything, an invisible hand slapped the fireball backward, where it hit the inside of the wall, the flames spreading harmlessly onto the green lawn. I noted there were three more scorched spots on the wall.

Three stories up, Cassiel waved to me from his perch on a balcony railing. The house wasn't built the way Humans would build it. The front looked conventional enough, but rather than one rich family, more than forty core pack members lived in the place. Along the back, with a view of the forest, three long balconies stretched the length of the building.

"You should come up," he called. "There are wolves roaming around down there." He swung his hand, and another fireball reversed its course.

A couple of furry faces peered through the open back gate a hundred feet away, and I fired a paintball in that direction. Tucking the gun into my bag, I leaped upward, most of the push coming from my good right leg. My feet hit the edge of the balcony, and I grabbed onto the railing with my right hand.

No sooner had I steadied myself than several wolves showed up, and one leaped at me, snapping at my ankle. I guess he didn't notice the sword in my left hand. It was his last mistake, and his body fell in a heap, knocking down one of his fellows. The rest of them decided not to jump at me, and I scrambled over the railing.

I put my hand in my bag, and my fingers curled around the paintball gun, then I thought better of it. Setting off sleepy gas directly below me didn't seem like the best idea. I set my sword aside and pulled out my bow and quiver.

"Are you all right?" Cassiel called.

"Yeah, I'm fine," I replied. "I cast the spell to protect the front of the house. How far did you and Isabella get on this side?"

"Up to the ends of the balconies on both sides."

That left a fairly large space that still needed to be covered. "Have they tried anything other than the fireballs?" I asked as I watched him reject two more.

"No. They've been amazingly uncreative. Or maybe that's all they can do."

I peeked over the railing and saw one of the wolves start to shift. He had a small bag around his neck, but it was too small to carry much in the way of clothing. It was large enough to hold a pistol, however. The sound of gunfire came from all over the compound, and I worried that Cass was an easy target.

"Maybe you should be a little more discreet," I called. "Or can you dodge bullets?"

The spaces between the balusters holding up the railing didn't elicit a real feeling of security, and Cass was sitting on the railing in plain sight.

The wolf finished changing into his Human form, slipped the bag's strap over his head, and reached inside. My arrow took him in the chest.

The rest of the wolves scattered, but one of them grabbed that bag on his way out of my sight.

The nearest door into the house was unlocked when I checked it. I left it slightly ajar, in case I needed to exit the balcony in a hurry.

The witch or witches beyond the wall continued to launch fireballs, and Cass continued to reject them. I didn't know how many of Vance's pack were on the grounds, but the invading force contained over a

112

hundred wolves that I had seen, plus witches and mages. I wondered what they hoped to accomplish. Vance's Chesapeake pack had more than two thousand members scattered from Philadelphia to Richmond, and I was sure a lot of them were currently on their way to the estate.

Movement at the gate entrance drew my attention. A man—a clothed man—stood there. I fired a couple of paintballs, and the pink mist hid the gate. A minute later, the man stepped through the mist, which didn't appear to touch him, and walked toward the house. He was dressed in some kind of ceremonial robes, like a priest of some religion. As he approached, I was able to tell he was a mage, not a witch, and he radiated considerable power.

The mage stopped about fifty feet from the building. His head was completely bald, or shaved, and he appeared to be a Human in his fifties or sixties. I judged him to be around six feet, and though the robes hid his body, he didn't appear to be either thin or fat.

I sketched a rune and said the Word to invoke a protective shield. "Cass, shield yourself!" I yelled.

The mage raised his hands, and fire poured forth, expanding with distance and bathing the balcony where I stood. I watched the wooden railing and balusters char, and while I was protected, I could feel the heat.

I sketched a different rune and tucked my hand behind my back as I said the Word to invoke the spell. I felt the drain of energy immediately. Although the house was surrounded by forest and lawn, I stood on a concrete slab, and couldn't draw energy from the plants. The spell would be so much easier and more powerful if I stood with my back pressed against an oak or yew or rowan tree, but all I had to pull from was my own life energy.

The flames seemed to roil about me forever, but the burst probably lasted less than half a minute. As soon as the flames died, I dissolved my shield and hurled the ball of pure life energy I held at the mage.

I ducked, and so I didn't see the instant when the energy hit, but I heard the explosion. Peering over the railing, I saw a small, shallow crater, and about ten feet away a pile of bloody, dirty, priestly robes that didn't move.

"*Danu merde*," Cass's voice came from above me in Elvish, "what kind of spell was that?"

"Life energy," I shouted back.

"Goddess, girl, that's dangerous!"

I slumped against the wall behind me and muttered, "Don't I know it."

Chapter 12

The attack on Vance's estate—home den of the Chesapeake pack—lasted about half an hour. When members of the pack that were called in to defend the place arrived, the attackers faded into the surrounding forest.

Members of the Chesapeake pack hunted the interlopers, and caught a few, but by nightfall even the most dedicated hunters had straggled back.

Cass was kept busy healing the injured, and Vance called in his usual doctors and healers. The final toll came to fifteen members of the Chesapeake pack killed, and thirty injured. We found fifty-five bodies that no one could identify, including the flame-throwing mage.

I took a potion and stood for about an hour leaning against a tree near the house. I would have liked to sit down, but the strong odor of wolf urine around the base of the tree discouraged me. I felt somewhat restored by the time Moretti called me into the house. Vance's wife had sent out for some food other than raw meat, and I gratefully ate a couple of pieces of fruit and a few slices of cheese pizza.

"It seems like a rather high price to pay for delivering a message," I said.

"Without you, it would have been a lot more than a message," Vance snarled, pacing the room. The normally suave, condescending crime lord was barely under control, and a lot hairier than normal. "They would have burned the house, and probably slaughtered all of us. That attack comprised more than two hundred wolves and a dozen witches. They truly meant to cut off the snake's head and absorb my pack."

"So why now?" Isabella asked. "Just coincidence that we were here?"

Moretti shook his head. "I don't think so. I think they had this planned, and when Miss Rogirsdottir showed up, they decided they could take her out as a bonus. What they didn't count on was the reason she came."

"And why am I so damned important?" I asked.

"I'm not sure they could tell you themselves. Do you know what a catalyst is?" a woman's voice came from the door of the room. I turned to see one of the healers Vance had called in, a witch named Gretchen Schneider who ran a paranormal emergency room in Fairfax County, across the Potomac River from DC. She had a slight German accent, and when I had spoken to her in German, she answered in the same language.

"I'm an alchemist," I answered.

"People can also be catalysts," she said. "They tend to be present at inflection points. The gods often work through them to accomplish their goals."

I chuckled. "That's a bunch of bullshit. Rulers have sycophants write their histories to make them seem heroic, or to justify all the people they slaughtered to gain power. The gods don't give a damn."

Isabella barked out a laugh and everyone turned to her. "Don't mind me. I don't know anything about gods and goddesses," she said.

I glared at her. As the demigod daughter of a goddess and an archdemon, she probably knew more about the inhabitants of the upper realms than almost anyone on Earth.

"You're not buying into this nonsense, are you?" I asked.

Isabella shrugged. "Occam's razor. If the shoe fits, and you don't have another, you either have to wear it or go barefoot."

"Is this your attempt at philosophy?"

"Things tend to happen in your vicinity, and often the resolution revolves around you."

I rolled my eyes. "So, all of this carnage is my fault?"

"No," Cassiel said from behind Gretchen, "but I wouldn't be surprised if you're involved in solving the problem."

I wanted to kill both of them. "I don't want to be involved at all."

"And that's why you came to see us?" Moretti asked with a raised eyebrow and a sardonic grin. "I believe your non-involvement almost got you killed."

With five hundred Werewolves patrolling the property and its accesses, we obviously weren't needed anymore. I told Vance we'd return the following day to finish the spell. True to his word, he sent six cars full of Werewolves with us.

We dropped off two cars at the nursery. "You can't go into the property," I told the men we left there, "but patrol the outside, both close around the fence, and also look for anyone who might be watching the place." Two of the Weres stayed in their Human forms with their cars, and the rest shifted.

Cass helped me pull a trough out of the nursery, set it next to the fence, and fill it with water. We put another trough in the truck, drove home, and I set it up in my back courtyard. I might not particularly like Werewolves, but that was no reason to deprive an animal of water.

As we crawled into bed that night, staggering from exhaustion, I asked Cass, "You don't really believe in that catalyst of the gods crap, do you? I mean, I studied basic cosmology, as did all students in our schools, but your father was an Angel." According to the Angels, they had a direct pipeline to some of the gods. "So, I assume you studied that sort of thing more than a farmer's daughter."

He sighed. "You know I never lived in Heaven or attended Angelic schools. But, yes, I've studied the gods and their legends. Are there people who are favored by the gods? People chosen to advance the gods' will? Possibly. Are there people who appear at specific times in history that change the course of history? Absolutely."

Cass rolled over so he faced me. "Why did Isabella decide you were the person to find an artifact of the gods? Why did the Icelandic and Irish Elves choose you to find a Dragon's egg? Why do a bunch of crazies think you're an impediment to their plans for global conquest, or whatever in the hell the local paranormals think is going on? And why do another bunch of crazies think it's important to keep you alive? I don't know, and I don't know that the gods have anything to do with all this, but you have to admit there's a pattern."

I tried to force a shaky smile. "Are you one of the crazies trying to keep me alive?"

Cassiel took me in his arms and kissed me. "I'm just crazy about you," he said as he slid a hand down my body.

We didn't talk much after that.

I arrived at the nursery the following morning as the sun broke the horizon. As I expected, a small mountain of paperwork awaited my attention. I took care of it, spoke with Ed and the kids we had recently hired for our summer crews, and checked on the greenhouses. Ed and Maurine had the business under control, and the Gnomes and Fairies had all the plants in the nursery doing fine.

Isabella, Cassiel, and I showed up at Vance's place mid-morning, and I finished the spell to protect his house. Working all day, I also fireproofed two warehouses and the strip club he used as his business headquarters. I was afraid to ask what the warehouses contained.

The day after that, Cass, Ed, and I helped Isabella move into her new house. Trucks from two different stores delivered her furniture. She was so much shorter than the rest of us, that it was awkward to carry things with her, so I told her to spray the walls of her house with flame retardant while the rest of us dealt with the furniture, and when she was finished, I invoked the protective spell.

Then I spent an hour spelling the trees Ed and I had planted. Isabella looked a little disappointed when I finished and the saplings hadn't changed.

With a laugh, I said, "Don't worry. You'll see the results fairly quickly. These trees grow about two feet a year naturally and reach maturity in thirty or forty years. But with the spells I used, they'll grow about five times that fast."

I expected the wild Fairies to find me, as they always did, and it happened mid-afternoon. A Fairy flew by and saw me. An hour later, about twenty Fairies showed up. When they discovered that "Mama Cat" was moving into the property, and she gave them some chocolate, they launched into a celebration. By evening, their number had swelled.

"You won't need a night watchman," I told Isabella. "They'll keep watch for you." A tipsy Fairy flew by upside down. "It's probably better if you give them fruit juice, though, and save the chocolate as a special reward."

I figured I would come by and plant some of the Fairies' favorite flowers as well.

Chapter 13

"I hear you're having more Werewolf problems," Sarah Faire said when I picked up the phone.

"Is there anywhere that you don't have spies?" I asked.

"If it's any consolation, I haven't had any luck recruiting any of your Fairies."

I had to laugh.

"Kellana, you should think long and hard about getting involved with Harold Vance. That could cause you real problems with the FBI."

"I need numbers. The army isn't volunteering to deploy a regiment to protect me and my property." I cringed as soon as I said it, dreading her response.

"I offered to help you if you help me," she replied. "What makes you think you can trust Vance? If you're not careful, you'll be in over your head before you know it."

"I'm not going into business with Harold Vance. We have an understanding about a limited amount of cooperation."

She snorted. "And you think your understanding of the relationship is the same as his understanding of the relationship? Kellana, I've asked David Torbert to meet with me tomorrow. Will you come?"

"Where's the meeting?"

"At my office."

I hesitated. "Can you get me in the building without being searched?"

"Come in with Torbert as a PCU contractor. Kellana, Beltane is only two weeks away."

With that ominous warning, I agreed to come. For all I knew, Faire had spies in the upper realms.

I left my furry escort outside the Rayburn Office Building. I didn't know why the Weres seemed to think they were inconspicuous. Six burly men, each with a wolf on a leash no thicker than a piece of twine, seemed a little obvious to me.

Despite Torbert's vouching for me, the nosy guards insisted that while I might enter the premises armed, they still had to look in my bag.

"No. That's not going to happen," I told Torbert.

He looked thoughtful, glancing back and forth between the guards and me. "What is the largest thing you have in your bag?"

Torbert had seen me pull a number of things out of the bag, and though I had never explained it to him, he had to suspect what it was. I thought about it.

"I have a couple of blankets, my cloak, two complete changes of clothes, including a spare pair of boots, a cook pot and a skillet, several pounds of food, four water bottles, my sword and a spare, my bow and quiver, and a spare, and a boar spear. Along with some miscellaneous this and that."

He blinked at me, then asked, "A boar spear?"

"Well, I haven't used it in a long time. Since the war, actually. But you never know—"

"When you'll run into a wild boar in downtown Washington?" Torbert finished my sentence.

"It would probably work on a small demon," I protested.

"I think the boar spear will work perfectly for what I have in mind. Turn around and pull it out. You can find it in there, can't you?"

The boar spear was about seven feet long, the narrow leaf-shaped double-edged blade comprising a foot of that length. Two broad wings, about four inches long, extended from the shaft behind the blade. They kept the blade from penetrating too far, so a boar couldn't climb the shaft to get at the hunter.

As I pulled it out, and it kept coming and coming, the guards' eyes got wider and wider.

"Are you sure you want to look in that bag?" Torbert asked. "You're never going to see the bottom of it unless you crawl inside. It's magic." Dropping his voice to a whisper, he said to me, "Pull out one of the bows or swords, whichever is longer."

"Here, hold this," I said to a guard, shoving the handle of the spear at him. Startled, he took it. I reached into the bag and grabbed Alaric's longbow, as long as the spear. Next, I reached for Alaric's sword, eight inches longer than mine. When I had it halfway out of the bag, the guards capitulated.

As we walked down the hallway toward the stairs, Torbert pointed to a ragged hole in the wall. "A demon materialized in this hallway last week. Killed three people before the guards nailed him with demonbane."

"And they want people to walk around unarmed? This isn't a civilized society anymore, you know. The cities are war zones. Is it any better out in smaller towns and rural areas?"

Torbert didn't answer.

It didn't surprise me that all of Faire's staff were Vampires. We were shown into her inner office and asked if we wanted coffee, tea, or water. Both of us declined.

"Thank you for coming," Faire said, indicating chairs for us to sit. "I'll get right to the point. Some of my intelligence indicates a major blowup on Beltane."

"And?" Torbert asked. "Every Beltane and Samhain the past two years has been a catastrophe."

"I'm talking about something worse, possibly as bad as three years ago. Indications are the epicenter of the problems will be here in Washington."

Torbert glanced at me. I shrugged. Hell, I had no idea what she was talking about.

"It might help if you gave us some inkling of where you're getting your information," I suggested.

Faire looked uncomfortable, something I had never seen before. Finally, she said, "I have the exact same prophecy from twelve different clairvoyants, all of whom have proven reliable in the past. These are people who don't know each other and live in different parts of the world."

Torbert looked at me again, skepticism plain on his face. I didn't blame him.

"You'll have to forgive me," I said, trying to be diplomatic, "but I have little experience with such talents."

Faire bolted from her chair, clearly agitated. She turned and looked out the window a long time. Without turning, she said, "I can understand that clairvoyance or precognition is hard to accept, especially when the predictions are usually so vague. But the past two times these people were unanimous in their warnings was just before Beltane three years ago, and last June. Before that, I was as skeptical as you are."

Beltane, when the veils shredded. Then two years later, an artifact of the gods displaced a major chunk

124

of metropolitan Washington and more than ten thousand people to someplace out of Earth's realm.

"What do the astrologers say about the celestial alignments?" I asked. For most witches I knew, that had been the harbinger of doom three years before.

Faire turned back to us. "Ah, there's the issue. People tend to assume that the celestial alignments happened on Beltane three years ago, and then things returned to normal. We're talking celestial here. Such things take a long time to come together, and a long time before they completely resolve. They are still concerning, although different than three years ago, of course. I expect the worst rupturing of the veils since that time, but some of the other alignments signal different problems—more violence and death. One interpretation I've heard links ruptures of the veils with geological and meteorological events in this realm."

"You mean like a volcano or earthquake coinciding with a breach?" Torbert asked.

I took a deep, ragged breath, and both turned to stare at me.

"Earthquakes and volcanoes are so common in Hel that the inhabitants there don't pay any attention to them," I said. "Volcanism in Transvyl is so heavy that it's dangerous for non-natives to stay there for very long without filter masks. Nasty sulfur dioxide concentrations."

"Shanghai," Torbert said, and Faire nodded. I must have looked puzzled. "Kellana," he continued, "there is an open breach in the veils near Shanghai, China. That is an area which has always been geologically stable, but since the breach, they've had a number of major earthquakes. Scientists aren't sure why."

I nodded, understanding. "The earthquakes may be happening in Hel. Well, that's all very interesting, but I don't have any magic that will prevent a tidal wave from drowning Washington."

"That's why I asked you here," Faire said. The predictions I'm getting concerning Washington aren't of the geological variety. The clairvoyants are foreseeing a war."

I snorted. "Hell, that doesn't require clairvoyance to predict. It's already started."

I walked with Torbert, flanked by my Werewolf escort, back to the FBI building.

"Have you eaten lunch?" he asked.

"No."

"The Dubliner? My treat." He named an Irish pub that was a favorite with generations of politicians.

"Sounds good."

We looped around the east side of the Capitol and crossed the park next to the Hart Senate Office Building. Suddenly my escort all started growling. A dozen wolves, some in Human form, appeared from behind bushes and trees.

Torbert seemed surprised, and other than stopping, he didn't react until I drew my blade. The Human-form members of my guard detail weren't that slow, pistols appearing in their hands as though by magic.

A man stepped forward, dressed in a designer suit. He was immaculately groomed, with his dark hair slicked back, and his mustache as precise as if a computer had drawn it. I recognized him from television.

"Senator," Torbert said.

"Good afternoon, Deputy Director," Senator Richard Bowman said. His eyes shifted to me. "Miss Rogirsdottir."

I didn't acknowledge him, keeping my eyes on the wolves threatening us. A silence stretched, and I finally figured out Bowman was staring at me, waiting for my attention.

"Is there something I can do for you?" I asked.

"Mind your own business. I assure you that your association with Harold Vance will bring you nothing but trouble."

Everyone always underestimated Elves, especially our speed. Before anyone could move, I had grabbed Bowman by the hair and pressed my sword blade against his cheek next to his eye.

"You must have missed history class the day they talked about Elves," I said. "We aren't fond of rude people, and making threats before we're even properly introduced counts as rude. In fact, every interaction I've had with your pack has started with some of the rudest behavior I've ever seen. So, let me give you a lesson in manners."

I let the sword bite into the side of his face. An Elven spell-forged blade contained steel, titanium, and silver. That last component was what made it so effective against paranormals who were sensitive to silver. The cut bled, then it sizzled, the blade cauterizing the wound even as it sliced his flesh.

Bowman's scream probably scared a few people casually strolling through the park. I let up on the pressure, but I didn't remove the blade.

"If you don't stop harassing me," I said, "I'm going to kill you, and I won't promise to make it fast. Now, I really don't care about your pissing match with Vance and his pack. Leave me out of it, and I'll be happy. But if you continue to attack me every time I turn around, I'll see if I have more luck trying to reason with your heir. Do we understand each other?"

"You don't dare. I'm a United States Senator. You'll go to jail for the rest of your life."

I laughed and saw the first sign of fear in his eyes. "As if one of your jails could hold an Elf. Now, tell your puppies to go away, and I'll let you live another day."

He growled something, and his wolves backed off. It took several minutes, but eventually all of them were out of sight.

I released him, pushed him away from me, and kicked him as hard as I could between the legs. He fell to the ground and vomited.

"It hasn't been nice meeting you, Senator," I said, then turned to Torbert. "We really should get out of here. I don't know how long his goons are going to stay gone."

As we walked, me having to slow down and Torbert almost trotting, he said, "He's right, you know. You can't just kill him."

"You're assuming anyone would see me do it or figure out how I did it."

"Did anyone ever tell you that you have a bad attitude?"

I turned to him and grinned. "You say that like it's a bad thing."

"We do have warded cells for paranormals, you know."

I stuck my tongue out at him. "My boyfriend's a realm walker. Top that, Mr. FBI Agent."

I had two tickets for a performance that evening at a Shakespearean play downtown. Cassiel had heard of Shakespeare, but never read or attended one of his plays. It was too late to get a ticket for Isabella, but she said she was a big girl who could entertain herself.

I left work early so I could put on a nice dress for a romantic dinner and the play. But when I walked in the door of my house, I found Cass dressed for travel, including a sack of food.

I stood there blinking at him like some sort of idiot, then finally said, "Did you forget about dinner and Shakespeare?"

He bit his lip, which was a bad sign. "Kellana, I'm terribly sorry. Paladin business. Hopefully, it won't take more than a few days. Maybe a couple of weeks."

"Maybe a couple of months, or a couple of years," I said. In theory, one could traverse the entire three hundred and sixty realms in a day. It had taken Alaric and me five years to pass through half of them.

Cass walked over and took me in his arms. "I hope not. It's my sister, Kel. I have to go."

I took a deep breath, then pulled his head toward me and kissed him like I had never kissed a man before. When I felt his knees begin to buckle, I let him up for air.

"You can't wait until morning?"

He shook his head. "The message I received is that it's urgent. You know I'm not usually tapped for my fighting skills." No, his fighting skills weren't that great, but he was a powerful healer.

"Come back to me," I said. "Don't you dare get yourself killed. Understand me?"

"Yes, your highness," he said, a smile playing around the corners of his mouth. "I promise."

Then he pulled me into another kiss.

He didn't go out the door, but instead climbed the stairs to the roof. I followed and watched him spread his wings and launch into the air. He rose almost straight up for a minute, then veered a little to his right and disappeared.

"Absolutely amazing," Isabella said from behind me. "He walked, or flew, I guess, to another realm?"

Turning, I said, "Yes. Do you like Shakespeare?"

I stopped as we entered the theater, unprepared for the wave of magic emanating from the audience.

Isabella looked up at me. "Is something wrong?"

Steadying myself, I said, "No. I think out seats are over there." First row of the mezzanine.

Once we were seated, she asked, "Are you sure you're all right? You look a little shaky."

I laughed, and even to my own ears, I sounded shaky. "Remember when people could smoke anywhere they wanted to?" I asked. I liked hanging out with Isabella because she was even older than I was, and if I mentioned something that happened fifty years before, she knew what I was talking about.

"Yeah?"

"Walking in here is like walking into a rock concert in nineteen sixty-nine," I said. "Only instead of smoke, it's magic, so thick I can hardly breathe. Like walking into a magic bazaar in Europe."

"Someone has cast a spell on the theater?"

"No, not a spell, although I can detect a lot of personal protection spells. There are just so many magic users—witches and mages and magical creatures."

"Maybe they're all critics and they want to make sure Shakespeare got it right."

I laughed, since the play was *A Midsummer Night's Dream.*

"Isabella, I've been living in this city for almost sixty years, and I've never seen this many magic users in one place. Hell, three years ago I didn't even know there were this many."

I spent the time until the lights went down people watching, trying to zero in on the strongest magical signatures. And there were a number of strong ones.

"Are they all Human?" Isabella asked as the lights dimmed and the curtain went up.

"Oh, no, it's like a stew," I said. "A little bit of everything."

The play was well acted and funny as it always was. I enjoyed it immensely. I understood that Humans had legends and myths dating back to when the veils last fell apart. Elves had ruled most of Europe for almost three thousand years. But for a Human to take those thin rags of information and craft a wholly new story from thin air always boggled my mind. No Elf could do what Shakespeare, or any other author of fiction, did.

As we left the theater, I asked Isabella, "Can you make up stories?"

She gave me a wary side-eyed look. "I'm not sure what you mean."

"Can you create, in your mind, a story? Populated with people who never really lived, doing things that never really happened? Like what Shakespeare did. I mean, he never met Titania. She was long dead before he was born."

Isabella blinked at me. She opened her mouth a couple of times, but no sound came out. Then her face changed as though a light had gone on, and she said, "Elves can't lie."

"No, of course not."

"And you can't create fiction?"

I shook my head. "I have no idea how Humans do that."

"You can't imagine something that isn't true?"

With a shrug, I said, "I've tried. When I first came here, I thought the fiction I read were true stories—histories and memoirs. Confused the hell out of me when I saw that the same author had published numerous memoirs about different people. A librarian in New York finally explained it to me. Once I understood it, I thought it should be easy, but all I could think of were things I already knew about. All of our tales are about things that happened. I can't imagine that a character might do something other than what they did."

"You can extrapolate what a person might do," she said. "Can't you project more than one path or outcome from an action?"

"Oh, yes, I can imagine probabilities based on a given set of facts, but I can't imagine a place or a setting or a person that doesn't exist or hasn't existed, let alone what a person who doesn't exist might do."

Isabella stared at me for a full minute, then chuckled. "Yeah, I can create stories. They probably wouldn't be as entertaining as Shakespeare's, though."

A man and a woman stood on the sidewalk

132

speaking to each other in savage tones, anger apparent in their faces. Both were accompanied by other people, who stood and watched. I expected blood would soon flow, since he was a Werewolf and she was a Vampire.

We stopped to watch the argument between Richard Bowman and Sarah Faire. Physically, he loomed over her, his size and masculinity giving him an apparent advantage.

"I saw him on TV the other day," Isabella said, "and he didn't have that scar on his cheek. Makeup, I guess, but it looks like it would be hard to cover up." The scar was still inflamed—red and puffy.

"It's a new scar. It will take a while before it settles down due to the silver poisoning."

Isabella gave me a long look. "I see. Busy day?"

Out of the corner of my eye, I saw Faire's hand shoot out and grab Bowman by the throat, her nails digging deeply. She shook him like a naughty puppy and several of the people standing around them jumped forward to intervene. Before anyone actually touched either of them, Faire let go.

"You'll pay for that," Bowman gasped, staggering backward clutching his bleeding throat.

Sarah Faire licked her fingers. "I look forward to seeing you try to collect."

"The man does have a talent for pissing people off," I observed as we walked to the metro station.

Chapter 14

It was my week for strange phone calls from people I didn't want to know. Shawna Greene called me at work wanting to meet with me. I tried to put her off, until she said that Gretchen Schneider suggested the meeting. I was tired of meeting with people on their turf, so I told her to come by the nursery at three o'clock.

When Greene arrived, she had Schneider with her. The two women appeared to be about the same age—Human early sixties—but that was always difficult to determine with magic users.

Schneider greeted me in German with a big smile, and I responded in the same language. Both women oohed and ahhed over the nursery, so I gave them a quickie tour, including a couple of the greenhouses where I grew vegetables and common medicinal herbs.

Along the way, Greene said, "Gretchen told me about the conversation out at that Werewolf's mansion. About you being a catalyst or nexus, and all of that."

My expression must have expressed my exasperation, because she burst out laughing.

"You're not serious, are you?" I asked.

"Oh, the look on your face. Hell, I don't know, but what I think doesn't matter. That's why I wanted to meet with you. Maddy Crowell thinks you are, and that's what matters."

"Who in hell is Maddy Crowell?"

"The leader of the Bluegrass Coven."

"Oh, sweet Goddess. Where did she get that idea?"

I looked at Gretchen. "Does she have a spy out at Vance's? Or did you tell her?"

Gretchen shook her head. "Actually, I heard about it from Shawna, who heard it from a spy inside the Bluegrass Coven. But when I met you at Vance's, I didn't know you were the person she was talking about."

"Things are a bit twisted, dear," Greene said. "I don't think you were introduced to me that day at the mall, and if you were, I wasn't paying attention. I had other things on my mind."

I took a deep breath. "Would you ladies care for some tea? I think I need to sit down to hear this."

I led them to the cottage, where I made tea, set out some banana bread, and sat down.

"Okay, let's start with who is Maddy Crowell— other than being daft and leader of a bunch of pyromaniacal, psychotic hillbillies—and why I should care."

Greene took a bite of banana bread and said, "This is really quite good." Then she took a sip of tea, and finally, before I strangled her, said, "Maddy Crowell is a very powerful witch, about a hundred and fifty years old, and she's been running things up in the hills since the end of the nineteenth century. The Bluegrass Coven has always been pretty strong, with maybe two hundred members when the veils shredded." She took another sip of her tea. "Maybe quicker than the rest of us, she figured out that we were in a whole new world. When the first witch-hunts and lynchings started, she took a couple of circles of her strongest witches and went into the areas where it was all happening, put a stop to it, and recruited everyone with even a smidge of power."

"That was a two-edged blade," Gretchen said.

"They grew rapidly, but the economy up there is rather lousy, and you can't eat magic. She's had an alliance with the Savage River pack for decades, and with all the new Werewolves coming through the veils, they started recruiting. Together, they took over the magical and criminal communities in Morgantown, then they moved into Pittsburg and Charleston. But that's small time in comparison to Philadelphia, Baltimore, and Washington. All they had to do was displace the Chesapeake pack, and they'd control all the criminal businesses in the Mid-Atlantic."

Greene picked up the story again. "I'm afraid that I threw a wrench in the works. When Maddy approached me about combining forces, I said no. She got the same answer from the Ravens up in Baltimore." Shawna shook her head rather vigorously. "I may have lived my life in the shadows, but I'm not a thief, I don't lust after power, and I have no use for dark magic."

"From what I've heard, it's worse than dark," I said, and told them the story I heard from Linda. The looks of disgust and revulsion on their faces told me all I needed to know about them.

"So, how did this Crowell woman decide I'm the key to everything?" I asked.

"A prophecy, one handed down from England before white witches ever came to this country," Shawna said. "Oh, it didn't specify a green-haired Elf, but it did talk about two witches who would oppose each other at a moment when the world teeters between order and chaos. I think Crowell tabbed me as her opposition at first, then when Grace Hopkins of the Raven Coven refused to join her, it confused her. Grace is much stronger than I am. That's when the Ravens started recruiting new members. Then she discovered you, and read up about your exploits, and became convinced that you are the one person who can prevent her from reaching her destiny."

"So, she is daft," I said.

Gretchen nodded. "Very much so, and not getting any saner by eating beating hearts."

"Lovely." I pondered what they had told me. "Are you on friendly terms with this Grace Hopkins?"

"Grace and I have known each other for decades," Shawna said. "I wouldn't call us friends, but we're cordial. I do respect her, and know she has no truck with the dark arts."

"She runs a shop in Baltimore called Raven's Roost Magical Supplies," Gretchen said.

"Do you know the woman who runs Magical Secrets up there?" I asked.

Shawna nodded. "Alicia Hopkins, Grace's twin sister. She's an unrepentant independent. When their mother died, and Grace assumed leadership of the coven, Alicia bailed out. I don't know what their personal issues are, but I've never heard either of them utter a bad word about the other."

I told them about the predictions Sarah Faire had shared with me without naming the source.

"That's disturbing," Shawna said. "Not surprising, considering everything else that's going on, but not good news. I think I'll be telling my members to batten down the hatches and prepare for the worst." She looked out the window. "Based on what you said at the mall, I take it that you're sufficiently warded here?"

"Yes, I think so, but that depends on what's thrown at me. If Crowell is batshit crazy enough to call a greater demon, all bets are off."

Gretchen shook her head. "She's not strong

137

enough to do that. She's not a mage. But I don't doubt she would do it if she could."

Shortly after Greene and Schneider left, a Fairy came to tell me that 'one of the hairy men' roaming around outside the nursery was asking to speak with me. Since the Weres couldn't cross my wards, the Fairy queen agreed to provide some English-speaking messengers in case Vance's guardians needed to communicate with me.

I met a young man at the nursery gate. Among my security detail, he and three others, who always stayed in Human form, were invariably polite and struck me as far more intelligent than the majority of Vance's thugs.

"What's up, Mike?"

"Miss Kellana, there are four men who seem to be scouting the place. They aren't shifters, so I wondered if they might be witches. I thought you'd like to know."

"Very definitely. Thank you. Can you show me one of them?"

"They're acting very skittish," he said. "Anytime one of us makes a move in their direction, they duck out. Individually, they seem to come and go, but all of them have been here on and off all day."

"If you spot one, leave him alone, but tell the Fairy where he is and have the Fairy come tell me."

"Yes, ma'am."

I wondered how the kid got mixed up with Vance, but then realized the pack was probably all he'd ever known. It wasn't as though a Werewolf had a lot of career choices.

The Fairy came to get me half an hour later. I donned a glamour and trekked over to a huge oak that marked one of the back corners of my property, climbed to a limb that hung over the fence, dropped to the ground, and shrunk to my smaller one-foot size. Then the Fairy led me to a man hiding behind a tree on the American University campus, less than a stone's throw from my fence.

The man was definitely a witch. In fact, he was one of the witches the PCU had arrested at my place before. More proof that the concept of bail was a bad idea. In Midgard, if you assaulted someone—and came out of it alive—you would end up doing something useful, such as working in the Queen's mines. Elves would never consider simply locking someone up in a tiny stone cell. An Elf would go quickly mad locked up like that.

I slipped around behind him and reverted to full size. Drawing my athame, I slipped my other arm around his neck and clamped down, lifting him off the ground. To ensure he didn't fight me, I held up the knife in front of his face and whispered, "If you struggle, I'll have to shove this in your eye."

He didn't struggle.

"Good boy. Now, we're going to have a little chat. In addition to not struggling, the other rules of our relationship include not yelling, no magic, and you will answer my questions truthfully, and completely. Your reward for obeying the rules shall include the ability to continue breathing and waking up in the morning with all the bits and pieces that you currently have attached to your body. Any questions before we get started?"

"Uhhh, no."

I set him down on his feet but didn't loosen the

pressure on his neck. "All right. How many magic users are with you, watching me and my property?"

He didn't respond immediately, so I moved the point of the knife closer to his eye.

"Six!"

I moved the knife away by several inches. "See how easy that was? Are there seven of you all the time, or does the number vary?"

"Sometimes one or two less, sometimes one or two more."

"Is Maddy Crowell here in Washington?"

He hesitated again, and I moved the knife closer.

"Yes!"

"What is her address?"

He gave me an address in Woodley Park.

I moved the knife down and pressed the point against his pants between his legs.

"What are your plans for Beltane?"

He stiffened, and I pressed the knife against him a little harder. "Remember what I said about all the bits and pieces?"

"I don't know much," he said, his words so rushed they stumbled over themselves. "All I know is they are going to open a portal into another world, and then we're going to crush the Sunrise Coven and kill that Werewolf out in Silver Spring. Honest, lady, I don't know no more than that."

I believed him. Sketching a rune, I said a Word, let go of him, and he slumped to the ground. Cass had taught me the spell, and to my surprise, it worked for me. If it hadn't, I would have resorted to my old method of putting him to sleep, but the spell was easier than figuring out how hard to hit him in the head. I dragged him into some bushes where he couldn't be seen and left him there. He would be unconscious until at least the next day, even if his friends found him.

I went back to my office and called Linda in West Virginia. When I told her about Crowell and Beltane, she said, "I've been hearing some very dark rumors. Rather than deal with it all, I'm closing shop and going on vacation."

"Linda, Beltane will happen all over the world," I said.

"I know that. My grandfather left me a cabin up in the mountains. It's got a creek on one side, and a small lake on the other. The nearest neighbor is a mile away by road, about half an hour by boat. I'm going to go up there and let the world go to hell without my participation. And if a demon shows up, I'll just row out into the lake and read, and knit, and wait for him to go away."

I had to laugh. "That sounds like a good plan."

"I'll email you directions in case you decide to come," she said. "No electricity, no cell phone connectivity. If the sun still comes up in the morning a week after Beltane, I'll go back home."

"I have responsibilities."

"I knew you'd say that. The invitation still holds."

"Linda, do you have any idea where Crowell might want to open a breach? I mean, to what realm?"

"Hmmm." Silence for about a minute. "She's always been fascinated with Norse mythology. That and the Bible. Her first husband was a fire and brimstone preacher. Those are the only things I can think of."

After work, I drove over to Isabella's house. When I got out of the car, Fairies swarmed around me calling greetings. A movement drew my eyes upward. Isabella, in her jaguar form, lounged on the apex of the roof, one paw languidly hanging down. She yawned, showing two-inch canine teeth, slowly got to her feet, stretched, and without warning dropped two stories to the ground in front of me, and shifted to her Human form.

I tried to be nonchalant, but in truth, the moment she stepped off that roof and fell toward me, my heart rose into my throat, my mouth went dry, my palms started to sweat, and I felt light headed.

"*Buenas tardes,*" Isabella said. "I was just taking a little nap in the sunshine."

I swallowed hard, took a deep breath, and said, "Uh, hi. I had some interesting visitors today, and I was hoping I could bounce some things off you and hear what you think about them."

"Sure. Have you eaten yet? Maybe we could try that Salvadoran place Ed told me about." In other words, she was hungry, and probably all she had in her kitchen was raw meat. Isabella could cook, but rarely did so simply for herself.

Bess expected me for dinner, so she would grumble at me when I didn't show up. But she refused to acknowledge the technology of the telephone, so I couldn't call to tell her.

I once took Isabella to a trendy Mexican restaurant in Georgetown, and she declared the food inedible. "Bastardized east coast Tex-Mex," she called it. But she had a couple of Central American places that she liked. "The *Centro Americanos* are cooking for their own people, so the food is genuine," she said.

We drove down to the Adams Morgan

neighborhood, and I took the opportunity to drive by Maddy Crowell's place in Woodley Park. Along the way, I told Isabella about my meeting with Greene and Schneider, and my encounter with the witch at my nursery.

After ordering at the restaurant, I said, "What I can't figure out is where Crowell plans to open a breach. You wouldn't open one to Daemon or Draegar. Demons and Dragons would start creating havoc by eating the members of her circle. Hel, maybe? But that would mean she has contacts with some Devils there, and we haven't seen any evidence of that. And no matter how much she thinks she's binding herself to the forces of chaos, archdemons don't need her to travel to the lower realms."

Isabella nodded. "That's all very logical. Are we dealing with a group of logical individuals? What about Were or Transvyl? She already has some Werewolf allies. Maybe some of their cousins want to join them? Transvyl is a chaotic realm, Congresswoman Faire's desire for order notwithstanding."

"Yeah, you've got a point. If Crowell's wacky enough, she may think opening a portal to Draegar is a good idea. Good luck with that one." Draegar was home of the Dragons, the most chaotic, powerful, and dangerous race in all three hundred sixty realms.

Our food came, and I discovered I was very hungry. When we got back in the car, I said, "My friend Linda suggested Crowell was interested in Norse and Biblical mythologies."

Isabella chuckled. "Maybe she's going to call Leviathan. As to the Norse stuff, you know how much that got twisted here on Earth. Maybe she thinks she can open a road to Niflheim or Muspelheim and command an army of frost giants or fire giants."

"Isabella, that's not funny. There really is a Niflheim. Not as its own realm, but a region of Jotun, which is a realm."

"Oh? Who lives there?"

"In Niflheim? Frost Giants, which are a kind of Troll, and most of the rest of Jotun is occupied by ordinary Trolls. You really don't want to meet either kind. But there are some Aesir and Vanir who live there—Aesir with a weird cult-like religion dedicated to chaos."

"Have you told Dave and Karen about any of this?"

"No, not yet."

"I think they should be watching the Bluegrass Coven a lot closer than they are."

Chapter 15

"Only one week until Beltane," the newscaster on TV said.

I about spilled my coffee. Three years before, every magic user on the planet had been on edge, and the mundane Human world was totally oblivious. The talking head went on to detail what governments and paranormal organizations all over the world were doing in preparation. Beltane fell on a Tuesday, and the authorities ordered all schools in the DC area to close that week. A lot of businesses also planned to close.

When I went in to work, I called everyone who worked for me together.

"Beltane is next week. Now, I'm not going to make this a requirement, but I'm going to strongly urge all of you to take this seriously. This nursery is warded. A demon can't get in, and neither can most other paranormals. I'm calling all of our customers and letting them know that we are closed next week. What I'm offering is if you bring sleeping bags or bedding with you on Sunday, you can stay here through Wednesday night. You can bring your families or significant others as well. We'll figure out someplace everyone can sleep. Probably put a lot of you in the greenhouses, but there are also the sheds if we can clear enough floor space."

Mostly young faces stared back at me, looking very serious, and some of them scared. That was a good thing.

"I'm going to bring in a couple of port-a-potties, and we'll set up some camp showers. The kitchen in the cottage is small, but we also have the charcoal grill. I'll buy the food, so if anyone has any dietary restrictions, let me know, and let me know by Friday if you're coming so I can buy groceries."

"You expect it to be bad," Jamie said into the silence.

"I expect it to be very bad. Maybe worse than three years ago. And if I'm wrong, then we'll have a fun time cleaning up the nursery, painting the buildings, and drinking beer with our hot dogs and hamburgers. You'll be paid for the hours you work."

I dismissed them to go about their work.

Maurine approached me. "I'll be bringing my husband and daughter."

"That's fine. Your family and Kathy and her husband can sleep in the office."

As I turned away, I found Jamie waiting for me.

"You're the best boss in the world," she said. A tear leaked out of one eye and rolled down her cheek. She grabbed me into a hug, then let go and ran off to join her crew.

To my surprise, Dave Torbert called and asked me to come in to the FBI headquarters downtown. My Werewolf escort wasn't too happy when I told them where I was going.

Torbert met me in the lobby and ushered me past the security checkpoints. He led me through several corridors, then down a set of stairs, then another one into the sub-basement. There we took an elevator and came out in what looked like a subway tunnel. I recognized it immediately.

We walked about a quarter of a mile until we came to another empty station platform. He used his

146

badge to open a couple of doors and an elevator, and soon we got into a different elevator that took us to the Attorney General's office.

I hadn't seen Attorney General Matthew Adair in almost a year, but he hadn't changed much.

"Miss Rogirsdottir, how nice to see you again," he said, coming around his desk and shaking my hand. "I am sorry that terrible circumstances are the reason for this meeting. Won't you please have a seat?"

A single overstuffed chair sat on one side of a coffee table, and couches finished the arrangement on the other three sides. A group of mostly men seemed to be waiting on us. In addition to the AG and three other men wearing suits, there were a couple of generals in military uniforms, and the Director of the FBI—Torbert's boss. The surprise participant was Alicia Hopkins, owner of Magical Secrets in Baltimore. She gave me a nod as I sat down.

"Kellana, would you please tell these gentlemen what you have heard about Beltane?" Torbert asked.

"How much do you gentlemen know about what's going on with the paranormals in DC right now?" I asked, trying to organize my thoughts.

"Why don't you assume we're totally ignorant and start at the beginning," Adair suggested.

"All right. Well, there are two Werewolf packs, each with more than two thousand members, fighting a war to control a number of crime enterprises in the Mid-Atlantic area. Three covens of witches are recruiting members and competing for power and control. One of those covens is allied with one of the criminal Werewolf packs and is responsible for all those fires we saw a couple of weeks ago. That was an attack on one of the other covens." I looked around the group. "Everyone with me so far?"

147

The expressions on their faces ranged from grim to uncomprehending. I took special note of those people. No one asked any questions.

"Okay. As you know, Beltane—May Day—is coming soon. On that day, the veils between the realms will thin. Three years ago, those veils shredded, and beings were able to cross between realms. From what I'm told, it may take centuries for the veils to heal."

That got their attention.

"Centuries?" one of the generals asked.

"The last time it happened, it took centuries for the veils to fully re-establish their integrity. Are you aware that Elves ruled most of Europe for almost three thousand years? All of your myths about gods and goddesses, demons, Vampires, Werewolves, and yes, Elves, come from those times when the veils ruptured and different beings crossed between realms. Almost every realm had Humans who crossed in the other direction as well. In my own realm of Midgard, Humans make up almost ten percent of the total population."

"And the rest are Elves?" another man asked.

"No, Elves are about fifty to sixty percent. Trolls, Goblins, and Dwarves make up the rest."

The stunned looks on their faces told me that the Humans in charge were not keeping up with what Humans had learned about the cosmos. Hell, Ed had shown me a Wikipedia article that had all the information I had just told them.

I glanced at Torbert, and he said, "Go on, Kellana, tell them the rest of it."

I took a deep breath. "I heard this second hand, but I have no reason to doubt it's true. Maddy

Crowell, leader of the Bluegrass Coven, has been practicing Human sacrifice. Blood magic encourages chaos, rather than order. Blood mages were responsible for what happened in Arlington last year. Now I hear that she is planning to open a door from another realm into Washington on Beltane. This would not be a door that closes."

"From what realm?" Adair asked.

"I don't know. I've been wracking my brain trying to figure it out."

"It won't be from somewhere we'll like," Alicia Hopkins said.

"Kellana, do you know Ms. Hopkins?" Torbert asked.

"I met her once, a couple of months ago."

Torbert's face assumed an expression just short of a smirk. "She told us almost exactly the same story. Who were your sources, if I may ask?"

"Shawna Greene and Gretchen Schneider of the Sunrise Coven."

"And I heard it from my sister of the Raven Coven," Alicia said. "As far as I know, my sister and Shawna Greene haven't exchanged a civil word in decades."

"So, how are these people able to know what's going on in this Bluegrass Coven?" one of the military men asked.

Alicia snorted. "All three of them have spies in each of the others."

The general shook his head. "If the other two covens know that much, can the information be trusted? One would think an operation of this magnitude would have better security."

"These aren't military organizations," I said.

149

"These people are charismatic leaders, but they're amateurs. And Crowell is crazy. I imagine she doesn't watch her tongue, and she probably brags."

Adair and the generals looked to Torbert.

"Yes, that tracks with what we know. We have spies in all three covens, also, but ours haven't been in place as long. My reports say that Crowell is becoming increasingly unstable and aggressive."

"Blood mage," Alicia and I said almost in unison, and then smirked at each other.

"Well, what do we do about it?" Adair asked.

They spent the next hour talking without figuring anything out. Alicia watched with a stony expression, and I wasn't sure if she was angry or falling asleep. I grew increasingly frustrated and considered just walking out.

"Why don't you just declare the Bluegrass Coven a terrorist organization, round them all up, and throw their asses in jail?" I don't know who was more surprised, the men in the room or I. I didn't mean to say that out loud.

"Go on," Adair said.

I glanced at Torbert and he nodded. Beyond him, Alicia also nodded.

"Look, we know they set those fires. You have plenty of witnesses. How many buildings?" I looked to Torbert.

"Sixty-seven, plus your house."

"And how many dead?"

"Seventeen, including the witch at your place."

"Okay. Sixty-eight terrorist attacks, and planning another, larger attack. I watch television and you guys are taking people down for less than that all the time."

"Someone tried to burn your house?" Adair asked.

"Yeah, but it was warded. Their fireballs didn't penetrate."

He nodded. Looking around the room, he said, "Well, what's wrong with her idea?"

"We don't even know all of their members," the FBI Director said.

"So that means you do nothing?" Alicia asked.

Another hour of discussion, argument, and passing the buck. I finally figured out that no one wanted to take responsibility for making a decision.

"Mr. Adair," I finally said. "I'm going home. If no one here is willing to do anything, I'll just barricade myself and my employees, arm everyone, and pray to the Goddess. I wish you luck, and hope there are more survivors than casualties."

With that, I picked up my bag and headed for the door. Behind me, I heard Torbert laugh, and then Adair joined him.

"Kellana, come back," Torbert said.

Turning back to them, I said, "I have things to do."

"Miss Rogirsdottir," Adair said, "is that really what you plan to do? Barricade yourself inside your nursery?"

"Absolutely. I've already told my employees to bring their families on Sunday and plan to stay through Wednesday. The butcher will deliver three hundred pounds of meat on Saturday, the fish market will bring a hundred pounds of fish, and I've ordered a dozen crates of vegetables and fruit. Three port-a-potties are being installed tomorrow, that's in addition to the two I usually have, and my foreman said he'll install the camp showers on Saturday. As long as my wards hold, we'll ride it out."

"And why wouldn't your wards hold?" Torbert asked.

"I have no idea what Maddy Crowell has in mind. If she manages to call and bind a greater demon, I have no idea what will happen."

Alicia gasped. "You don't think she can do that, do you?"

"I don't know. I've never met her."

Chapter 16

Isabella, Karen, and I crept up the street under the cover of Karen's illusion spell. The PCU had the street—a long cul-de-sac—blocked off, and Crowell's house was in the middle of the block. No alley in the back—one way in, one way out.

An hour before, I had walked down the street with Isabella on a leash, acting out Karen's illusion of a teenage girl walking her dog. As we approached the house, a feeling of dread began to grow, and then the dread turned into the stench of blood magic. I didn't have to look at addresses to know which house was our target.

We walked to the end of the cul-de-sac, then back on the other side of the street to where Torbert and his troops waited at the main street. Karen dissolved the illusion and Isabella shifted to her Human form.

"Blood magic," I said. "The stench is very heavy. They have conducted ceremonies in there. I count seventeen magic users, and there's a demon."

"The smell of Werewolf is very strong," Isabella chimed in.

"Is Crowell in there?" Torbert asked.

I shook my head. "I've never met the woman, so I have no idea. Someone in there is a very strong witch, but it could be her, or someone else. For all we know, there could be multiple witches in the coven who are stronger than their leader. It's not like a pack where the strongest wolf is the alpha."

The PCU had significantly bolstered their paranormal roster over the previous year. Torbert assigned twelve witches, fourteen Werewolves, and a dozen Vampires to the operation. Across the city, more PCU, ATF, and FBI agents waited for our signal to close in on members of the Bluegrass Coven. A battalion of Army paratroopers sat on a runway waiting to drop into the Pendleton-Seneca Rocks area in West Virginia.

While I was surprised that the government had gone all out to control the coven, what surprised me the most was that I had succumbed to Torbert and Wen-li guilting me into getting involved.

We were after Human witches, not nocturnal paranormals, so we had waited until twilight. The street had a lot of trees, and when we reached the house, Isabella flowed across the neighbor's lawn like a pool of ink, bounded into a tree, and then onto the roof.

A couple of men came out of the house and got in a van parked on the street. As they drove away, Karen spoke in a low voice into her phone.

"Got a couple of customers in a van coming your way, Dave."

I shrank down into my smaller size.

"Oh, my God!" Karen gasped.

"Shh. Keep your voice down." I realized she had never seen me do that. Elves tended to keep that ability secret.

I scampered up the driveway until I reached the garage, grew to my full size, and leaped up on the garage roof. From there, I could look into the second-floor window in the back of the house. Donning a glamour, that's what I did.

The blood magic stench almost gagged me, but what I could see inside was rather innocuous. A woman appearing to be in her thirties sat on the bed in a large bedroom with three doors. I assumed one led to the hallway, the others to a closet and possibly a bathroom. She was a blood mage, but not a very strong one. That confirmed my suspicion that the covens were incorporating mages as well as witches into their ranks. That mage magic would be handy in helping to bind a demon.

I could feel the demon below me, and assumed he was in the basement. The strongest blood magic feel was also in the basement, but the strongest magic user was a witch on the first floor. Pulling out my phone, I reported all of that to Torbert.

"Wards?" he asked.

"Yes, but not active. I think they have too many people going in and out. If you can get into the house before they shut things down, I think you can prevent them from invoking them. Hell, Dave, the window I'm watching isn't even locked. I don't think they're particularly worried about security."

My eyesight was a lot better than any Human's. I watched as Torbert's force, dressed in black, ghosted into position around the house. They quietly evacuated the houses on either side, and the houses bordering on the backyard. Another man came out of the house and got into a car in the driveway below me. After he started the engine, a woman emerged from the house and joined him. They drove away toward Torbert's waiting jail cells.

The woman I was watching spent most of her time doing something with her phone. After about forty-five minutes, she went to one of the doors and opened it to reveal a bathroom. When she closed the door, I slipped my athame under the window frame and pried the window open. I slipped into the room, lowered and locked the window, and shrunk to my smaller form. By the time she came out and sat on the bed again, I was seated on the floor under the bed.

The disadvantage of my position was that I was out of touch with Torbert and the rest of the team. My bag shrunk with me, but all the stuff inside it did not—cell phone, knives, swords, and all that useful stuff. On the other hand, I was inside, and could easily disable the young mage when the action started.

I entertained myself by thinking about a new dress I could make to surprise Cassiel when he came home.

A crash downstairs told me it was time to pay attention. The mage leaped off the bed and faced the door. I rolled out from under the bed, came to my feet behind her, and grew to full size. Wrapping my arm around her, I pulled her to me and cut her throat with my athame. My sympathy for a blood mage was zero, and I didn't want to give her a chance to use her magic. Blood sprayed, and she fell when I released her.

On the other side of the door, I could hear chaos. It was tight quarters to use a sword inside the house, so I kept my athame and drew my paintball gun. Prior to starting the operation, I had loaded the hopper with sleepy gas.

Opening the door, I stuck the gun out the door and fired a paintball in both directions, then peeked to see what was going on.

A mage stood at the top of the stairs firing bolts of energy at someone below him. I steadied my gun and fired. The paintball hit him in the side of the head. He swayed as a pink cloud enveloped him, then pitched head-first down the stairs.

I could feel two witches in the room at the end of the hall, so I trotted down the hall and kicked in the door, then fired two paintballs inside. A few gunshots downstairs convinced me to raise my shield.

The strong blood mage was still downstairs, so I cautiously worked my way down the steps. That's when I heard a demon roar, then a scream, and a fusillade of gunfire. The demon's roar was answered by that of a jaguar in the backyard.

Since I didn't think sleepy gas and an athame were appropriate accessories for meeting a demon, I stopped and swapped out the hopper on my paintball gun with one filled with demonbane.

I reached the bottom and glanced into the living room. Karen and another witch were fending off an attack by three witches and a mage. Two FBI agents lay unmoving on the floor. I fired a paintball at the nearest witch. He turned to me with a startled look on his face, then screamed as the demonbane began to burn his skin.

Demonbane was a mixture of cinnabar, mandrake root, and torbernite in a beet juice solution. Cinnabar, or mercury sulfide, was so nasty it couldn't be handled with bare hands. Torbernite—a crystal formed from phosphorous, copper, water and uranium—was found on Earth but was more common in Hel. Mandrake root contained hallucinogenic neurotoxins. It was very nasty stuff, and I used leaded glass for the paintballs.

The mage turned toward me, and I shielded myself. Someone fired a gun from outside on the front porch. The mage spun around and fell.

A demon snarled behind me, and I turned in that direction. I was facing the kitchen but couldn't see the demon. Edging around the corner, I saw a scene of bloody mayhem. The demon had its back to me, so I dropped my shield. I fired at its back at the same time as an FBI agent popped up from behind the kitchen island and also fired a paintball.

The demon screamed, leaping over the island and reaching for the agent, who managed to get off another shot. I fired again.

At first, I thought the agent had managed to escape, but when I came around the island, I found the dying demon with its hand on the agent's crushed skull.

A sound to my right caused me to duck, and I felt a slight breeze as something passed over my head. I turned to see a woman coming out of the basement stairwell. I recognized her as the woman from Elise Rosenthal's projected illusion, the one who beat the girl's mother to death in front of her. The woman reeked of blood magic. Powerful blood magic.

She was holding an iron rod, and realizing she'd missed me, she swung back. I blocked the blow with my paintball gun and staggered backward. The woman didn't pursue me, but instead dashed to the door leading from the kitchen to the backyard.

My paintball gun was trashed, the barrel bent and the body containing the firing mechanism partially crushed. I dropped it and drew my sword, then followed the witch out the door.

The crackle of fire and a growing light alerted me, and as I reached the door, I dove rather than run through it. The fireball passed over my head, enveloping the doorway and spilling flame into the kitchen.

For a woman as old as she appeared, the witch was amazingly spry. She hurled another fireball across the backyard, and it hit the jaguar who was chasing her.

"Isabella!"

I pulled water from the air, grass, trees, and a small pool beneath a fountain in the backyard, then let the water go. It looked as though someone had turned a giant bucket upside down over the area. The force of the water knocked me off my feet.

As I struggled back to my feet, I saw the witch, soaked to the skin, slip between two trees and climb over the back wall.

I didn't care. I rushed over to where Isabella lay. As I reached her, she rolled over and tried to crawl to her feet. Half of her fur was burned off, along with one ear, and blisters were evident on her bare skin.

"Stupid cat! Lie down! You can't chase her in that condition!"

She snarled at me.

"Shut up!"

I reached in my bag and began pulling out potions and poultices. Twisting the top off a bottle of pain killer, I held it out. When Isabella snarled at me again, I poured it down her throat. She choked, and when she recovered enough to snarl at me again, I poured a bottle of healing potion in her mouth.

It was amazing that she was still alive, but she was more than twelve hundred years old. I once asked her if she could be killed, and she answered, "I assume so, but no one has managed it yet."

I pulled my phone out and called Torbert.

"Kellana! Are you all right?" he answered.

"Yeah, but I need a healer for Isabella. Maddy Crowell escaped over the back wall. Look for a soaking wet woman who looks like she's in her seventies. And watch out—she's nasty. Fireballs."

"Got it."

I hung up the phone and started unpacking

poultices. Isabella watched me, panting in pain. I applied the first poultice to her face and ear, and wrapped it in place. I didn't know if the ear would grow back after she shifted and healed, but luckily the flames had missed her eye on that side. As soon as I applied the poultice, she sighed, and some of the tension went out of her body.

Torbert called back. "Is it safe to send a non-combatant in?"

"The healer? Have her come around the side of the house. It's clear back here, but there was still a fight going on when I was inside last."

About ten minutes later, I looked up and saw Doctor Evans, a healer who worked with Torbert's PCU. I moved away from Isabella so the doctor could see her.

"Oh, my. Kitty, I'll bet that hurts."

Isabella curled her lip and gave us a weak snarl.

"I've already given her a healing potion and a pain killer," I said.

Evans unwrapped the poultice on Isabella's head and lifted it. She sucked air when she saw the wound.

"What about her other side?" Evans asked.

"The fur's intact. I didn't bother to see if she has any other wounds. Usually, when she gets in a fight, any blood isn't hers."

Evans nodded. She worked on the cat for half an hour, healing her head first, then her neck and chest area, then her side. As she finished each part, she replaced the poultices.

"Do you have a good burn cream?" she asked when she finished. Isabella lay still, her breathing more normal.

"Yeah, should I apply it now?"

She shook her head. "I think the poultices are good for now. When she shifts, I'd use the burn cream."

"So, she'll be okay?"

"She'll live. Give me an address, and I'll stop by tomorrow for another treatment."

I wrote my home address on the back of one of my business cards and handed it to her. "I'll tell the Brownie to let you in."

Her head snapped up. "You have a Brownie?"

"Yes. She just sort of moved in."

"Lucky you. If she has any friends, I'd love to have one."

I chuckled. "Be careful what you ask for."

Karen found us after the battle was over. Doctors, paramedics, the forensic teams, and some self-important looking people in suits were roaming around by then. Thankfully, the news media was being held beyond the entrance to the cul-de-sac.

"Is she going to be all right?" Karen asked, kneeling down by Isabella.

"I think so. Doctor Evans thinks so. I think her anatomy is fairly normal, but who knows? She's sleeping, which is a good sign."

"Why is it so wet out here?" she asked as we watched the paramedics splash through a puddle, carrying a body away.

"I had to put out the fire."

She blinked at me. "You made it rain?"

"No, I just concentrated all the water in the area in one place."

"I see," she said in a tone that conveyed complete bafflement. I didn't try to explain.

"We're going to need some help getting her out of here. If you can commandeer a stretcher and someone to help me carry her, I would appreciate it."

"I think we can manage that."

"Karen, that woman who killed Elise's mother? That was Maddy Crowell. She tried to brain me with that same steel bar tonight."

"That helps. It seems that she has no pictures on file, no driver's license, never paid taxes. That explains the paintings we found in the house here that were stolen from the Rosenthal's."

I snorted. "She's well over a hundred years old. I'm sure she's always lived in the shadows, and living up in the hills like that, she's been able to slip under the radar. Your parents, me, we wanted to be part of society, so we had to establish identities. Her society didn't care."

Torbert and his boss splashed through the yard, and after surveying the carnage, stopped by us.

"Is that mostly the jaguar's doing?" Torbert asked, nodding toward a pair of witches who looked as though they'd been through a blender.

"Yeah," Karen said. "The ATF agents who came over the back wall got ambushed. A couple of them survived. They told me Isabella saved their lives."

"She tried to take on Maddy Crowell," I said. "It didn't turn out well, but she'll live. How did all the other raids turn out? As big a clusterfuck as this one?"

Torbert's boss answered, "More than two hundred members of the Bluegrass Coven have been arrested, and almost a hundred Werewolves. Other than here, seventeen Humans killed along with about fifty

162

Weres. We lost five of our own."

"And here?"

"A dozen dead, twenty injured. A couple may not make it."

"Have you heard anything from the operations in West Virginia?" I asked.

Torbert shook his head. "Nothing yet."

Chapter 17

The veils were thinning already. The TV news was full of reports from all over the world of mysterious disappearances and even more frightening appearances.

Inside my nursery, a single bewildered Pixie from another realm winked into existence. He was so afraid and lost that the Fairies took pity on him, and I didn't have to intervene to keep them from killing him. They took him to a Pixie nest a few blocks away.

Many of the incidents were more serious than mine. A hellhound appeared in the middle of a small town in Mexico and slaughtered the entire population. A mage eventually hunted it down and banished it.

The day after the raid, Karen came by. Isabella was still asleep but appeared to be healing rapidly. Doctor Evans had already visited and done another healing. She also applied healing magic to my arm and leg, which felt much stronger afterward.

"The operation in West Virginia was declared a success," Karen said. "Only about fifty or sixty known members of the Bluegrass Coven are still at large."

"Crowell?"

She shook her head. "No, she and some of her closest associates are still missing."

"So, the best we can hope for is that she opens her portal out in the forest somewhere, instead of in the middle of the city."

Karen stared at me for a moment. "You're certainly cheerful today."

"Worried."

Her expression turned grim. "Yeah, I hear you.

164

Some of Crowell's followers have been rather forthcoming when we questioned them. It seems that this move out of the hills into the city was sparked by a new friend of hers—a mage from another realm."

A realm walker seeking a power base. An adventurer with dreams of grandeur and wealth. I had traveled to Earth with such a man, but Alaric was much too flighty and too much of a good-time boy to seriously work for power. And while he had no qualms about theft or working a con, he would never have stepped over the line into dark magic.

"That explains her plan to cause a rupture," I said. "Is this mage Human?"

"No idea. A couple of people who have met him seem to think he's not truly Human, although he looks Human."

I shrugged. "Could be Aesir or Vanir or a halfling. All the other races would be noticeable unless he wore a glamour all the time."

"A couple of other things," Karen said. "Since the raids, the battles between the Chesapeake and Savage River packs have escalated. Vance has taken advantage of the chaos to strike back. And our informants in Ivy City are getting increasingly antsy the closer we get to Beltane. One woman I talked to said she feels as though the whole area is about to explode."

"You should talk to Sarah Faire about that. The Vampires might know what the demons are planning," I said.

"The scars will fade," Isabella said. "I've had worse. As soon as my skin heals, the fur will come back when I shift."

"Did it ever occur to you to duck?"

She just shrugged.

Her resilience and healing prowess were phenomenal. Only forty-eight hours after the raid, she was up and about, complaining that she was starving. Bess seared a chunk of beef the size of her head, and Isabella ate it all, then ate another one. To my amazement, her ear was intact when she shifted to her Human form.

On Saturday morning, I left Isabella to Bess's care and drove over to the nursery. Preparations there were almost complete. Ed and Jamie were taking deliveries and dealing with last-minute stuff that I hadn't considered. Elves didn't feed milk to their children after they were weaned. Why Humans thought cow's milk was necessary for their children was beyond me. Shouldn't the cows be feeding their calves instead?

Kathy and her husband showed up at midday.

"A couple of demons rampaged through a grocery store near our house this morning," Kathy said. "Close enough for me. I'd rather hang out with the Fairies."

That evening, several Fairies flew up to me and, all talking at once, told me that a fight was going on outside the nursery. It took me a couple of minutes to sort out the problem. My Werewolf guards were under attack by other Werewolves. The Fairies were quite excited, and the whole nest was jostling for the best views of the action. They didn't care who won, viewing it as a sporting event.

I rushed toward the side of my property where the main battle seemed to be in progress. I climbed the nearest oak tree and tried to make sense of the scene below me. Even in daylight, it would have been difficult to tell one wolf from another. The wolves, of course, knew by smell whether the wolf they faced was friend or foe.

Turning to the Fairy sitting on my shoulder, I asked, "Can you tell which ones have been here all week, and which ones are new?"

She assured me that she could. I wondered if I should take her word for it.

"The one with the white streak on his shoulder likes to sleep under this tree," she told me. "He's lazy, but he doesn't snap at us if we get close."

He was also fighting for his life against three other wolves.

"You're sure?"

"Yes. Those three are new."

I pulled out my bow, drew an arrow, and when one of the attackers backed away from the scrum for a moment, loosed. My aim was good. His buddy dying distracted one of the others, and he turned to look first at the arrow, then lifted his head as though to find the source of it. I helped him in that search.

The white-streaked wolf took advantage and tore out the throat of his remaining foe. He might have been lazy, but he was no slouch when it came to defending himself.

Using the Fairy's spotting skills, I shot six more of the attacking wolves. Somebody on their side finally got the message, and suddenly the fight was over on that side of my property. I could hear at least two savage dog fights going on elsewhere, however.

I changed trees and shot another wolf. Almost like a miracle, silence descended around me, then the Fairies started booing as their entertainment ended.

As I climbed down from the tree, a naked man walked up to the fence.

"Thank you, Miss Rogirsdottir," he said. "We've called Moretti, and he's sending some reinforcements, but they'll take some time to get here. Evidently it's a busy night."

That made me think about the next few days. It really wasn't fair to keep Vance's Werewolves outside once I locked down my wards. At that point, I would be in more danger from a realm walker appearing inside my property than from an outside assault.

I went back inside the cottage and turned on the TV. Over the past three years, Human news organizations had become a little calmer when reporting paranormal events, but the sheer number of incidents told me the Were was right. It was a busy night.

Around midnight, I slipped out of the nursery and took a path through the park to go home on foot. I walked with my sword in my hand, but I didn't encounter any problems.

Bess greeted me when I walked in the door, and she didn't look happy. "The cat says you're going to abandon the house."

"No, that is not correct. I'm going to reinforce the wards and seal the house until after Beltane. I will be moving Isabella to the nursery, and I'll be staying there as well. I will be protecting almost fifty people there, and that is too many to fit here. If you wish to go, you are more than welcome, but I think the house will be safe."

She sniffed, looked me up and down, then turned and walked toward the kitchen. "If you're hungry, there is stew on the stove."

It was delicious, too. I watched news of the latest incursions on TV while I ate a bowl of it, then checked on Isabella, and went to bed.

By noon on Sunday, thirty-five people had taken up residence on the nursery grounds. One thing I hadn't thought of was the amount of space two dozen extra cars would take up. I made everyone park out on the street, and hoped their cars survived anything that might happen. I knew from experience that insurance companies didn't believe in—or pay for—demon damage.

Maurine's husband had served in the army when he was younger, so I gave him a paintball gun and fifteen minutes of instruction on using the gun and the different types of paintballs. Two of my crew and two 'significant others' played paintball on weekends, so I issued guns to them, too. Along with Ed, Jamie, Isabella, and me, that made nine of us armed. I told everyone else to simply run and hide if an inimical beastie managed to get into the compound.

We were grilling ribs and Ed had just tapped the first keg of beer when a car pulled up in front of the closed gate. I went out to see who it was and discovered Karen and Meagan.

"Hi," Karen called. "We've been assigned to guard you this week. Can we come in?"

"Do you plan to stay?"

"Dave said we were to stay here through Wednesday. We brought sleeping bags and food."

"And wine," Meagan added.

"Then come join the party." I certainly wasn't going to refuse two additional magic users. Paintball guns were fine, but Isabella and I were the only

169

warriors, and neither of us were at full strength.

Including the PCU agents, there were forty-five of us, two bathrooms, five port-a-potties, four kegs of beer, and three camp showers. I had a clothes washer and a dryer, but I hoped we wouldn't be there long enough to need them.

Ed had brought a portable TV, and after dinner, he put it on the porch of the cottage so everyone could sit around in a half-circle and watch the news. The reporters provided updates on a continuous stream of scattered incidents from all over the world.

"It's still more than two days until Beltane," someone said. "Why is stuff happening already?"

"The veils don't give way all at once," I said. "They've been thinning for a couple of weeks, and since they are in bad shape already, breaches and ruptures start even before Beltane. You're right that Beltane doesn't officially start until Tuesday by our calendar, and that's based on London time. But the actual start is based on celestial alignments, not our calendar."

"So, it's just going to get worse and worse until Tuesday?"

"No, it's going to get worse and worse until long after Tuesday. But hopefully the veils will thicken and the surprises appearing from other realms will stop. Then we'll just have to deal with whatever has already come through."

When it got late, I hung magelights in each of the port-a-potties, pulled the plug on the TV, and told everyone to go to bed. The Fairies on night patrol would alert me if there were any strangers outside the fence.

The excited chattering of Fairies and the distant sound of fireworks woke me. It was still dark outside. Grabbing my bag, I tiptoed out the back door to avoid waking those sleeping in the front room.

A lot more Fairies were out than the normal night watch, and many of them were flying very high above the compound. The firework sounds came from the east, and I could see some flashes of light in that direction.

I climbed about fifty feet up the nearest oak and settled on a limb. A soft growl behind me led me to turn and find a large jaguar who butted me with her head. I stood and jumped to the next branch over. She took my place on the limb and shifted into her Human form.

"*Que pasa?*"

"It looks like a magic battle."

Off in the distance to the southeast, I could see flashes and streaks of light—white and red—along with the fire and smoke of explosions. Whether it was near the Capitol or farther away was impossible to determine.

We watched for about two hours until a pair of airplanes swooped in and each fired two missiles. As they pulled up out of their run, a beam of white light shot up from the ground, and one of the airplanes exploded at the same time as the missiles exploded on the ground.

The fireworks suddenly stopped.

"I always said the best way to swat flies is with a shotgun," Isabella commented.

"Yeah. What good are a lot of big, expensive, noisy toys if you don't get to use them? I think that's what they call a surgical strike. At least it's better than other things they could have done."

"Such as?"

"Carpet bomb the city with incendiaries."

"Dresden? That would have never occurred to me," Isabella said.

"That's because you don't have a military mind set."

After ten minutes of quiet, we climbed down and went back to bed.

Chapter 18

The first room I built when I bought the land for the nursery was now the kitchen and the dining room. I had almost no money left over from the land deal, no place to live, and was mowing lawns with the one piece of equipment I owned just to feed myself. The dining room wasn't a dining room then, but part of the kitchen. It was the dining room, bedroom, sitting room, and the office. And literally every meal I ate for three years was prepared in that kitchen.

So, it always struck me as odd when people commented on the size of the kitchen, how nice it was, and how efficient. What other kind of kitchen would a hearth witch have?

But it was a kitchen for a single cook. I realized I was starting to get grouchy with people who asked if they could help. I sent them all out of the cottage with orders to build tables, set the tables, and pour drinks for everyone. Finally left alone, it took me little time to fix breakfast for forty-five. Actually, compared to working as a short-order cook in a New York fast-food breakfast joint, it was remarkably relaxed. And no one yelled at me if I ate a piece of bacon or two while I cooked.

I told Karen and Meagan about the show the night before, and Karen called Dave. After talking to him for a while, she motioned me over and handed me her phone.

"What happened last night?" I asked.

"I was hoping you might be able to tell me."

Huh? "Dave, I was here at the nursery. I was talking about that wild fireworks display, complete with fighter jets, over on the east side."

I heard a deep sigh. "I should have been more specific. I don't suppose I could talk you into meeting me over there. No one on my staff—no, wait—what I should say is that everyone on my staff has an opinion, and none of them match."

My deep sigh echoed his. "You'll send an armored assault vehicle for me? Including a battle mage for a driver?"

It was hard to tell over the phone, but I think he laughed. "I'll send something as secure as I can manage."

Isabella wanted to come with me, but she still wasn't a hundred percent, and besides, I wanted her at the nursery.

Dave actually did send an armored personnel carrier, or APC, but with five Human soldiers instead of a battle mage. Their expressions were pretty grim, and their demeanor all business. I knew from the TV that a curfew was in effect and all non-essential traffic was banned. I didn't know whether the government planned that after my little speech to them, or they finally figured it was a good idea after they had to bomb their own citizens.

The car itself had eight wheels, bristled with guns, and looked like it could climb over or through almost anything. They tucked me inside, and all I could see was the driver's screens, and through a thin slit to the outside.

The President had declared martial law, then evacuated to Camp David. The only vehicles I saw out on the streets were those of the police, various official government agencies, and the military. It was Monday, less than ten hours until Beltane officially started at midnight, London time. Of course, it was already Tuesday in Australia. I wasn't an astrologer, and such things made my head hurt.

The insanity of Beltane was apparent as we drove. An Imp chased a squirrel across the street in front of us; and another block along, I saw a Sylph sitting on a mailbox looking rather confused. A satyr snuck across a lawn and peeked through the window of a house.

Then a demon ran into the street in front of us. Instead of trying to dodge it, the driver stepped on the gas.

"No! Don't!" I shouted, but it was too late. I threw up a shield and braced for impact.

The demon flew about thirty feet, rolled, and came to his feet laughing. The armored car careened off the road and hit a light pole. As soon as things stopped moving, I released my safety harness and opened the hatch to the outside. I managed to get my head and shoulders out about the time the demon reached us.

The poor guy sitting with his head out of the forward hatch never had a chance, but while the demon was killing him, I shot it with three balls of demonbane. It screamed, staggering away from us and trying to claw at its back. When it turned to face me, I shot it again.

What I didn't see was his girlfriend, who came up behind me and swiped at me. I ducked, but she hit my paintball gun, and it spun out of my grasp.

I dropped back inside the APC and fumbled around inside my bag for a weapon. My hand closed on my athame, and when the demon tried to stick her head through the hatch, I shoved the knife into her eye. She lurched backward, ripping the knife out of my hand.

A machinegun started firing, close and deafening. I clapped my hands over my ears and curled up in the bottom of the APC. It seemed like the firing went on forever, and I realized why all the soldiers wore helmets with ear protection. They hadn't offered anything like that to me, and I hadn't thought to cast a spell.

When the noise stopped, I didn't notice at first because the ringing in my ears continued.

"Hey! Girl! Are you all right?" a soldier was very close to me and shouting, but I could barely hear him.

"Yeah. Did you get the demon?"

"Yeah, we got the bitch."

"Can one of you drive this thing?" I pointed to the driver, hunched over the controls. He was breathing, but unconscious.

"Yes, ma'am, we can drive it, but we should call this in and wait for reinforcements."

I reached out, grabbed his shirt, and pulled him close to my face. "Do you know how many demons came through a rift near here?"

"Uh, no, ma'am."

"It could have been only two, but suppose it was twenty, or two hundred. Get him out of that seat and get us the hell out of here."

"Yes, ma'am." Goddess, he was so incredibly young. "Uh, how do I know I won't hurt him more by moving him?"

"I'll take care of him. Just get us moving."

I helped him wrestle the driver into the back of the APC and lay him down. I dribbled a healing potion slowly into his mouth, and his breathing evened out. That seemed to reassure the other soldier, and he started the engine, backed the car away from the pole, and started off down the street.

"Don't try to run over any damned demons!" I

176

shouted over the sound of the engine.

As soon as we were underway again, I called Torbert and told him what happened. After I hung up, I asked the driver, "How did you kill the second demon?"

"Paintball. We were issued paintball guns with some funny glass balls this morning. Shot the hell out of that son of a bitch with a machinegun, and it barely fazed it. Then Jim shot it with one of them damned paintballs, and it just curled up and died."

"You didn't happen to pull my knife out of her eye, did you?"

"Jim did. He said you'd probably want a fancy knife like that back. Gotta say, that was pretty damned ballsy sticking that thing with a knife."

"It was all I had at hand."

We drove on a few miles before the soldier spoke again. "What are those little guys? Blue and green and round, bouncing around like they're made of rubber?"

"Imps. They aren't dangerous, just irritating as hell, and they're thieves. They'll steal your teeth if you aren't paying attention."

"What about a shaggy dog, sort of colored like a Doberman, and the size of a pony?"

"A hellhound. Where did you see one of those?"

"Right up there on the edge of that park."

I bolted for the hatch and stuck my head out. Sure as taxes, a hellhound. Dear Goddess.

Dropping back inside, I said, "Tell all your buddies to keep their heads down. If they can get in here, that would be better."

"That thing's dangerous, huh? How do you kill it? That paintball stuff?"

"Goddess only knows. Maybe the demonbane will kill it. Cutting its head off will probably do it, but I'm not very keen on getting that close to it. Its saliva is acid, and its body temperature is close to that of boiling water. How fast can this thing go?"

"Top speed around sixty."

I shook my head. "Too slow. What does that big gun shoot?"

"High explosive incendiary rounds."

"Well, if it tries to eat us, you might try that. We're best avoiding it."

Without even slowing down, he took a right turn down the next street and accelerated. I couldn't see to the rear, so I cringed and waited, but after a few minutes decided the hellhound hadn't followed us. A hellhound was bad news, and I hadn't seen one since the first Beltane when the veils ripped.

Some time later, the driver slowed markedly, and the road became very rough.

"What's going on?" I asked. "Where are we?"

"Reached the edge of the trouble last night," he answered. "We're just passing Howard University."

I stuck my head out through the hatch again. The buildings around us showed some battle damage, as did the road. The damage got progressively worse as we drove, with rubble and destroyed cars littered about.

"I'm going to take us to our unit command post," the driver said. "There's a medical unit there."

"Yes, that's a good idea. I'll ask Deputy Director Torbert to meet us there."

Once I set my feet back on the ground again, and retrieved my athame from the other soldier, I took a good look around. It had been a hell of a battle. It wasn't Dresden, or Berlin, but I had seen similar damage in many small cities as I made my way west after the war.

Torbert showed up, chauffeured in the same kind of APC. After my trip to meet him, riding in the armored car struck me as a false sense of security. We rode back to the place where he had awaited me.

I saw immediately what concerned him so much. A hole in reality gaped wide where a building used to be, half-way down the street. Surrounded by damaged buildings, looking like a painting with a ragged frame, was another world, one that looked vaguely familiar.

The rift was about ten feet high, and eight feet wide. The view through the hole showed rocks and forest with white mountains in the background. In contrast to that, the sounds coming through were those of surf pounding a shore.

"Any idea what we're looking at?" Torbert asked.

"Agent Torbert, if you know anyone who still doesn't believe in multiple dimensions, bring them here. It could be any number of realms. There are probably places on Earth that are similar to this, but you are looking at another world."

"Yeah."

"What's on the other side?" I asked.

"We haven't been brave enough to find out."

"Oh, no, I mean, if you walk around it, what's on the other side? I've always been curious."

Torbert gave me a strange look.

"I've never seen an open breach before," I said. "This sort of thing is not normal."

He chuckled, and said, "Feel free to check it out."

I walked around the rift. From the front, it looked like a movie screen. I walked behind it, and it disappeared. I could see Torbert standing in front of me.

"Weird," I said when I rejoined him. He nodded.

He led me to a half-shattered house nearby. "Does this look familiar?"

The body was humanoid, about eight feet tall, and I guessed about four or five hundred pounds. "That's a Troll. Was Maddy Crowell involved in all of this?"

"I don't know. One more thing, but I can't show it to you. What would you say if I told you that the being that did most of this damage was about fifteen feet tall, shaped like a woman whose head was like a cross between a Human and an alligator, and covered with silver scales like a snake."

"I'd say you have big problems. That sounds like a greater demon. What was she fighting?"

"A bunch of Human mages, some Werewolves, and a hell of a lot of those Trolls. As you can imagine, there is a shortage of living witnesses. Also, in addition to the snake woman, we have had a major demon problem since all this erupted."

"So, what happened first? The snake demon appeared, and the Humans attacked her?" I doubted that sequence but wanted to hear what Torbert had to say.

"From what we can piece together, there was an earthquake—a small one—and that hole over there opened. Shortly thereafter, some Humans and a lot of Trolls came through and met up with some other Humans. About half an hour later, the snake woman showed up and started slaughtering everything in sight. The Humans fought back, more demons showed up, the Trolls scattered, and things escalated from there. We've removed most of the body parts."

I pulled out my phone and called my expert on gods and archdemons. "Tell me about snake gods," I said when Isabella answered. I put her on speaker so Torbert could hear.

"There are a number of them," she said. "Kukulkan is the Mayan god of war. The Aztecs called him Quetzalcoatl. Apophis or Apep is the Egyptian god of chaos. Then there's Jörmungandr, the so-called Midgard Serpent, who supposedly will trigger Ragnarok."

"All chaotic," I said.

"The Naga is a god of death and rebirth, as is Selket. The concept of destruction preceding a new start. Why?"

"A fifteen-foot, scaled, magic-wielding demon with a reptilian head."

"Sounds like a greater demon to me. If it was an archdemon, that fight wouldn't have continued that long."

"Thanks." I hung up and turned to Torbert. "She agrees it was probably a greater demon. You know, most of the paranormal businesses in Ivy City are controlled by a greater demon. I feel it very strongly at *Fang* and *Sensual Labyrinth*, but its presence hangs over that entire area." *Fang* was run by a Vampire, the other club by that Jayne-Mansfield-look-alike succubus that he had once mentioned.

Torbert looked even more unhappy. "Any chance that we killed it last night?"

"You mean with those airplanes? Anything's possible, I guess."

Chapter 19

To my relief, Torbert conveyed me back to the nursery by helicopter. I had missed lunch and arrived in time to eat a hamburger and some fruit for dinner.

People sat around the TV again, but also gathered around the computers in the office and the laptops several of them had brought. I went into the cottage and turned on the TV there, poured myself a glass of *agavirna*, got out some sewing to keep my hands busy, and sat back to watch.

Isabella came in and sat with me. "So, what did Torbert have to say?"

"You nailed it. There's an open rupture between the realm of Jotun and Washington, D.C. A group of Human-looking people led a lot of Trolls through and met up with Humans on this side."

"Crowell."

"Probably. And her Human-looking mage friend."

She thought about it. "You said there was a weird cult of Aesir living in Jotun."

"Yeah. I thought about that. The mage is probably a realm walker. He hooks up with Crowell, feeds her Norse fantasies, and she builds a circle to open a portal to his world when the veils thin. Now, he and his homies can take over a new kingdom with Troll enforcers."

"So, what went wrong?"

"Poor planning, I guess. They opened their doorway too close to Ivy City. The greater demon who controls that area evidently felt they were encroaching on her territory."

Karen and Meagan came in and joined us. I

offered them *agavirna*, but both refused, opting for beers instead. We watched the chaos reports together in grim silence.

If all someone saw was the TV, they would have thought the whole world had gone crazy. We watched reports of breaches and battles and weird incidents from all over the world. Outside my fence, it was quiet and deserted.

At six o'clock in the evening Washington time—midnight Greenwich Mean Time—Beltane officially began. The world did not immediately change.

Fifteen minutes later, my little corner of it did. The Fairies went nuts, and I rushed out to see what was going on. Near the rear of the property, two imps cavorted by the pond. Breathing a sigh of relief that I had imps and not demons, I hurried back there and banished one of them, but it took me ten or fifteen minutes to corner and banish the other one. My banishment spell worked well on minor demons, such as imps and young succubae, but not at all on stronger and older demons.

"Kellana! Come see!" someone shouted back by the cottage. I rushed back, expecting another incursion, but everyone pointed at the TV.

The pictures were evidently broadcasted from a drone. I couldn't imagine Torbert or the military allowing an airplane or helicopter to fly over the breach. We saw a picture of urban ruins—the one I had traversed earlier that day. A steady stream of Trolls, seeming to appear from thin air, spread out across the area. In the short time I watched, I estimated that hundreds of the creatures crossed into Earth.

"Is that a Human?" someone asked, pointing to a spot on the screen.

"Aesir," I answered. "A race related to Humans and Elves. That's who's doing the thinking behind this invasion."

The picture suddenly went black. I wondered who had taken out the drone. It wasn't to either the government's or the coven's benefit to have that drone broadcasting.

"What were those things?" someone asked.

"Trolls," I answered. "There's a rupture in the veils southeast of Howard University."

I spent the next half hour explaining about Trolls and their realm of Jotun. My audience was far more attentive than the idiots I usually dealt with in the government.

"What happens now?" Ed asked. "There were hundreds of them."

"We only saw a few minutes," Jamie said. "There wasn't anything stopping them."

"When I was down there earlier today," I said, "the military had a lot of armored vehicles and tanks in the area. Dave Torbert told me that additional troops were on their way. Trolls aren't magical, so conventional weapons will kill them."

"But you said they're eight feet tall," Jamie said.

"Oh, they're tough and hard to kill, but it's not like having to fight hundreds of demons."

My statement had a hollow ring, even to me. Trolls weren't very intelligent, ranking with Goblins at the bottom of what was generally considered sentient. But they controlled fire, made weapons, and could master simple mechanical tasks. In the wild, they were ambush hunters, and ate anything they could catch. That included fish, birds, animals, Humans and Elves.

A couple of hours later, a TV station broadcast another video from a drone. It showed a force of Trolls assaulting a line of APCs and a tank. It was difficult to watch as the Humans' automatic weapons slaughtered the invaders. The fight was quick and ugly, and the Trolls withdrew. Then the station switched to a different video, showing the same setting, only with Trolls coming at the vehicles from all directions, overwhelming their crews. I watched in dismay as a Troll grabbed a machinegun and ripped it from its mount on an APC, then cradled it in its arms and started shooting at the APC next to it.

By midnight, we couldn't find a single station showing any drone footage. I assumed the government cracked down.

Most of my employees were young and had lots of energy. At least a dozen of them still watched the TV, and several more surfed the net on their computers, as I said good night.

Wednesday morning, the day after Beltane, dawned bright and warm. I stood on the porch of the cottage and smiled at the pristine-white newly-painted buildings, and how neat and tidy the nursery appeared. At least I got something out of the money I spent and the revenue I missed by being closed.

Unfortunately, that last part wasn't over yet. The TV news reported that DC was still locked down, and the fighting had spread. The biggest news from my point of view was an interview with Maddy Crowell on one of the local stations. Obviously, they didn't know she was wanted by the FBI.

"Humanity is under attack by these monsters from other worlds," she said. "The government is powerless to stop them. Magic is loose in the world, and our only hope is Humans with magic. But the government is intent on holding onto their power."

The station then switched to Senator Richard Bowman, who essentially echoed what Crowell said. "I've introduced legislation to enable us to meet this magical otherworld menace," he said, "but reactionary forces are blocking it. What happened yesterday underscores that we need to act now."

Karen called Torbert.

"He says their estimate is ten thousand Trolls came through in the past forty-eight hours," she reported after she hung up. "There's heavy fighting along a line extending from the Anacostia River to Howard University, and south along Sixth Street, but so far we're containing them."

"Containing them?" For some reason, I couldn't see Trolls fighting like a normal army.

"Yeah. I mean, there are some that have gotten through our lines to other parts of the city, but mostly we've held them back."

I wasn't so sure. For one thing, Trolls liked water, so I didn't think the river would constrain them the way it would demons. For another thing, why would the Trolls care about capturing territory? From what I knew about them, they were interested in finding something to eat, and they couldn't eat dirt.

I also noted that she didn't talk about what would be at the Trolls' backs—Ivy City and the snake demon. Had they forgotten about her, or did they think she simply stopped caring about the Trolls and their mage allies? My bet was that the snake demon was the reason the Trolls and their Aesir masters hadn't moved southeast to escape the city.

Of course, the real question was why they created

the rupture right in the middle of the city. The sounds of surf I had heard from the other side of the breach tickled at the back of my mind. The geography between realms didn't always match, so the Aesir might have had a problem with that. The mountains I had seen through the rupture would be in the middle of the Atlantic Ocean on Earth, and the surf sounds came from a direction that on Earth would be the National Mall, Georgetown, and the main landmass of North America.

Still, there had to be a reason for targeting Washington, D.C. Crowell's and Bowman's statements seemed to be aimed at scaring the government by scaring the voters.

"Karen, are there any reports of Trolls that are different than those we saw on TV?"

She gave me a puzzled frown. "Different how?"

"Larger, whiter."

"No, not that I've heard. How much larger?"

"Oh, ten to twenty percent. Nine or ten feet tall as opposed to eight?"

"What would that mean?" she asked.

"Frost Giants, another race of Trolls, like the difference between a Viking and you."

"Oh. I'll ask Dave."

"What about other invaders? Demons, hellhounds, Vampires, you know, the typical run-of-the-mill predators that tend to eat people without asking their permission?"

"Oh, yeah. Lots of that kind of thing. That's going on all over the country."

She reported back that all of the Trolls seemed to be of a homogenous phenotype, differing only slightly in skin color and clothing. I thought that was good news but didn't consider it the last word on the subject.

After breakfast, Meagan approached me, looking rather worried. She drew me off to the side and said, "I need you to lower the wards so I can leave."

"Okay. What's up?"

"I take medication, and I need it twice a day. I didn't expect to be gone so long, and I took my last pill this morning."

"I have a number of general healing potions, and I can always make something more specific."

She shook her head. "It's genetic, a metabolic issue. I don't think you could synthesize it."

I shrugged. "So, where do you need to go to get more?"

"My apartment."

I remembered her telling me that she lived about a mile away from my house in Georgetown. "Where is it, exactly?"

"Over between DuPont Circle and Logan Circle."

That placed her apartment between two and three miles from my house, and almost five miles from the nursery. Something didn't make sense, but I decided I was just being picky. Considering what I'd seen traveling with the army guys, the route to get there was a nightmare of other-realm predators.

"Do you want me to come with you? Believe me, I've been out there, and it isn't very pretty. I didn't tell all the kids because I didn't want to worry them, but we were attacked by demons that wrecked an APC, and I saw a hellhound."

"Would you? I didn't want to ask, but it's scary to think about going out there alone. I thought about asking Karen, but I don't know how demons react to illusion magic and," she cast a glance over her shoulder, "I would really rather she not know about my condition."

"Your superiors don't know?"

"No. If they did, they'd take me out of the field."

I hunted up Isabella. "Meagan needs to go out, and I said I will go with her. I think you and Karen and the paintball crowd can handle most anything until I get back, don't you?"

"Probably. I'm feeling like my normal self." The burns had disappeared without leaving any scars. Her powers of recuperation were beyond anything I'd ever seen. "There's just one thing," she continued, "I hate to sound like a downer, but how do we get out if you don't come back? You don't have a slipknot on your wards, do you?"

I didn't.

"Let me construct one and show Karen the key," I said. Isabella nodded.

As the name implied, a slipknot on a spell was a backdoor way of dissolving it. The catch was to create one that Karen's magic could activate. Not only were Human and Elven magics different, but an individual magic user's talents might enable one type of trigger and not another. We found Karen and explained the problem.

"Why does she need to go out?" Karen asked, then said, "But I think having more than one person with a key to the wards is a good idea. How much food do we have left?"

"Another couple of days. After that, it's what's ready to eat from the greenhouses, although the Fairies and Gnomes could haul some supplies in for you."

"If anyone could speak with them," Isabella said.

"Oh, Ed speaks Low Elvish. He's quite fluent, and a few of the Fairies speak English."

I took Karen to the gate and sketched a rune at the gatepost. "Can you see that?" I asked her.

"Very faintly. A pale-yellow glow."

To me it was a bright, fiery red. No matter. I sketched it again. "Can you copy that? Draw it in the dirt."

It took her three times to get it correct. Isabella took a picture of it with her phone.

"Good. It needs to be exact, proportions and minor curves matter. Now, draw that in the air, about an inch from the gatepost, and feed as much magic into it as you can. Then say this word." I spoke the High Elvish word to trigger the rune. She spoke five languages, so she got it on the second try.

"Okay, now draw the rune."

She did, and a yellow rune appeared. I was impressed. "Now, say the Word."

To any non-magic users, nothing happened. To me, and to Karen, the ward between the gateposts dissolved.

"Go get Meagan," I told Isabella. She sprinted off, and I turned to Karen. "That is only the ward for the gate. The rest of the fence line is still intact. If you have to do this, and you want to seal it off again, you'll have to construct your own ward."

She nodded. "I understand."

Meagan and Isabella came up to us, and Karen asked, "Why do you have to go out? Did Dave contact you?"

Meagan looked uncomfortable. "It's a personal matter. Can we leave it at that?"

190

Karen didn't look very happy, but she nodded. "Be careful, you two."

We stepped through the gate. I turned and set the ward, then headed for one of my pickups that was parked on the street.

"Let's take my car," Meagan said.

"I think the pickup will be better. It's more rugged." Her sports car had zero in the way of protection and ground clearance, and I didn't think speed would save us if we were confronted with a hellhound. What I didn't want to say was that I trusted my reactions and instincts driving far more than those of a Human. I didn't want a repeat of some stupid move like that soldier trying to run over a demon.

While I could tell she was reluctant, I ignored her and got in the pickup.

I purposely took a route to go by the Naval Observatory and the Vice President's residence. As I expected, the military presence was heavy, and we were stopped four times. I found it comforting. Meagan showed her credentials each time, and we were waved along.

It also wasn't a surprise to see a lot of military vehicles as we drove along beside Rock Creek Park and the Kalorama neighborhood. Those in charge of the U.S. government talked a lot about equality, but a person's wealth seemed to determine how much equality they received.

We parked on the street in front of Meagan's apartment building. The electricity worked—something that wasn't true in some parts of the city—and we took the elevator to her fourth-floor apartment. I didn't know much about apartments, but I had been to Karen's for dinner once, and Meagan's building seemed nicer.

She opened the door and ushered me inside, then closed the door and locked it.

"I won't be a minute," she said, brushing past me even as the stench of blood magic rolled over me.

"Meagan, wait!" I shouted as she rounded a corner. She didn't come back, but a man stepped into my sight at the end of the hallway. He was almost as tall as I was, with reddish-brown hair down to his shoulders and a matching beard. He was dressed in a traditional Aesir style—a fur-trimmed robe open to show a leather cuirass, and leggings—and he was the source of the blood magic I detected.

A weight pressed inexorably down on me, and as it slowly forced me to the floor, things grew dimmer until darkness enveloped me.

Chapter 20

"Tell me the spell."

The voice seemed to come out of a void. Everything was dark, but I wasn't sure if my eyes were open. I couldn't move. I tried my arms, legs, fingers, toes, and figured I probably couldn't move my eyelids, either.

"What is the spell to open the bag?" the voice came again. A woman's voice that was vaguely familiar.

Pain shot through me—a shattering, electric pain that touched every nerve in my body.

"What is the spell to open the bag?" A male voice, with an accent. In Low Elvish.

I tried to open my mouth to tell him that I couldn't open my mouth, but I couldn't open my mouth. I didn't know whether I wanted to laugh or cry. The pain lanced through me again. After a couple of more jolts that made me want to die, they got tired of the game and left me alone in the dark.

I could hear and feel, but I couldn't move. The man torturing me was the blood mage from Meagan's apartment. The woman was Meagan. For some reason, I thought we were still in her apartment. A few minutes later, I heard them having sex. That went on for over half an hour, then they quieted.

A while later, I was picked up and carried. Whoever did it wasn't gentle and banged various parts of my anatomy against things—walls, doorjambs, possibly other things. I had the impression of going down an elevator, then I was dumped on something hard. A car engine started, and I felt motion. Since I couldn't hear either Meagan or her companion, I decided I must be in the car's trunk.

We drove for about an hour. The car stopped several times, and I could hear Meagan use her credentials to get us through the checkpoints. The last of them was followed by a passage over water. I wasn't sure why I was so sure we had crossed a bridge, but I was.

When we arrived at their destination, the vehicle stopped, the engine shut off, a door of some sort opened near me, and I was picked up and carried again. My transportation dumped me on a hard floor and left me alone again.

I had no idea if I was tied in any way, or how long I had been out. I wondered if they planned to feed me. I wondered if I could pee while under the spell, or maybe I had and didn't know it. I didn't pursue that line of thinking any further.

The spell that held me didn't seem to affect my posture, and I didn't feel stiff. I thought I had been sitting at Meagan's apartment, then I was carried over someone's shoulder, laid on my side in the car, and then dumped in what I thought might be a basement, lying twisted on the floor, with an arm under my torso. It wasn't uncomfortable, but it should have been.

Pushing against the spell with my magic produced no results. Then I heard a thump, as if something hit a door. That was followed by Meagan cursing.

"The damned thing just follows her around. I swear, I left it in my apartment, but here it is."

I inwardly wanted to smile. Their questions suddenly made sense. They wanted to get into my bag and see what kind of goodies I had. I hoped they never got in it, because if they did, it meant I was dead. The binding spell I had put on the bag was keyed to my life energy.

"Don't worry about it," the male voice said, his accent even more pronounced in English, "the bag isn't sentient and can't do anything on its own. She's bound it to her, but it's just a bag."

The time I spent blacked out at Meagan's apartment was far preferable to the time after becoming aware. I had always had a good sense of time and distances. I didn't know if that was something unique to me, or if it was an Elven thing. I never thought about it until I spent a lot of time around Humans, and by then there weren't any Elves around to ask.

With a lot of time to think, I was glad Isabella made me create a way for Karen to open that ward. How I got where I was seemed to be simple bad luck. Meagan hadn't asked me to go with her; I offered to accompany her. I couldn't figure out why she decided she needed out, unless her story about the medicine was true. But it could also be that something had happened, or was going to happen, that I didn't know about.

When that kind of thinking got old, I thought about Cassiel. I wondered where he had gone in such a hurry, and I hoped his sister was all right. I hoped that I would get to meet her someday.

Obviously, I wasn't very important to Meagan and the Aesir, since I lay there for more than forty hours before they came back to check on me. There was a scraping sound when they opened the door, and Meagan cursed. I realized it was my bag when it bumped up against me.

"I'm not sure what to do with you," the male voice muttered in Elvish. "Meagan says you're dangerous, but you're only a hedge witch. Of course, it's highly unusual to see a hedge witch carrying a Dragon-skin bag. In another realm that would be worth a prince's ransom."

He walked around me. Studying me, I guessed. It was easy to keep track of him because of the stomach-turning blood-magic emanations. He was a man who was deep into the dark arts. I wondered how old he was. Many centuries, probably.

"What should I do with her?" he asked.

"We should wait for Nana," Meagan said. "She was the one who was so fixated on her."

"Yes, that's true," he said.

"She hasn't eaten or drunk anything in a long time," Meagan said. "She's not in total stasis, is she? I mean, her metabolic processes haven't stopped, have they?"

I realized then what had been puzzling me, what had been tickling at the back of my mind. Meagan didn't have any whiff of blood magic about her. She wasn't one of the coven's inner circle. But if she wasn't part of the Bluegrass Coven, none of what was happening made sense.

"No," he said. "I guess we should feed her, or at least give her a drink if we're not going to kill her."

The blackness lightened, and true feeling returned to my body. The concrete floor I lay on was cold, my right arm, which I was lying on, was asleep, and my twisted back was stiff and sore. I rolled over and had to bite back a scream as the blood flowed into my right hand. My bladder felt like it was ready to burst, and my mouth felt like it was stuffed with sawdust.

196

Struggling into a sitting position, I looked around. A basement, with a sump pump in one corner, and four legs attached to my captors. I crawled toward the sump pump, and when I reached it, I fought to my feet, unfastened my jeans, and squatted.

"I guess she really had to go," Meagan said. I wasn't sure whether I wanted to thank her or kill her. My feelings toward the Aesir mage weren't as ambiguous. Killing him was number one on my bucket list.

"We can't leave that bag with her," Meagan said. "The gods only know what all she has in that thing. Weapons for sure. For all we know, she could have a bomb in there. We didn't find her cell phone, either in the apartment or in her pickup."

"Go get her something to eat and drink," the mage said, "and I'll stay and watch her. After she eats, I'll spell her again."

Meagan went out, and I heard her climbing stairs beyond the door.

A million thoughts ran through my head, but my body was so stiff and weak that I knew I couldn't perform at my best. I needed to make sure I was in a relaxed position when he spelled me again. I planned my escape while my mind was still active.

They came back the next day, and there were more of them. I thought I could detect four people—Meagan, the blood mage, and two blood witches. One of them was the old woman who escaped the night of the raid on the Bluegrass Coven, Maddy Crowell. Thinking back, I hadn't seen Meagan that night, and didn't know if she was part of the raid at a different location.

"Here she is, Nana," Meagan said. "I'm not sure why you want her."

"Well, that remains to be seen," Crowell said. "Honey, be a dear and run out to the car and get the basket I have in the back seat."

"Sure thing," Meagan said, and I heard her go out.

As soon as she was gone, Crowell said, "So, an Elf and a witch. Her blood should be especially pleasing to the gods."

"I suppose," the mage answered. "I've never sacrificed an Elf before."

"Of course they'll be pleased," Crowell snapped back at him. "Bring her along, and we'll hold the ceremony tonight."

"Tonight? That doesn't give me any time to prepare her."

"Yes, tonight. As soon as possible. We need to do something. Your Trolls are getting slaughtered, and we need to take back the initiative."

"Well, we do have Doris Sanger. She's been through all the preparation rituals."

"We'll do the Elf. If that doesn't work, then we'll sacrifice Doris. Maybe the gods will favor us if we do two sacrifices at once."

"If I had known about that damned demon, we would have done all of this differently."

"The ceremony will take care of the demon," Crowell said. "Now, Arlen?"

"Yes, ma'am?" a fourth voice, a man.

"Take Meagan up to Franklin. I want her as far away from this business as possible. She needs to be ready to take control once the government falls."

"Yes, Miz Crowell."

198

Meagan came back down the stairs. "I put it in the kitchen," she said.

"Thank you, my dear. Now, I have a need for one of the family to take charge of things at home. Arlen will drive you up to Franklin tonight. I'll give you a call tomorrow."

They all left, and I waited. Sometime later, Crowell and the Aesir came back. He picked me up, threw me over his shoulder, and carried me up the stairs. Once again, I was dumped in the trunk of the car, or so I supposed that was my place. But this time, someone rearranged my body, my legs and my arms, into comfortable positions. I heard a soft thump next to me. Then I heard the trunk close.

We drove for an hour, and I wondered where we were going. I also wondered if they planned to leave me under that spell when they cut my heart out. That would ruin all my plans.

Chapter 21

Very smart people often make very stupid mistakes by simply not thinking things through. Maddy Crowell had not been with us when I was kidnapped, so she couldn't have known that we got out of DC only because of Meagan's FBI credentials.

Once again, I could tell when we passed over water, but the passage was very brief. I thought for a moment, then decided we must have crossed Chain Bridge, where the river was narrowest. Immediately, we came to a stop.

"The District of Columbia is under martial law," a voice said. "Please state your business."

A long pause, and then I heard Maddy's voice from the other side of the car. "My granddaughter needs her medicine. She called me, and she can't get out to the pharmacy. So, I picked up her prescription in Virginia, but I need to take it to her. She'll get sick and die if I don't."

I swore that if Meagan's illness wasn't real, I would kill her myself.

"We can't let you through," the first voice said.

"She'll die," Maddy wailed. "She's a member of the FBI. Surely you can do something."

"Wait here."

We all waited about ten minutes, then the man outside the car said, "What's your granddaughter's name?"

"Meagan Humphrey. She's an FBI agent," Maddy repeated.

"And you are?"

"Artur Hamundson. I'm a friend of the family. She

needed someone to drive her."

"And where are you going? Where is your granddaughter?"

Crowell gave them Meagan's address. Another twenty minutes of silence ensued.

"All right," the man's voice came again. "You're cleared to your granddaughter's place. But once you get there, this travel permit expires. Do you understand me? Once you get there, you stay there. Your approved route is marked on that map. Do you understand it?"

"Yes, I understand it," Hamundson said.

"Do not, under any circumstances, deviate from that route. We'll send an escort with you."

The car started again, and my hopes dropped. I started planning anew. From what I'd seen of Meagan's apartment, it was too small to fit thirteen witches and hold a sacrificial ceremony. That meant they would have to take me somewhere else after they thought the authorities had stopped following them.

I didn't know how the escort would take us to Meagan's from Chain Bridge, if that was where we were. One way would take us right by American University, and then along the same route I had taken days before. I might be practically close enough to spit on the nursery and have no way to contact anyone.

It felt as though we were driving slowly, and I could tell when we turned off Canal Road due to the sharp turn up a hill. That confirmed where we were, and how close we would come to the nursery. For the first time, I suffered a pang of self-pity.

We had been traveling for about ten minutes when Hamundson let out a curse in Low Elvish so loud I could hear it in the trunk. That was followed by four loud bangs. The car bumped and swerved, and I could hear the sounds of a flat tire rolling along the road. Maybe multiple flat tires. That was followed by a loud crash, and I was thrown into the front wall of the trunk.

The crackling sound of magical lightning was the next thing I heard, and I cringed, hoping I wasn't touching anything metal, but I was powerless to move. More lightning, then the whoosh of a fireball. The car rocked, and a jaguar roared. I was so shocked I didn't even mentally cheer.

Another fireball whoosh was followed by a scream so full of terror and pain that it froze my mind. Something exploded, then another explosion, then sudden silence.

I heard the trunk ripped open, and a voice yelled, "I found her."

Yeah, they found me. As my mind re-engaged, I pondered my situation. I was still enspelled, and if Hamundson lived, could he be convinced to remove it? And if he had died, could anyone lift it? There was a reason some people pursued blood magic. It conferred incredible power.

"What do you think?" a familiar voice asked very softly in Elvish.

"We can try," an unfamiliar voice replied in the same language. "I don't think we can hurt her by attempting to remove it."

"Would more power help?" a different familiar voice asked. "Some of us can link with you."

"I'm not sure power will be the issue," another voice said. "It really depends on if he tied off the spell. If she's in a complete stasis, we may have to call in a full-blood master to unravel it."

I felt magic, a different kind of magic than I was familiar with, but with a slight flavor reminiscent of Hamundson's. I imagined it as tentative, searching, then it strengthened and bathed me.

Air on my skin. I opened my eyes and blinked at blinding brightness. I stretched, and my muscles responded. Turning my head, I saw Cassiel leaning over me. It was too much, and I burst out crying.

He gathered me into his arms and lifted me out of the trunk, kissing me on the cheek and murmuring, "It's all right, Kel. It's all over. You're safe. You're safe."

I managed to suck it up after a minute or two and stop watering Cassiel's shirt. "Put me down. I think I can stand." He did but didn't let go of me, and I didn't object.

A woman standing in front of me had pointed ears. She was almost as tall as I was, but with golden hair and blue eyes. The woman next to her, with white-blonde hair and blue eyes, had round ears. Beyond them, short and stout for a male Elf, was a man whose face I recognized.

"Ser Miika," I said. "Your timing is impeccable."

Dipping his head and giving me a half-bow, he said, "Sel Kellana. Glad we could be of service."

"Are you all right?" Isabella asked. I realized there were probably twenty people standing around looking at me, including people in military uniforms and PCU combat vests.

"Yes, I think so. Hungry, thirsty, and a bit disoriented. How in the hell did you find me?"

Someone handed me a water bottle, and I gratefully drank all of it.

"The Bluegrass Coven may be powerful," Karen

said, "but they're amateurs. I can't believe that they used a car registered to Madeline Crowell and gave their real names at the checkpoint. Then they used Meagan's name, and we've had an all-points bulletin out for her ever since you two disappeared. You wouldn't happen to know where she is, do you? I have a special interest in seeing her again."

Karen's smile looked more feral than friendly, and her eyes were black stones.

"Try Crowell's place in Franklin, West Virginia," I said. "That's where she was headed last time I heard."

Karen's grin widened, and she jerked a nod.

Looking around, I saw that the car had four flat tires and had skidded into a stone wall after jumping the curb. About fifty feet behind us, I saw a spike strip laid across the road. A couple of Army Humvees sat on the other side of the strip.

"You set them up and laid an ambush," I said. Duh. My brain still wasn't working properly, and I was having trouble catching up to the obvious. "What happened to Hamundson?"

Miika shook his head. "The blood mage? He disappeared."

Even I knew that Maddy Crowell hadn't escaped. Her ravaged body lay in a large pool of blood by the side of the car. Isabella hadn't been gentle.

I retrieved my bag from the trunk. I pulled out a healing potion and an energy potion, and downed both of them.

They took me to the nursery, and Karen fixed a quick shrimp stir-fry in my kitchen while I took a shower and changed clothes.

"Where is everyone?" I asked in between mouthfuls.

"All of your employees and their families were evacuated to Fort Meade," Karen said. "DC is still a war zone, and the military provided some better accommodations for them up there."

"We had a battle with a bunch of stupid Werewolves," Isabella said. "Torbert and the military came by after you disappeared, and the Weres sprang an ambush when Karen dissolved the ward on the gate."

I looked around and turned to Cassiel. "You should introduce me to your friends."

"I am Naleema," the golden-haired woman said as she wrapped a territorial arm around Miika's waist. She was a half-Elven Nephilim, like her brother. The family resemblance was striking.

"Cassiel's sister," I said.

She dipped her head in acknowledgement. "His older sister," she said with a grin.

Her posture made me wonder if she knew Miika and I dated while she was gone the year before. Hell, I never even kissed him.

"Angelique," a woman with white-blonde hair, blue eyes, and round ears said, pronouncing it with a French accent. A half-Human Nephilim.

"I'm Faida," said a dark-haired woman sitting on a chair in my sitting room. She had pointed ears and appeared to be very young.

"I'm Angelo," a standing man said, "and this is my brother Giuseppe." Other than the color of their shirts, I couldn't tell the two of them apart. They were halflings—Aesir and Human.

"I assume I should thank the two of you for

205

freeing me from that spell?"

They shrugged in unison.

"So, the Paladins resolved their problem and came home?" I asked Cassiel.

He shook his head, his expression grim. "Our problem came here."

I must have looked as puzzled as I felt, because he said, "We came through the rift from Jotun yesterday. That's where we've been. Unfortunately, we're quite familiar with Artur Hamundson."

Finally feeling full after two bowls, I pushed back from the table. "We have a problem."

"Only one?" Isabella asked.

"One major one, and Hamundson is a large part of it. From what I overheard, the snake demon is back?"

"Oh, yes," Karen said. "She showed up two nights ago and blew up the Trolls' battle formation."

"Crowell said she slaughtered a lot of them," I told them.

Karen shook her head. "Not that many, actually. They broke ranks and scattered. Now, instead of a bunched mass of Trolls in one part of the city, we have Trolls all over the city, and scattered reports of them in Virginia."

"How do Hamundson and the demon figure in?" Miika asked.

"He plans a ceremony to counteract the snake demon. I don't know if he's going to try and bind her, or banish her, or call and bind another demon to fight her. But he has a sacrifice prepared to go. Crowell wanted to include me in the festivities, before you disrupted their plans, and she wanted to hold the ceremony tonight."

That information drew the Paladins into a

brainstorming session in my sitting room.

I went outside and walked around the nursery, reveling in being alive. I said hello to the Fairies, dropped by to chat with Fred and Kate, smelled the newly-bloomed flowers, and breathed in fresh air. Simple things that seemed so far away just a few hours before.

Trolls. Blood mages. Greater demons. It made me almost nostalgic for simpler times when all I had to worry about were Werewolves and Vampires. Maybe an occasional incubus trying to pick me up in a bar. Simpler times when the greater demon stayed behind the scenes in Ivy City instead of coming out in the open to kill Trolls and fighter jets and scare the piss out of me.

I pulled out my phone and called Sarah Faire.

"Kellana, what a surprise," she said when she answered the phone.

"Are you in the city?" I asked.

"Hell, no. I scatted over to Virginia as soon as the Air Force started firing missiles at civilian neighborhoods."

"Sarah, can you get a message to the demon in Ivy City?"

"What?"

"The greater demon who controls all the paranormal businesses in Ivy City. Can you get a message to her?"

She hemmed and hawed, and tried to deflect.

"Sarah, I know she's there. Every time I get near *Fang*, I can feel her. Or is that a different greater demon than the snake woman I've seen on TV? Or does she have a boyfriend? I know that two greater demons aren't going to exist in the same space unless they're very friendly."

"No, there's only one," Faire grudgingly admitted. "What do you want with that kind of chaos agent? You haven't gone over to the dark side, have you?"

I explained the situation. "I'm not fond of demons, but a greater demon who keeps a low profile is preferable to a blood mage who wants to disrupt everything," I said when I finished.

"When you put it that way, I think I agree with you," she said. "Yes, I'll convey the message. Any ideas about where he plans that ceremony?"

"None, unfortunately. I suppose he could hold it in Jotun, on the other side of the rift."

She was silent for a full minute. "That would make all kinds of sense and be the worst-case scenario."

Chapter 22

"Jotun," Miika echoed when I went back inside and told them my guess. Everyone quietly mulled over that for a while, looking around at each other.

"Would you know where to find him there?" I asked.

Another round of thinking and everyone waiting for someone else to say something.

"The cult has a temple there," Naleema finally said. "That's where they conduct their filthy rituals. But whether they would use that, I don't know."

"Why not?"

No one seemed to have an answer.

"The house where they breached the veils is gone," Isabella said. "There's nothing there now except a big hole in reality."

"According to what our prisoners tell us, all the sacrificial sites the coven used are across the Potomac," Karen said, "either in Virginia, or West Virginia. He would have a problem getting to any of those, and we have military units sitting on all of them if he showed up."

"But how important is the site?" I asked.

"Fairly important," Faida said. It was the first time I had heard the young halfling's voice, and it was like a little girl's, almost as high as a Fairy's. "The blood that soaks into the site prepares it for further atrocities. A sacrifice on virgin ground is difficult, and if Hamundson is trying something as tricky as calling a greater demon, he'll want everything to be as perfect as possible."

We bounced ideas around for a while, and then

Isabella asked, "What happens if we guess wrong? He calls a demon, and then his troubles really start. He has to bind it, right? That isn't guaranteed."

"True," Miika said.

"Mythologies of many worlds tell cautionary tales about mages who weren't strong enough to bind a called demon," Faida said.

"And since we don't have a politician's clue as to where he might be on this side," Isabella continued, "we take our best guess and try to intercept him in Jotun."

"Makes sense to me," Naleema said. "If he's gone back there, we know where to find him."

The Paladins asked for a travel permit, which Karen procured, and then hitched a ride with the Army to Naleema's house in Chevy Chase.

"Grab all the food that's left," I told Cass as I started gathering my things together at the nursery so I could go home and get ready. "Bess has probably eaten everything we left there, and she'll be cranky if we don't feed her."

I headed for my house in Georgetown with Cassiel, Isabella, and Karen. The plan was to meet that evening at a command post the Army had set up at Howard University Hospital.

"What's a Paladin?" Karen asked. We were in my lab where I was preparing a batch of healing potion.

"An ancient organization devoted to advancing order and obstructing chaos," I answered.

"My, I feel so enlightened."

I laughed. "Karen, I've known about them for more than six months now, and I'm still not really sure. As far as I can tell, they're a bunch of magic users, a lot of them halflings, but not all, mostly realm walkers, but not all, who run around the realms acting as a kind of quasi order police. Sort of like paranormal vigilantes who have trouble holding a real job."

"Oh. And Miika is a member?"

"Evidently. I didn't know he was a member. He never told me." Of course, he never told me about his relationship with Naleema, either. He made it sound like they were just friends.

"Sounds exciting."

A wistful note in her voice stopped me, and I turned to her. "Do you know what an adventure is?"

She gave me a puzzled look and shook her head.

"An adventure is something terrible happening to someone else a long ways away. In other words, to someone in San Francisco, we're having an adventure. But when it's up-close and personal, it's dangerous, scary, dirty, and doesn't pay for shit."

With a chuckle, she said, "I guess that's true. Well, at least I'll get a taste of it."

"What do you mean?"

"Getting to see another realm, even if just for a short time."

"Did Dave assign you to go with us? I don't think that's necessary."

She stared at me with big puppy-dog eyes and didn't say anything.

"Karen, you could get killed. That is a very dangerous place."

"Unlike Washington, D.C., in the midst of a post-Beltane Troll invasion with snake demons blasting fighter jets over the city? Please?"

I sighed. Her logic was irrefutable. "If Dave Torbert ever asks me, I'm going to tell him you snuck along over my objections. And since Elves can't lie, be sure to sneak really good. Dress warm. Jotun is a much colder place than here."

"Will my pistol work there?" she asked.

I paused. From what I knew, gunpowder did not work in Alfheim or Midgard. It burned, it fizzled, but it did not explode. Fireworks there were entirely constructed with magic. Likewise, petroleum didn't burn. We used magelights and magefire for cooking, heating and light. On the other hand, those things did work on Earth. It could be very confusing at times.

"I think so. We can ask the Paladins." I had my hands full, but I motioned with my elbow. "Take one of those paintball guns over there, with the red hopper. It uses carbon dioxide for propellant. If you can't recharge the bottle, I can, or probably any of the mages can."

Karen picked up the gun and looked at it. "I should be able to recharge it."

As I filled the potion bottles, I thought about what else I could give her. "Can you use a knife?"

"To fight with? Sure, I have some training. I'm also a black belt and have weapons training with nunchakus and sai."

When I finished with the potions, I reached into my bag and pulled out Alaric's off-blade. The bag had been his—not originally, but after he stole it—and I had kept it when he died, along with his weapons and a few other things. His sword would be far too long and heavy for Karen to wield, but the off-blade was only eighteen inches long and slender.

"This is a spell-forged blade," I said, sliding it out of its scabbard.

"It's beautiful," she breathed. It was. Alaric was the younger son of a noble family, and the blade was engraved with elaborate scroll work.

I handed it to her. "A spell-forged blade is almost unbreakable, and it will cut through steel or rock. It never needs sharpening. Take this. Even if your gun works, you won't have an endless supply of bullets, and it's not much good if an enemy is too close."

"Yeah, that's true. Maybe we can drop by my place and pick up my nunchakus as well."

The Army guys dropped us off at their command center in the middle of an attack by two demons. I was impressed at the improvements the military had made in weapons technology. Instead of using paintball guns to deliver doses of demonbane, someone had created a glass-tipped bazooka rocket with the demonbane inside. Not only did it have a much longer range, but the results were spectacular when the rocket hit a demon.

The Paladins arrived shortly after we did. I wondered at the talents of those I would potentially be depending on in battle. Miika I knew. Halfling he might be from my home realm of Midgard, but he was a battle mage, skilled and powerful. To him I would trust my life.

I assumed Naleema's magic was similar to Cassiel's, but I knew she wasn't a healer. Most Nephilim were powerful, but Angelique's magic would be different from that of the two half-Elves. Aesir tended to have heavy battle-oriented magic, and the twins both carried massive two-handed swords. As to Faida, half-Elf, half-Human, young and frail looking, I had no clue. I noted that she carried a bow and quiver and a short sword, as did all three Nephilim.

As we trekked over to the rupture, I realized that it was directly across the street from a cemetery. I wondered if that was just chance, or if Hamundson had chosen the location for that reason. I mentally shrugged and let it go. I knew far more about dark arts practitioners than I ever wanted to.

Picking our way through the rubble of what had been a nice neighborhood of row houses and older apartment buildings, we came to a concrete canyon, and I realized it was North Capitol Street.

"We'll have to find an overpass that's still intact," I said. I gave Cassiel a mock frown. "Assuming those with wings are going to slog along with the rest of us."

Things had been quiet, but a sudden absence of any sound at all drew my attention. A silver hand, large as a bushel basket and tipped with claws the length of short swords, clasped the wall in front of us. A second hand followed. And then the head of a being—so disturbing and terrible it froze me in my tracks—peered over the wall. It pulled itself up to the street in front of me.

At least fifteen feet tall, covered in silver scales, the demon had two short, thick hind legs, and long, almost delicate arms ending in hands tipped with four-inch claws. Her tail extended beyond her legs and was almost as long as her body. The impression was female, with three pairs of breasts. The top of her head and eyes also resembled a Human female, but the nose extended into a blunt snout a foot long above a mouth loaded with sharp teeth. A sharp crest ran from the top of her head all the way down her back to her tail.

Out of reflex, I drew my sword from its sheath. The demon stood and looked down on me.

"So hostile, little Elf?" she said in High Elvish. Her voice had the quality of a sharp knife through flesh, her pronunciation sibilant, the esses drawn out and almost slurred. "I was told you have a message for me."

"I-I," I stammered, then shut my mouth, swallowed, took a deep breath, and started over. "We believe that he who opened the breach into Jotun plans to call a demon to contest with you." I clamped my jaw shut to keep my teeth from chattering.

"Very interesting. And why do you tell me this? Do you wish to worship Apophis?"

"N-no. I mean, not really." That couldn't really be Apophis, could it? A god, or more accurately, an archdemon?

She leaned closer, and the sword I held out in front of me looked like a toothpick.

"Then why?"

"I prefer the way you've treated the city to the way the mage, Hamundson, has."

Her eyes were the size of dinner plates, silver irises slit like a cat, or an Elf. I could see my reflection in them, a disturbing double image.

"And how do I treat this city?"

"You don't destroy. You don't hunt."

"Ah, you prefer a lazy agent of chaos. A case of enlightened self-interest?" she practically purred. "Interesting. I like that. Do you understand why?"

"N-N-No." I wasn't sure I wanted to, either.

"The three strongest emotions are lust, fear, and anger," she said. "I find lust the most satisfying. It's just a personal preference. That is a spell-forged blade, is it not?"

"Yes."

"Do you think you could hurt me with it?"

My teeth started to chatter again. I fought for composure and finally said, "I don't know, but I will try to defend myself."

She threw back her head and laughed. The sound chilled me to the bone, and I almost peed my pants. My hands were shaking so hard it was difficult to continue holding the sword.

"I wonder. I've never encountered a spell-forged blade," she said. "Well, every life needs a little mystery, don't you think? So why don't you and I leave that question for another time. And I think there shall be another time, little Elf. I rather like you."

She disappeared.

My legs wouldn't hold me any longer, and I sank to the pavement.

Cassiel rushed up and knelt beside me. "Are you all right?"

"I think so."

"What happened?"

I blinked at him, feeling stupid. "Didn't you see?"

He shook his head. "See what? You just whipped out your sword and stood there. I called to you and you didn't respond. Then we discovered there was an invisible shield around you, and we couldn't reach you."

"Then you collapsed, and the shield dissolved," Isabella said.

"You didn't see her?"

They both shook their heads. "See who?" Isabella asked.

"The snake demon."

"No," Isabella said. "Here?"

If anyone should be able to see a demon, I thought it would be Isabella.

Cass helped me to my feet.

"No big deal," I said. "Probably just a lack of sleep or something."

"Probably delusional," Naleema said. "Not a terribly unusual condition for those setting forth to save the world. Shall we proceed?"

I shot her a look, and she winked. As we walked along, she matched her pace to mine.

"Is it something we need to know?"

"I don't know. The snake demon. I told her about Hamundson." I had trouble organizing my thoughts.

"You told her we're going to Jotun?"

"No. I don't think so." I shook my head, trying to clear it. "I said that he was trying to summon a demon. To fight her." I let my breath go in a whoosh. "*Danu merde*, she scared me."

"I would imagine. Well, if we have to fight a greater demon, or two greater demons, then that's what we have to do."

"You're crazier than I am!"

"Probably." The look in Naleema's eyes made me believe her.

Chapter 23

The gateway to another world was still there, halfway down the street. Torbert and his team of witches had set up across the street where they could watch it. Two heavy machine guns, one on each side of the rift and about fifty feet away, were manned by soldiers and aimed to catch anything coming through in a crossfire.

"We tried to set a shield across the opening, and then we tried setting wards around it," Torbert said. "So far, nothing we've tried has made any difference. But we haven't had anyone wanting to come through to this side in about eight hours."

I remembered Cassiel telling me that the Angels were unable to close a breach between Heaven and Earth.

"Has anyone gone the other way?" I asked.

"We've sent several scouting teams through, all volunteers. They haven't explored very far. We didn't want to trap anyone if it suddenly closes."

"Unfortunately, I don't think that's very likely," Miika said. "But if that does happen, tell your teams to stay close to the area where they came through, and we'll go get them."

I drew Karen off to the side. "Once we're through, stay behind me. If I have a sword in my right hand, stay behind to my left. If I have a sword in my left hand, stay behind to my right. Understand?" She nodded, wide-eyed. "If we're attacked and you find yourself between a Troll and one of us, hit the ground. And for the Goddess's sake, be careful around Miika. That man is a one-man army. Karen, I don't doubt you can take care of yourself on Earth, but you are much slower and weaker than any of us. All of these people are seasoned warriors, so if they tell you to do something, do it."

"Yes, ma'am." She glanced toward the breach. "It's beautiful, isn't it?"

I smiled. "Yes, it is, and very deadly."

"How many realms away is it? I mean, it's not one of the ones next door to us, is it?"

I turned to look. "If I remember correctly, about thirty. It's been a long time since I went through there."

Alaric and I had spent a couple of weeks in a village in Jotun. Just long enough to get a good idea of how weird their religion was. They used blood magic— animal sacrifices—during their major celebrations. So, I could easily see how the more extreme members of their cult might drift into something darker.

We gathered, everyone checked their gear and each other, then we crossed. It was a bright sunny day on both sides, but the temperature dropped from eighty degrees Fahrenheit to fifty with a single step.

The sounds of surf crashing against the shore caused me to walk around the breach and gaze out at the ocean beyond. We had come out about fifty feet from a cliff. I walked to the edge and looked down about a hundred feet to where the surf pounded rough boulders. The ocean spread in front of me to the horizon. The cliffs rose to the north and descended to the south where I could make out a sandy beach almost out of sight.

Isabella shifted and moved out in front at a lope to scout the area. Naleema and Angelique spread their wings and took to the sky. Angelo and Giuseppe spread out to the flanks while Miika took the point. They did all of that without a word, and it was obvious the group was experienced and comfortable with each other.

I turned to Karen and said, "Move up there with Faida and Cassiel. I'll take the rear."

The ground around the breach was pretty trampled down, and we had to move quite a distance before distinct trails resolved themselves. It appeared the Trolls had come to the area along three main routes.

The mountains rose steep and white about a hundred miles in front of us. Dense forest lay around us on all sides. The position of the sun told me we had about six or seven hours until sundown.

I breathed the clean air, reveling in the freshness unpolluted by cars and airplanes, and the rest of Earth's technology. I knew Isabella enjoyed it. She was born at a time when Earth was that unsullied.

One or the other of the Nephilim circled back over us on a regular basis. They appeared to be flying at high altitude in two interlocking circles, and if I didn't know what they were, I probably would have mistaken them for birds.

We had traveled for about three hours when we came over a rise in the trail and found Isabella in her Human form sitting on a huge log. The rest of us plopped down and broke out trail rations and water bottles. I offered some jerky and water to Isabella.

"No, thanks. I ate some sort of a rabbit thing about an hour ago, so I'm fine. There's a band of Trolls coming this way. They should get here in another half hour, so I thought we might discuss what we want to do."

"How many?" Miika asked.

"Forty or fifty. They don't act like they're in a

hurry, so I doubt they know we're here. Probably just headed for the breach so they can plunder the new hunting grounds."

"Arms?"

"Mostly clubs, some have spears or bows. It doesn't appear their technology is very advanced."

Miika shook his head. "They're definitely on the low end of the low-tech side. Some of them have knives or axes they traded the Aesir for, but those become rarer as you travel away from the Aesir villages."

He looked around our little circle, then said, "Cassiel, please go find the ladies and ask them to join us. Any good spots for an ambush?" That last was directed at Isabella.

"Right here," she said. "At the other end of this clearing, the trail makes a swing around some large rocks. We catch them between the rocks and this log; it will slow them down and make it hard to run in both directions."

Isabella shifted back to her cat form and trotted off down the trail. She planned to camp out on one of the large rocks and drop in to cut off the Trolls' retreat. Faida scampered up a tree. I deposited Karen up a tree outside the killing zone, then took a tree of my own opposite Faida's, and we both strung our bows. Miika waited on the side of the log away from the approaching Trolls.

Naleema and Angelique winged in a while later and conferred with Miika, then took off back aloft. While we waited, I ate some dried fruit and admired everyone's glamours. Other than Isabella, not a one of our party was visible except Miika, and only his head and shoulders could be seen by the approaching Trolls.

The lead Troll was halfway across the small clearing when he caught sight of Miika. He stopped dead and looked around. Some of his followers fanned out a little from the trail, and those in the rear began to bunch up as the last of their party passed Isabella's rock.

I saw her stand and stretch, then she roared and dropped off the rock onto the back of a Troll below her. She bit his head as she rode him to the ground, then stood on her back legs and raked the chest and abdomen of the next closest Troll with her claws.

Faida and I both began loosing arrows into the crowded clearing. Miika held up his hands and channeled energy bolts into the front of the group.

Suddenly the snake demon was there, standing in front of the group of Trolls and towering over them. They froze in their tracks, staring in awe. I knew the feeling. I wasn't sure what to do next. Then one of Faida's arrows passed through the demon and struck a Troll in the throat. That's when I realized I was looking at one of Karen's illusions.

The sound of wings overhead caused me to look up in time to see the three Nephilim diving toward the Trolls. As Naleema reached the treetops, she loosed a blast of lightning, then pulled up. Angelique followed her, with Cassiel acting last.

But Naleema wasn't done. She completed a loop and dove to strafe the Trolls with lightning again.

I mentally shook myself and directed my attention back to the Trolls. Only half of them were down, so I knocked an arrow and shot another one.

It was over in less than five minutes. It took us almost an hour to collect our arrows, drag the bodies away from the trail, and dump them in places that couldn't be seen. That taken care of, we continued on our way.

Miika called a halt at twilight. We ate and rolled up in our blankets as the temperature plummeted. Miika, the Aesirian twins, and I agreed to take watch. Miika made sense when he said that the Nephilim expended far more energy flying than those of us on the ground did walking. Karen was never in the conversation for night watch.

Cassiel and I curled up together, and it felt so good to hold him again.

"So, this is where you've been since you left Earth?" I asked.

"Most of the time. Here and Vanaheim."

"What's going on? Why are the Paladins interested?"

"The Paladins in Vanaheim called us in," Cassiel said. "Hamundson's blood cult originated on Vanaheim and spread to Valhalla. About three hundred years ago, they were purged and exiled to Jotun. But they didn't completely stamp it out in Vanaheim. The moneyed interests there cooked up a scheme with Hamundson to open a breach into Earth. Their plan, as best we can figure out, is to establish a black magiocracy on Earth. Hamundson recruited two or three more hedge kings, and they promised the Trolls new hunting grounds."

"They think they can take over the U.S. government?"

He kissed me on the nose. "They've been a little clumsy about it. I would have used money instead of force. That seems to have worked for those currently in power."

When Giuseppe woke me for my shift in the early

morning hours, he told me, "A herd of wild pigs came down the trail about an hour ago. They didn't seem interested in us, and I was happy not to draw their attention. Angelo heard a couple of wolves howling on his watch, and I think Isabella is out hunting." He grinned. "And with that, I'll say good night."

I entertained myself by wishing I could start a fire and thinking about what I could cook if I did. The Trolls' diet consisted almost wholly of meat and fish, but I knew wild grains, mushrooms, and a variety of wild berries would be available in season, as would pine nuts. The Aesir who lived in Jotun had imported a number of grains and vegetable crops from Asgard, Valhalla, and Vanaheim. Except for the Trolls, I found Jotun pleasant enough, but if given a choice, I would have chosen Vanaheim over all the other Aesir-ruled realms. I had enjoyed the time Alaric and I spent there.

Shortly before sunrise, Isabella padded into camp and flopped down next to me. Without even a nod, she leaned against me and fell asleep. Since her body heat was far higher than mine, I didn't mind.

Our destination—the Paladins told Karen, Isabella, and me—was a large town another day's travel from our resting spot. That was where Artur Hamundson was the king, and the main temple of their religion was half a day's travel farther from there. Thus far, we hadn't encountered any sign of Aesir, but we were warned that might change at any time.

Our trail widened, and then came to a road, with the choice to continue straight or go left. The road showed horses' hoof prints and cart tracks.

"Our destination is straight ahead," Miika explained, "and there is another village to the left. As you can see, they chose that site for the breach very carefully. The ocean is in front of them on both sides of the breach."

"Horses and wagons?" Karen asked.

Miika chuckled. "Yes, but not necessarily together. Some of the wagons are oxen pulled, some are magic driven. They use horses mainly for riding. What they do lack is anything other than magic and hand power for clearing forests or building roads. Keep in mind, fossil fuels are used in few places besides Earth and Transvyl. Were primarily uses solar and wind power."

"It's not that the people in other realms can't or don't use technology," I said, "but in Alfheim and Midgard, the technology is fueled by magic. Much of the technology you use in Earth is unnecessary."

Isabella twice warned us of traffic on the road ahead of us, and we hid in the forest until the Aesir passed. At midday, Naleema warned us that we had followers coming from the village we had bypassed. We ate quickly and pressed on.

In mid-afternoon, Miika led us away from the road. An hour of wandering through the forest brought us to the edge of a valley. From a rock formation that provided some concealment, we looked down on the town. A wide creek ran from the head of the valley to our right, through the town, and out the other end of the valley to our left.

"Welcome to *Brunhilobaenum*. That creek runs into a larger river in about thirty miles, and the river empties into the ocean about a hundred miles north of the breach," Naleema said. "In fact, if you get separated and can find where this creek joins the river, turn ninety degrees left and walk straight to find the breach."

"You said that Hamundson is king here?" I asked. "Are there a lot of kings? I never heard of one when I was here before."

"King Artur," Miika said with a smirk, "controls an area about a hundred miles long and seventy miles wide, although he claims about five times as much land. As best we can determine, there are only about a hundred thousand Aesir in this realm, with about three hundred thousand Human slaves. Compare that to about a hundred million Trolls, and you can see who really controls things."

"When I was his captive, Hamundson said he had a sacrifice prepared, all the pre-rituals completed. If he has Human slaves, why would he need to worry about a sacrificial victim in Earth?" I asked.

Miika and Naleema both shrugged, but Faida said, "Probably a witch. Many of the *Jotunblod* rituals involve absorbing the magic of the sacrifice. Any Humans in this realm who show any signs of magic powers find themselves on an altar rather quickly. Ergo, no local witches."

I caught Karen's eye. "If any young man tries to walk you to the altar, just say no."

She laughed.

Faida used a mirror to scry the town. The Nephilim's eyes were much sharper than mine, but I pulled out a pair of binoculars and studied the place. I figured about three or four hundred houses, all two or three stories, plus another fifty other structures. One building in the center was very large and the only one more than three stories tall. Miika walked up beside me and placed a hand on my shoulder.

"May I?" he asked. I handed him the binoculars.

226

"Where is the temple?" I asked.

Without lowering the binoculars, he gestured up with one hand. I looked at the opposite valley wall, my eyes tracking higher and higher. Three-quarters of the way up sat an obvious stave church, looking more like those with onion domes I had seen in Northern Russia than those in Scandinavia. The path up the mountain was steep and looked treacherous.

"I hope we don't have to climb that trail," I said.

"At worst, only halfway. See the bench?"

About halfway to the church, there was a level area, probably fifty to a hundred yards wide, then the path went up again.

"Yeah?"

"Great place for an ambush."

Chapter 24

We camped out at the valley's edge overnight. By noon of the following day, we still hadn't spotted Hamundson or anyone heading in the direction of the temple. Fearing that we might have guessed wrong, the Paladins sent Angelique back to the breach.

Naleema and Cassiel flew out to reconnoiter. Naleema reported that large numbers of Trolls were headed in the direction of the breach. They seemed to be coming from all over the continent. Cass flew up to the temple and reported back that four guards and a caretaker—maybe a priest of some kind—were the only people up there.

For my part, I waited, and fidgeted, and worried. If we guessed wrong and Hamundson held his ceremony somewhere else, things in Earth's realm conceivably might be worse when we got back.

I sought out Miika and Cassiel.

"If you can get me close enough, I can sneak into town and try to get some information," I told them.

"By playing squirrel?" Cassiel asked. When he and I conducted a rescue in Transvyl, I had found the prisoners by shrinking to my one-foot height and donning a squirrel glamour.

"Something like that."

"Can you fly at night?" Miika asked.

"Sure," Cassiel said. "That won't be a problem."

I shook my head vigorously and Miika asked, "What's wrong?"

"His night vision is crap."

Miika snickered. "But you can tell him when he gets near the ground, right?"

"Hopefully."

"Dropping her on one of those roofs will be easy," Cass said. "There's plenty of magelights, and no one will see us."

I listened to them make plans as though I had turned invisible. Somehow, my idea had become theirs.

Naleema walked up and put her hand on my shoulder. "It makes them happy to think they're in charge," she whispered in my ear. "You're right, he has crappy night vision, but I don't."

"Can you carry my weight?"

"Aren't you going to shrink first? You don't still weigh the same at Fairy size, do you?"

I hadn't thought of that and felt pretty dumb. "No. I don't know where the mass goes."

"Magic, is what my mother always said." Their mother was an Elf, but the ability to change sizes never carried through to Elves' halfling children.

I laughed. "That's what my mother said, too."

We worked out a set of signals in case I needed to be picked up, and also in case they needed to assault the town. That would be a last-ditch option. Aesirian mages were no slouches, and according to Naleema, magic occurred in the population of Jotun at a higher-than-normal rate.

We informed Miika and Cassiel that we were leaving and listened to five minutes of admonitions to be careful, then I shrank, and Naleema tucked me inside her bodice.

She glided silently down into the valley. Dressed in black, she was practically invisible against the moonless sky. I felt her level off, then slow. Suddenly our orientation changed, and I realized she was back-winging, coming almost to a stall in the air.

"Out you go. Quickly, now," she whispered.

I clambered out, took one look at the roof below me, and jumped. The fall was only about four feet, or the equivalent of a couple of stories in my larger form. Looking around, I could barely discern her form rising into the sky above me.

She had dropped me on the largest building, which she said was Hamundson's home—the 'royal' palace—the only government building and common gathering place for the town's populace.

I crawled around the roof, checking out the town from every angle. Most of the houses had lights on, but few people were out on the streets. The tavern across the street to the north from the palace was an exception, and it appeared quite lively.

I dropped down to the roof on the next level, then climbed the wall back up to the eave, where I slipped inside the building through a vent. That led to a shaft which took me down another level. As with similar Elven architecture, even though the building was heated with magic, there was a need to vent to the outside, allowing carbon dioxide and various odors to escape. I had been in castles built at a lower technological level, and they tended to be pretty stinky.

After spending half the night exploring the building, it became clear that few people lived there, and most of them were absent. I found a nice cozy bedroom that had a layer of dust on the floor inside the door and went to bed for the night after warding the door.

The sounds of activity woke me a couple of hours after dawn. I broke my fast, then shrank down again and climbed through the vent system until I found the source of all the noise.

Quite a bit of activity was going on in three different areas of the building. One area seemed to be governmental, with scribes writing, issuing documents, collecting money, and gossiping. A second area seemed to be some sort of market. It took me a little time to catch on that the goods being bought and sold were Humans. The third area was the most germane to my business. Several Aesir, dressed in clothing a little too fancy for hunting or slopping the pigs, sat around a large table.

The topic of discussion was Hamundson, the breach, Trolls, concern about a possible invasion from Earth, and concern about invasion by their Jotun neighbors to the south and east. While those present seemed all to agree that the breach was a good thing, most were not happy that the other side opened into a large city.

Those who supported Hamundson and his plans were in the minority, but I noted that the group who opposed him did so in rather passive and measured tones. While they were unhappy, they didn't openly oppose him. What everyone had in common was a deep concern, mixed with curiosity, that Hamundson was missing, and no one knew where he was.

For the rest of the day, I hung around eavesdropping in various parts of the building. Naleema wouldn't be able to pick me up until after dark, nor would I be able to leave the town on my own until then.

Close to sundown, Artur Hamundson walked into town on the road coming from the east. A few people acted happy and excited to see him. The people I took to be the ruling class were also excited, but not all of them were happy. To me, the interesting thing was his direction. He didn't come from the breach. Of course, as a realm walker, he could have crossed realms anywhere, but Earth was thirty realms away.

He went straight to the palace, spoke briefly to three or four people he met, and brushed off everyone else who approached him. He then went to what I guessed were his private quarters on the third floor.

I knew from my earlier inspection of the building that seven people resided in that section—four women and three children. Guards stood watch on the door around the clock, and I hadn't seen anyone go in or out before Hamundson arrived.

Watching through various vent grills over the next four hours, I saw Hamundson bathe, eat, and have sex with two of the women. Then he left and went downstairs.

My guess proved correct when he entered the room with the long table I had observed earlier. All of the men from the earlier meeting awaited him.

"You've been gone a long time, my lord," a man said as Hamundson seated himself.

"The work has been more complicated than expected," Hamundson said. "The plan does move forward, however. The portal is stable, and the path before us is clear. The gods favor us. Tomorrow, I will perform a series of ceremonies, and then we shall take the last step. Gather your armies and be ready to march at sunrise the day after tomorrow."

He soon dismissed them all and called in six other men. These men were older, and while they once might have been warriors, I doubted they still participated in battles with a sword. My suspicions were soon confirmed. They planned out a series of ceremonies, each ending with the sacrificial death of a Human. The final ceremony they planned was different. Wielding the power of a circle of seven, they planned to sacrifice a woman named Doris Sanger and use the magic released by her passing to call and bind a greater demon.

I had never been so sorry in my life to have guessed correctly. Hamundson and his buddies were stark raving mad.

Chapter 25

I waited until the sun set, then made my way out of the building on the side away from the tavern. Growing to my normal size, I donned a glamour mimicking one of the men I had seen earlier that day. I walked down to the creek, then followed it upstream out of town.

Well past the reach of the town lights, I could see outlined against the starry sky the rock outcropping where my companions waited. Kindling a small bright white magelight in my palm, I forced it to cycle through blue to green, yellow, orange, and red, then cycled it back to white and extinguished it. After five minutes, I kindled the light and cycled it again.

A dark shape grew above me, blotting out the stars, then I heard the sound of wings. Naleema landed next to me.

"We saw Hamundson," she said.

"Yes, he came back. I know their plans, the question is, what can we do about it?"

I shrank, she tucked me away, and we flew back to our camp.

Everyone gathered around, and I told them what I learned in the town. No one asked any questions until I finished.

"Only seven of them?" Miika asked.

I knew why he asked. Traditionally, across all branches of magic, a full circle was considered to be thirteen witches or mages.

"Thirteen is traditional," Faida said, "but maybe seven is all they think they need."

I nodded. "Yes, all very powerful, all blood mages.

They didn't mention using any more people for their ceremony, but who knows what their ceremonies require."

Miika shrugged. "Maybe. If I was going to call a greater demon, I'd hedge my bet."

"They said they would use the sacrifice's magic to bind the demon," I said. "What I know about summoning demons could be fit in a thimble, but I've seen black mages attempt a lot of strange things by themselves."

"Did any of them live?" Miika asked.

"No, but my sword had something to do with that."

He gave me a smirk, then sobered. "You said they were powerful," Miika said. "Stronger than I am?"

Miika was a halfling but a full-powered battle mage and the strongest of our company, except possibly for Faida. She was so young, and I could tell she had yet to grow into her full power. I was curious about her magic, though. I had never met anyone with her particular flavor of magic.

"I think the six were once of your power or less, but the blood magic...it makes it hard to tell." I shrugged, and he nodded. "Hamundson is stronger than you are. Him, I would be very wary of." I looked to the Nephilim. "Is it true about Angels and dark magic?"

Angelique said, "That tale is exaggerated, and we are all halflings. But, yes, we have some immunity. The three of us can probably construct a shield even a circle of seven can't overcome."

"Who is this Doris Sanger?" Angelo asked. "Hamundson seems to think she holds the key to their plan. That's not an Aesir name."

"It's an Earth name," Karen said, "but I never heard of her."

"It could be she's a member of the Bluegrass coven that has some kind of special magic he thinks he can use," Cassiel said.

"Faida, do you think you could mess up that path to the temple?" Miika asked.

"Sure. I hope everyone brought their rain gear. I'll set things in motion now, and whoever is on watch at four o'clock should wake me up."

She moved to the edge of the valley and turned to face the direction of the ocean. Raising her hands in the air, she began to chant in High Elvish. A shiver ran through me as I realized she was a weather mage, but I had only heard legends of such magic. The strength of the magic she poured into the air was astounding.

After about fifteen minutes, she lowered her hands and walked over to where her pack lay next to a fallen log. She took a drink from a water bottle, then rolled into her blankets. Naleema went over to her and sort of tucked her in and used a little bit of magic.

It might have been my imagination, but I thought I felt a breeze I hadn't noticed before.

"Faida, it's time to wake up," I said, squatting a few feet away from her. Touching or even getting too close to a warrior when they were asleep was not a good idea.

Her eyes opened, and she stared at me for a few seconds, then said, "Can you fix me some warm tea, please? With honey."

"Sure thing. It feels like a storm is blowing in."

"I certainly hope so," she said, sitting up.

When Naleema had flown me out of the valley the night was starry and clear. But when Giuseppe woke me to take my watch, a steady breeze blew in from the sea, and low clouds covered the sky.

I already had a pot of tea made. Actually, half a pot of tea. I had drunk the other half. I poured Faida a cup and added a dollop of honey to it, also giving her a few slices of dried fruit and a piece of jerky.

She thanked me and sat in her blankets drinking the tea and nibbling on the food. After she finished eating, she made a short trip into the woods. When she came back, she stood on the edge of the valley surveying the clouds overhead.

With a sigh, she muttered, "And the weather has been so nice."

Faida threw her hands into the air, sketching runes with both hands, and shouted at the clouds, invoking the Goddess, the four winds, and finally Dagda, the god of weather. The amount of magic funneling through her thin body was staggering.

I watched in awe as the clouds darkened and began to boil. Faida shouted again, and lightning ripped through the air, followed by a deafening clap of thunder. More lightning, more thunder, and then the heavens opened, and a deluge of rain poured down.

I threw up a shield and managed to stay mostly dry. Glancing around me, I saw that all of my companions had done as I had—shielded themselves before going to sleep. I remembered Angelique speaking to Karen as she bedded down, and when I glanced at her, I noticed the rain hadn't touched her. The only one wet was Faida, standing with her arms spread wide and her face turned up to the sky with an expression of jubilant rapture.

237

That didn't mean everyone was still asleep. Even the dead couldn't have slept through that crash of thunder. We all sat in our own little bubbles watching the rain. Within minutes, I saw the creek start to rise.

"So, what's the plan?" I asked.

"We wait for the flood, then move down into the valley," Naleema said.

"Flood?"

She chuckled and gestured to the creek. "You haven't seen anything yet."

An hour later, I understood. With a roar, a wall of water came rushing down into the valley, washing trees and boulders downstream with it. The bridge above the town buckled and gave way, adding to the debris in the water. The bridge below the town soon followed. Only the arched bridge in the middle of town, next to the palace, still stood, but its ends on both sides were under water.

Soon, half of the valley was submerged.

"Time for us to go," Naleema said. The rain had tailed off from its earlier downpour and settled into a steady, hard rain.

We made our way down into the valley, and when we reached the river—now several times as wide as before—Naleema instructed Karen and me to harden our shields, making them air tight. She, Angelique, and Cassiel then took to the air. Each of them created magical hooks that attached to each person's shield and towed us all across the river to the other side like children's toys.

I had never seen a group with such divergent talents work together like the Paladins did. Hell, I had never seen a group with such divergent talents, period. Sometimes it felt as though Miika was in charge, at other times Naleema. I had the feeling that neither of them considered themselves to be the leader. Everyone just did what needed to be done, and sometimes that task was to lead.

We trudged through the soaked valley to the road leading to the temple. As the road began to climb, it turned into a series of short switchbacks. And it was a mess, looking more like a stream than a road. Giuseppe tried to walk on it and sank to his ankles in mud.

The Nephilim flew me, Isabella, Karen, and Faida up to the bench that Miika had pointed out to me before, then they used a makeshift sling carried by Cassiel and Naleema to ferry the three men.

"When we get back to Earth," Naleema said when they finished, "I'm putting all you boys on a diet."

We found places out of sight on both sides of the road and waited. Personally, I didn't have a lot of faith that anyone would be performing sacrifices that day. The river had inundated half of the town, and some people were clinging to rooftops in the rain.

"Maybe you overdid it," I said to Faida.

She blushed. "I'm still learning how to fine-tune things. You want a storm, you get a storm. Don't wish for dry weather unless you want a drought."

I chuckled. "I'll remember that. Any idea how long this will last?"

Faida rolled her eyes upward, then said, "Probably a day or two. It shouldn't get any worse, though."

It didn't, but it still made for a miserable night.

The following day at mid-morning, the rain started to abate, and the river stopped rising. Most of the town was still flooded, but a group of about forty or fifty people on horseback headed up the road toward us.

The lead riders in the procession were about halfway to where we lay in wait when another group set out from town. I pulled out my binoculars and scouted the two groups.

"We have a problem," Naleema said. Nephilim didn't need binoculars. "The men we're after are in the second group."

I had just figured that out. We were looking at a hundred people, most of them armed, and no telling how many with magic. Our party consisted of seven mages, two witches, and a jaguar. Those were the kind of lousy odds that would get us killed.

"We still need to try and stop them," Angelique said. "Time for plan B."

"Or maybe plan D," Miika responded. "A brute-force ambush would be suicide."

We brainstormed options for about ten minutes and came up with a plan. Cassiel flew up the mountain and took a station well off the road. Getting our healer killed sounded like a lousy idea to everyone. Naleema took Karen and me up to a place on the mountain a bit above the temple and off to one side. I grew to my normal size, and we waited. Our gambit would play only if every other trick failed and Hamundson's circle managed to get to the temple for its ceremony.

A huge bolt of lightning hit some rocks on the edge of the plateau as the first group neared it. The resulting avalanche was small, but destructive. At least a dozen riders and their horses were knocked off the trail. Unfortunately, a number of mages with the group cast shields and minimized the damage to the people and horses. The damage to the road was another thing. A number of the riders who were below the road damage abandoned their steeds and slogged on up the road on foot.

"I don't know why they're all coming up here," Karen said. "There's no way they're going to all fit in that little temple."

The temple would hold forty people at most, I figured. "Probably a lot of guards," I said. "Soldiers and guardsmen were everywhere in the town. I guess they're paranoid."

"Look closer," Naleema said. "At least a dozen of the people in the second group are Humans. The guards are to keep the guests of honor from running away."

She was right, the day's toll would be paid by Human slaves.

Our mages set off another rockslide on the trail from the plateau to the temple, and another one on the lower stretch, but that was as much as we dared do for fear of giving ourselves away. It slowed the *Jotunblod* crazies down, and it was late afternoon before Hamundson and his circle reached the temple.

Those who arrived earlier sat around outside under as much shelter as they could find, drinking, nursing their wounded, and feeling sorry for themselves. I thought it was very strange that no one tried to take shelter in the temple, but none of them even approached the doors. Two of Hamundson's mage circle were old men—for an Aesir to show white hair and a beard, that meant well over seven hundred years old—and they looked almost spent.

Hamundson simply looked angry. He ordered the slaves brought forward, and he marched toward the temple doors without hesitation. One of the slaves, a young girl with long blonde hair, dressed in a filmy white dress, looked somewhat different from the other slaves. As she drew closer, I could feel her magic, but I also realized something else.

"That's Doris Sanger," I whispered. "She's definitely a witch, but that's not all. The son of a bitch plans to sacrifice her because she's a virgin."

A silver snake demon suddenly appeared in front of the temple entry, and everyone froze.

My first three arrows took the mages following Hamundson in the chest. Naleema's arrows took two more. My fourth arrow, aimed at Hamundson, failed to find its target. He waved his hand, and the arrow took a sharp turn, going straight up into the sky.

"Run!" Naleema hissed and took off through the forest. I grabbed Karen around the waist and followed. I didn't turn to look at what caused an explosive crashing sound behind me.

I had to hand it to her. For someone with wings, Naleema could run, and knew how to make her way through a forest. I guessed that being half-Elf probably helped.

We didn't stop until we reached a cliff. Below us, a very long way down, was the bench, much narrower than where the road crossed it. I started looking around for a way down, when Naleema said, "I think it's safe to fly from here."

She flopped down on a rock, breathing heavily. "I don't think I've run that far since I was a kid. Do you think we did enough to disrupt his plans? Surely he can't still try to summon a demon with most of his circle dead."

"He's crazy," Karen said. "Who knows what he'll try." She shook her head as I put her down. "Thank you. I felt like a baby when you picked me up, but I figured out pretty quickly that I would never be able to keep up. I think it has finally registered that you aren't Human."

"Definitely," Naleema said. She looked up at me. "You aren't even breathing hard."

"Clean living," I said, and they both grinned.

Naleema flew us down to where Miika and the others waited. They signaled Cassiel, and he flew a long circle to rendezvous with us.

"What now?" Cass asked.

I looked back up the hill, somewhat reluctant to abandon the Sanger girl, then said, "There are several armies headed for the breach. I don't know how large, or what their makeup is, but I would guess a mixture of Aesir and Trolls. They don't know that Hamundson failed. I think we should at least warn people in Earth's realm that they're coming."

"She's right," Miika said. "We know that Hamundson's plans all revolve around Earth. It may take him a while to show up there again, but we're probably better off waiting for him there than hanging around here."

Chapter 26

Hidden in the bushes a few hundred yards from the breach leading to Earth, I whispered, "So, what do we do now?"

Miika's eyes slid toward me, then back to the scene before us. Out of sight for anyone peering through the breach from Earth were several thousand Trolls and at least a thousand Aesir. When Hamundson spoke of armies, he wasn't kidding.

"I assume they're waiting on Hamundson to show up and lead them to the promised land," Miika said.

"Not a bad guess. I wonder if he knows that."

"Probably," Naleema said. "I assume those people we saw on the trail were carrying messages back and forth."

It had taken us far longer to get back to the breach than it had to get to Hamundson's town. We weren't able to travel on the road much because of all the traffic, and when we drew closer to the breach, we discovered thousands of Trolls camped in the woods.

"This situation can't last," Isabella said. "They've stripped the area of game, and there's a limit to how many fish you can catch from the shore. They don't have any boats."

"These are Trolls from inland," Miika said. "I doubt they would know what to do with a boat."

"Can't we get someone through to warn Earth?" Karen asked.

Everyone looked at each other, then they all looked at me. I waited for them to look elsewhere, but no one did.

"Couldn't someone fly through?" I asked. My

voice sounded sort of whiney, and I cringed a little.

"As long as I didn't get blasted out of the sky," Cassiel said.

"Or shot full of arrows," Angelique said. "The Trolls do manage to kill game with their bows."

"Including birds, sometimes," Naleema said.

No one else jumped in with other ideas.

With a deep sigh, I asked the air, "Do you have any idea how far that is for someone whose legs are only six inches long?"

I didn't expect an outpouring of sympathy, and they didn't disappoint me. I tried to think up an excuse to delay, but Trolls saw as well at night as I did. They were somewhat sun sensitive, though, and since Faida's storm had passed, it was a bright, sunny day.

"You're all going to feel guilty when some Troll eats me," I said, then shrank down to my smaller size. I didn't bother donning a glamour. As Isabella noted, almost everything edible in the area had already been eaten. A squirrel or rabbit dashing across the open meadow would draw far too much interest.

Darting from bush to tree to tussock of grass, crawling at times, I made my way around the trampled meadow leading to the breach. A couple of times I was forced to work my way around campsites of either Trolls or Aesir by climbing a tree and jumping from it to another. Eventually, I got as close to the breach as I could and stared across fifty yards of open ground.

I debated whether I should cover that space at my smaller size, or at full size. Fifty yards at full size would take less than five seconds, but at least a minute at my smaller size. On the other hand, a blast of magic was almost instantaneous and could even follow me through to the other side.

Crouching low, I walked toward the hole in reality at a measured pace, ready to shift to my full size and sprint at any sign I'd been spotted.

I heard a shout in the distance but kept walking. The shout was repeated, and then several more voices joined in. I took off at a sprint but didn't shift.

One of the weirder things about a portal to another realm was what was behind it in addition to what was through it, as Torbert had shown me on the other side.

Two Aesir suddenly appeared in front of the breach, blocking my path. Since both were staring straight at me, there wasn't any question that I'd been detected. A thought flashed through my mind that maybe they didn't understand what I was. An overgrown Fairy? Some other kind of Fae? A magic user with a glamour? An illusion?

One of them drew his sword, then bent his knees to position himself lower. I altered course slightly to run straight toward him, but just before I got within reach of his blade, I darted to the side and dove between the legs of the other man. I hit, rolled, and leapt back to my feet. A howl of pain came from behind me.

I took a chance and glanced over my shoulder as I reached the breach and saw one of the men down, holding his leg. His buddy was leaning over him, holding a sword with blood on the blade. Sometimes you get lucky. I dove toward the hole and felt the weird ripple of reality as I passed through to Earth.

The image of the machineguns pointed at the breach had haunted me during my entire journey toward the gateway. Hamundson and Crowell had opened the breach from inside a house. That had since been destroyed, whether from the breach opening or the fighting in the area I didn't know. But part of a wall, about two feet high, remained standing. I rolled behind it and held my breath, half expecting to hear the rattle of guns.

Silence.

I shifted to full size, and yelled, "Hold your fire! Call David Torbert! I have news from the other side!"

The silence turned into a lot of people shouting. I picked out one that said, "Come out with your hands up!"

"I'm coming out. Hold your fire." I cast a shield and stood. No one shot at me, and I took that as a good sign.

"Move away from there," an officer said, waving me toward a place not covered by the machineguns. I was more than happy to comply.

Torbert soon trotted up. At first, he smiled, then frowned when he realized I was alone. "Kellana. Where are the others? Karen?"

"Everyone's fine, but they're trapped on the other side. Dave, can we go somewhere private?"

He led me to the abandoned house where his command post was set up and offered me something to drink. I took both water and coffee.

"So, what's the story?" he asked.

"We disrupted Hamundson's plan to some extent. At least, we think we did. But he's been thinking a lot bigger than we suspected. On the other side of that window is a fairly large army, and a lot of magic users. Their plan is to invade and take over the U.S. government."

"Hah! Good luck to them."

"Their plan might have already succeeded if it

wasn't for that demon," I said. "Richard Bowman and others would have provided some credibility for them."

"Bowman? Explain."

"Follow this line of reasoning," I told him. "The government is unable to stand against the invasion of demons, Trolls, and the gods know what else. What we need are our own magic users, people born here and true-blue patriotic Americans, to take charge and save us. People like the Bluegrass Coven and their friends from Savage River."

"You're joking."

"I wish I were. Didn't you listen to that TV interview with Crowell and Bowman?"

"No, but someone told me about it. I've been busy."

"Dave, they plan to set up a magiocracy, and since they control the Trolls, they could show some quick wins and prove they are more competent than the old government."

Torbert poured me some more coffee. "But we've destroyed the Bluegrass Coven."

"Not all of it. Have you captured Meagan Humphrey?"

"No, she's eluded us."

"And on the other side of that breach are thousands of Trolls and hundreds of mages, just waiting for the word to invade. What's happened here while we were gone?"

He got up and walked around the room as he talked. "Things seem to have stabilized, though they're still crazier than they were two weeks ago. The veils seem to be less stable than they were before, and we're seeing a lot more strange creatures and people than we've ever had."

"I thought you said things have stabilized."

"They have, in the sense that things stopped getting worse."

A half-dozen military men plus representatives of the FBI, various police agencies, and several government experts met in a large conference room at the Pentagon. Torbert didn't understand why I insisted on bringing in the leaders of the Raven and Sunrise Covens, who each brought two people with them, and Sarah Faire, who brought the Jayne Mansfield succubus.

"The Trolls are more a distraction," I told them at the end of my story. "The military could easily control them, especially since they will be coming through a bottleneck. Assuming the *Jotunblod* don't open another breach somewhere else."

"But Beltane is over," one of the government men in a suit protested.

"They opened this one before Beltane," I reminded them. "The veils are fragile. With strong enough magic, and using their methods, we should consider the possibility. But even if they don't, the problem is the Aesir mages. Have all of you seen the devastation from the battle the night before Beltane? That was only a few mages and one greater demon. How are you going to stop a couple of hundred mages?"

"Forgive me if I violate any top-secret, cross-my-heart intelligence things," Faire said, "but there are at least six other open breaches around the world, and no one has a clue about how to close them. I've been

249

told that the Angels in Heaven haven't had any luck closing the two breaches in their realm that provide access to Earth. It would appear that while stopping an invasion is the immediate concern, we need a long-term strategy for dealing with beings from other realms."

A couple of the suits glared at her, and she responded by smiling back and batting her eyelashes. I wondered if they knew what they were dealing with. If she got either of them alone, they would be purring like pussycats when she was finished with them.

Into the silence, Torbert turned to me and asked, "Do you have any recommendations?"

Huh? Who, me? Oh, dear Danu, we are in deep trouble, I thought. I bit my lip and looked across the table at Faire, who also looked far more alarmed than she had a minute before. The succubus leered at me, and I could tell she thought the whole thing was funny.

"We might be able to stop them from coming through," said Grace Hopkins, leader of the Raven Coven. "It would be a temporary fix, not a permanent one."

"That's what the Angels have tried to do with the breaches in Heaven," I said. "From what I understand, they've been partially successful, but their breaches are more complex. We only have to deal with one realm."

"More complex?" one of the suits asked.

"Each of the breaches in Heaven leads to three other realms. One of them has two entrances in Earth," I said.

The succubus spoke up, her voice a combination of smoke and silk. "From Earth, I can travel directly to twelve different realms. From there, I have no idea how far I could go, for each of those realms have multiple rifts." She turned and smiled at Faire. "There are three other rifts here on Earth you obviously aren't aware of."

Everyone started talking at the same time, and it took a while before the suit in charge—Torbert whispered to me that he was the Director of National Intelligence, as dubious a job as I'd ever heard of—could reestablish order.

"Okay, assuming we can't close it, and we can't keep the inhabitants of Jotun out forever, what do we do about the current situation?" The DNI Director asked.

Everyone looked around at each other, hoping someone would have a brilliant idea. I looked at Torbert, who raised an eyebrow.

I took a deep breath. "We need to cut off the head of the snake. We eliminate Artur Hamundson and his fellow kings in Jotun who are leading the invasion. We finish crushing the Bluegrass Coven, including Meagan Humphrey. Then we start approaching Humans' interactions with paranormals as a permanent issue that needs to be solved rather than something that needs to be conquered or ignored. We aren't going away."

I left the meeting feeling as though I had made some progress, at least as far as the government men understanding the problem. It didn't appear, however, that we were any closer to solving it, or getting Karen, Isabella, and the Paladins back to Earth.

Chapter 27

I walked out of the Pentagon feeling incredibly frustrated. Torbert was silent and grim. Faire and the succubus were ahead of us, walking toward a limo where the driver stood holding the door open for them.

"I'll catch you later," I told Torbert, then trotted ahead to catch up with Faire and her friend. "Can I get a ride with you?"

Both of them looked startled, then Faire said, "Of course." She held out her hand to the car, and I climbed in. I'd never been in a limo before and was surprised at the leg room. Faire and the succubus sat across from me.

"Where to?" Faire asked.

"I'm not sure. Probably my place in Georgetown."

She nodded. "I would like to take Lilith back to *Sensuous Labyrinth* before going to Georgetown. Do you mind?"

"Not at all." I turned my attention to Lilith. "You said there are at least a dozen worlds open from Earth. I would assume there are multiple rifts in those realms. Has anyone mapped all the connections?"

Lilith studied me for a minute, then said, "There was a map of sorts, but it's woefully incomplete following Beltane. People talked about the veils being shredded before, but it's much worse now. You're right, the situation here in Earth's realm is not unique. Heaven is experiencing such chaos as they haven't seen in millennia." She looked positively delighted about that.

"I'm wondering if there is another route into

Jotun, or at least into Vanaheim or another close realm."

Faire and Lilith both looked thoughtful.

"You want to get your friends out," Faire said.

"Yes, but if we can get the backing, we might be able to neutralize Hamundson and his backers. If we can take down the blood cult, the Trolls are only a minor nuisance. As long as they have full bellies, they aren't going to be interested in conquering anything."

"True," Lilith said, "but why should we help you?"

I grinned at her. "The chaos Hamundson is fomenting doesn't benefit you."

Faire burst out laughing. "She's got you."

The limo pulled up in front of Lilith's nightclub. She got out, then leaned down and said, "I'll see what I can pull together for a map."

"How about a guide?" I asked.

She drew back, staring at me. I could see something change in her eyes. "I might be able to do that."

"I'll supply the magic users," I said.

Lilith nodded. Reaching in her purse, she pulled out a card and handed it to me. "Call me tonight."

As we pulled away, Faire asked, "Georgetown?"

"Have you got a travel permit to go anywhere you want?"

"Yes. Where do you want to go?"

"Baltimore."

"Is Alicia in?" I asked the girl at the counter of Magical Secrets.

"Yes, who should I say is calling?"

"Kellana Rogirsdottir. Is she upstairs?"

The girl's eyes widened slightly. "Yes."

"Thanks. I know the way."

I climbed the two flights of stairs to the third floor. Alicia Hopkins awaited me. She didn't say anything, obviously waiting for me to speak.

"I need your help," I said.

She offered me a seat, then made tea and set out some British biscuits on a small table. After she poured and we each took a sip—all very European and civilized—she said, "Tell me about it."

So, I did. I talked for an hour, with Alicia interrupting with questions occasionally. When I got to the part about asking Lilith for a guide, she held up her hand.

"What did you promise in exchange for her help?"

I took a deep breath. "Nothing."

Alicia gave me a disbelieving look and started to push back from the table.

"There's something I didn't tell you," I said, and she settled back in her chair. I told her of my encounter with the snake demon.

"I see. And you promised the demon nothing?" I shook my head. "And you asked the demon for nothing?"

"All I did was warn her."

She leaned back in her chair and was quiet for a long time. Occasionally, she took a sip of tea or a bite from a cookie. Finally, she asked, "What can I do?"

"If we can get to Jotun and kill Hamundson, and disrupt his plans, then we can defuse this crisis. I need enough powerful magic users to stop the *Jotunblod*."

"How much time do you think we have?"

"Very little. I would like to be ready to move tomorrow."

"If I happen to find anyone crazy enough to join this venture, where should I send them?"

I gave her my business card.

Leaving Magical Secrets, I walked a block down to the fancy bar where I'd left Sarah Faire. I found her in a booth with a man on either side. She looked bright and happy. They looked happy, but listless.

"Enjoy your lunch?" I asked.

"I did," she said with a smile. "Ready to go?"

As we climbed in her limo, she asked, "Did you have any luck?"

"I don't know. Maybe."

She patted me on the arm. "Sometimes I think luck is an underappreciated talent. And girl, you may be the luckiest person I've ever met. Have you ever been to a casino?"

I slept at the nursery that night. If any magic users were crazy enough to show up, I didn't want to give them the chance to change their mind. But when I woke, the Fairies said it had been quiet and I hadn't had any visitors.

The quiet didn't last. The Fairies erupted while I was doing the breakfast dishes. A man stood outside the gate, so I went to see what was going on.

He looked like every sleazy, overdressed card shark anyone ever cast in a cheap movie, complete with slicked-back hair, a pencil-thin mustache, and a sneering smile. He made Richard Bowman look trustworthy. I tried not to gape. I couldn't see through his glamour, but I could clearly feel his magic.

"Lilith sent me. She said you need a guide." The quality of his voice alone made me want to hold onto my purse tighter.

"Okay, Mister...uh."

"Call me Luce."

"Lucifer?"

"Yeah. My mother was real religious."

"Hang on. I'm going to have to do something with the wards for you to pass," I said. He waited while I dismantled three layers of wards on the gate. I also had to tell the Fairies to leave him alone. They wanted to roast him and feed him to the neighbor's dog.

When I finally led him into my kitchen, I said, "Would you like something to eat or drink? And, well, you don't have to maintain that glamour if you don't want to."

Luce chuckled, and the glamour faded away. Other than the horns, tail, and red skin, he pretty much looked the same. "I'll take some coffee if you have some."

"Can you drink *dalesh*?"

His sneer turned into a delighted smile. "Yes. I would love some."

It turned out he was a realm walker and a trader, someone who could transport inanimate objects between realms. Cassiel could also do that, but it was a rare talent.

"I built the original map Lilith spoke of," he said, "but the past few weeks have totally changed things."

"You understand what I'm trying to do?"

"She explained it."

"And you don't think I'm crazy?"

"Oh, you're crazy all right. But I'm getting paid

256

very well. And I'll get paid even better if I haul your ass back in one piece. That part was emphasized." He motioned to the window. "You've got more visitors."

I saw Luce recast his glamour as I went out to let my new volunteers in.

By noon, I had a complement of fifteen witches and mages, every one of them more powerful than I was. That was when Alicia showed up with another twenty magic users.

"Can you lead this many people through the veils?" I asked Luce.

"I might have to take you through in groups," he said. "Ten at a time, no problem. But what we need to do is make it to either Sweden or Mexico."

"The rifts to Asgard?" I asked.

"Exactly. From Asgard to Vanaheim to Jotun. If I have to ferry everyone through every realm from here to Jotun, it's going to take a while."

I called Torbert. He called me back half an hour later and told me some military vehicles would come to haul everyone to Andrews Air Force Base.

"How long is this going to take?" I asked Luce.

"Depends. The problem with going through Mexico is it will put us in Asgard a long way from where you want to be in Jotun. It takes longer to get to Sweden, but you'll be near a major city, and you can pay at a portal to cross into Vanaheim, and then I'll take you into Jotun."

I understood portal travel. That is how I had visited Alfheim from Midgard. Portals existed on Earth, but Humans didn't produce realm walkers or portal mages. I called Torbert back.

"I need about a hundred ounces of gold."

"For what?"

"Portal fees. Other realms really don't understand paper dollars. They prefer real money."

"I'll see what I can do."

The plane waiting for us turned out to be one of the planes reserved for the U.S. President. Also waiting were Torbert and a lot of government and military types.

"What are they coming for?" I asked Torbert. "Hoping to set up diplomatic and trade arrangements with other realms?"

He gave me a sour look. "I don't know, to be honest. As soon as I requested an airplane, everyone wants in on the act."

"We're not taking anyone with us into other realms who can't cast a protective shield," I said. "I don't care what their rank is."

One thing I had to admit. They fed us well on the flight.

We flew into Gothenburg instead of Stockholm, as the rift was in one of Gothenburg's northern suburbs. One good thing about the military people being involved, they had called ahead, and the Swedish military had trucks waiting to take us across town.

The rift was in the middle of a children's playground for an apartment complex. The Swedish military and government had taken over much of the area, but since the rift didn't lead to anyplace nasty, there was a relaxed atmosphere to the place. They even had a customs office set up to handle visitors and trade coming across from Asgard.

Alicia and I had briefed all the magic users on the flight, and we divided into three circles, plus me and Luce. While I was capable of participating in any of the circles, I had de facto been placed in charge.

We crossed through the rift and found Aesir waiting for us. I tried to talk to them about hiring transportation to the nearest portal, but instead they pulled me into their version of a customs office. Since I was the only one who spoke High Elvish, everyone else stayed outside.

"Sel Kellana," an Aesir nobleman addressed me as he motioned me to a seat. In addition to the man behind the desk, several more nobles sat or stood around the office. "The Swedish authorities gave us some information about your mission, but perhaps the language issues left some things unclear. Can you please explain what you propose to do?"

So, I told my story again. When I finished, a man to my right said, "You intend to break the *Jotenblod* with a force of thirty-eight mages? We have been trying to do that for centuries."

"We intend to cut off their head," I said. "Those who threaten us in the Earth realm will be gathered in one place. Kill their kings, disrupt their command structures, and thwart their invasion. I may be a fool, but I'm not crazy. Hopefully we can take the war to their realm instead of just defending ours."

"Your governments are facilitating this initiative," another man said. "Why aren't they involved?"

I sighed. "Most of Earth didn't even acknowledge that magic existed until three years ago. Most Humans don't have any magic at all. There aren't any schools, or organized guilds, let alone governmental institutions dealing with magic. I pulled together as many magic users as I could on short notice. I'm hoping to get some help from the Paladins in Vanaheim."

I thought it was going to be another one of those

meetings where everyone looked at everyone else, but the Aesir surprised me.

"Well," the man at the desk said, "we can supply you with transportation, and a regiment of battle mages. I think you will find the Crown in Vanaheim equally cooperative."

I walked out with my head spinning.

"What did they say?" Alicia asked. "Are they going to let us through?"

"Yes, they'll give us transportation, and they're going to lend us a thousand trained warrior mages."

Chapter 28

When we reached the location in Vanaheim that corresponded to the rift between Jotun and Earth, our force comprised two thousand five hundred battle mages from Asgard, Vanaheim, and Valhalla. Another thirty thousand non-magical troops waited to cross the portal after the mage shock troops secured a beachhead. A hundred Paladins had joined our number, and I was, thankfully, no longer in charge of anything.

By my calculations, which were always tricky when passing between realms, I had left my friends in Jotun six days before. We also had no idea what was happening in Washington. The *Jotenblod* invasion might have already started, and we would be coming in behind the invading force.

What we weren't short on was transportation. A full thirteen portal mages stood in a circle holding hands around an arch built of rough stone. Another portal mage stood in the center of the circle. I had watched those mages lift the stones—each of which weighed tons—into place. I roughly estimated the portal at fifteen feet high and twenty feet wide. Large enough for a Vanaheim truck to drive through.

"They are creating a true portal," the mage next to me said in a low voice. "When they are finished, we'll have a way into Jotun that we control, that can be opened and closed at will."

"And what about the rift to Earth?" I asked.

"Nothing to be done for that, but you will be able to use the rift to reach this portal, and from here, the other Aesir realms. Alfheim and Midgard, even, if they ever reopen those portals."

I had asked, but the portals to my home were closed. No one wanted the Elven civil war spilling over into other realms.

My original objective had been to rescue my friends and prevent an invasion of Earth. The Aesir had far more lofty ambitions. They wanted to crush the *Jotenblod* religion, exterminate the blood mages, and occupy Jotun, turning it into a legitimate Aesir/Vanir colony. That it would open trade to Earth was viewed as a questionable side benefit.

The mage in the center of the circle began chanting and sketching runes on the stones forming the arch. Magic gathered and concentrated into the circle. Soon the entire circle began to glow. I had never been around any magical working so great, so I watched in awe.

The final culmination of the spell seemed almost anticlimactic. Suddenly the space under the arch shimmered, and then images flashed by so fast I couldn't focus on a single one. I knew there would be three hundred and fifty-nine of them, and then the shimmer faded, and I could see through to the other side again.

The man at the center of the circle sketched another rune, spoke a Word, and the space under the arch opened to the meadow in Jotun. I could hear the sound of the surf in the background.

The mages broke their circle and moved to the side. A phalanx of battle mages moved into the arch and disappeared from sight. More followed. By the time the third company passed through, I could hear the sounds of fighting filtering back through the portal.

Alicia stood on one side of me, and Luce on the other. I had to pledge my first-born for the Aesir to allow him to accompany us.

"When you came to me in Baltimore, I thought you were crazy," Alicia said. "I can't believe we actually thought we were going to challenge an entire army with three circles of Human witches."

"I can't believe you were crazy enough to buy into it," I responded. "But you know that I truly planned to succeed."

"I was right," she said. "You are crazy."

It took an hour for all the warrior mages to pass through, then the leader of the Paladins signaled to us, and we moved forward.

I drew my sword and cast the spell to set my shield. The ripple of reality as I passed through the arch was starting to feel familiar again. The portal sat about a hundred yards from the rift to Earth. On the Jotun side, nothing marked it, and I knew the mages would probably build an arch on this side, though they didn't need to go through the ceremony again. Any portal mage could open it by sketching the rune of his destination.

Bodies lay all about, most Trolls, but a few Aesir. None that I saw wore the uniforms of the battle mages who crossed from Vanaheim.

I made my way toward the area where I left my friends six days before, keeping an eye out for any of them, and also for any of the blood mages, kings, or generals I had seen in Hamundson's palace. I came across the body of one general near where I started my journey toward the rift. The arrow in his chest looked Elven, but short. The fletching was Faida's, and a feeling of elation bumped in my chest.

Inside the forest, near the path toward Hamundson's town, I found one of the kings. He had been mauled by an animal that bit his head hard enough to crush his steel helmet.

"Isabella!" I yelled. "Cassiel!" There was no reply.

"They were here?" Alicia asked. The Paladin leader hovered at her side.

"I left them here six days ago. That," I pointed at the dead king, "is Isabella's work." The man's blood was fresh, so he couldn't have been dead long.

"Goddess," Alicia breathed. "What—"

"She's a jaguar shifter," I said. "I saw another man killed with one of Faida's arrows."

The Paladin nodded, then gave orders to his followers. They spread out into the forest.

"They might be trying to work their way toward the rift," I said, and turned in that direction.

I hadn't gone very far when a band of Trolls burst out of the forest. I cut down the first one, and Alicia hurled an energy ball that took out three more. The Paladins with us moved to engage the Trolls, and we found ourselves in the middle of a melee. I ducked under an axe the size of a stop sign and cut at the Troll's legs. It felt like hitting a tree, but he stumbled away.

Beyond the Trolls, I saw a man sprint out of the woods in the direction of the rift. Dodging another Troll, I looked again and realized the runner was Artur Hamundson.

It took another pass to catch the Troll engaging me off guard, but as soon as I beheaded him, I backed out of the fight and took off running. Hamundson had a large lead on me, but I bet on my Elven speed.

He was most of the way across the clearing when a golden-winged Nephilim appeared from above and shot lightning at him. It appeared to sparkle and splash on his shield, and he stumbled. Catching his balance, he kept going.

Off to my left, out of the corner of my eye, I saw a jaguar racing after the running man, but I knew she was too far behind. I tried to push harder, adding a burst of speed, but I was already running as fast as I could.

Another Nephilim, this one with white hair, dove toward the man and unleashed more lightning, but again it was foiled by his shield.

As I ran, I drew energy from the forest around me, sketched a rune, and spoke the Word to trigger the spell. I held a ball of life energy in my hand but didn't know if I would get close enough to use it.

Hamundson reached the rift and slowed, turning to look behind him. I hurled the energy ball without breaking stride. It hit him, exploding on his shield, and knocked him backward. He fell through the rift.

I covered the last dozen strides and leaped low through the rift, too, my sword held in front of me. Landing on the other side, I rolled, praying I wouldn't hear the sound of machineguns.

Everything was unnaturally quiet. I rolled to my feet and looked around. A giant silvery presence dominated the area in front of the rift. Hamundson stood frozen in front of the demon.

Seeming to shake himself out of his shock, Hamundson sent a bolt of black plasma toward the snake demon. It splashed on her shield and she laughed. Leaning forward, she curled her hand around Hamundson and lifted him off the ground. I saw blood spray from where her claws penetrated his body.

She swung her head in my direction. "We meet again, little Elf. You are a rather surprising creature."

And then she was gone. Normal sounds resumed, and a voice shouted, "Stop right there!"

I held my hands above my head. "Don't shoot! I'm an American!" Even as I said it, I thought it was a stupid thing to say, but I didn't get shot.

A motion to my right caught my attention, and I saw a jaguar leap through the rift.

"Don't shoot!" I screamed. Too late. One soldier fired a three-shot burst. Isabella seemed to fade and become insubstantial, then solidified again. The bullets hit the ground behind her. She landed on the street and swerved toward me. Too relieved for words, I knelt and enveloped her in a hug when she reached me.

"Don't shoot!" I heard another voice call. Looking up, I saw Torbert running toward us.

Suddenly I was holding a short, squat, Mayan woman instead of a large spotted cat.

"I thought Elves didn't do public hugging," Isabella said with a grin.

I let go of her and stood up. "We don't hug people. Kitties are different. Cass?"

"He's fine. Faida took a Troll arrow in the shoulder, and he's with her."

"Karen?" Torbert asked as he came to a stop in front of us.

"She's fine," Isabella said. "You know, gunpowder doesn't explode on Jotun. Good thing you gave her that pig sticker and the paintball gun."

Another person joined us, and I turned to see Luce standing there, his card-shark glamour firmly in place.

"Say cheese," he said, holding up a cell phone and taking our picture. "Good. Need that to collect the rest of my money." He bowed to me. "It's been a pleasure, Sel Kellana. Let me know if you need my services again."

With that, he turned and walked off in the direction of Ivy City.

"Who was that guy?" Torbert asked.

I chuckled. "Believe me, you don't want to know."

Curled up on the couch watching the news with Cassiel, I couldn't quite identify what Bess was cooking in the kitchen, but the smell was making my stomach grumble.

The craziness was ongoing. A Troll and a demon got into a fight at an elementary school in Pennsylvania, but no children were harmed. A debate had started in Sweden over whether an Angel could be prosecuted for fraud. I was all for it, since he was accused of stealing an old lady's life savings.

An advertisement caught my attention. *Witches' World grand re-opening sale! The best in witchcraft supplies and other-realm goods marked down as much as fifty percent!*

"Shawna Greene told me the fire would bankrupt them," I said.

"Evidently they assumed a lease for the store the Bluegrass Coven planned to open," Cass said. "Any word on Meagan Humphrey?"

"No, and I think Karen would have told me if they found her. Some of the Savage River pack told the PCU that she'd gone to Canada."

The next commercial caused me to laugh out loud. *Make your next ski vacation an out-of-this-world experience. Book now for skiing in Vanaheim. This limited availability offer is filling fast. For a skiing experience you will never forget, call 202-555-0909 now.* The voice-over was accompanied by a video of handsome Aesir men and women skiing down snow-covered slopes with even-taller peaks in the background.

"Other-realm tourism," I said. "I had a feeling that would be coming. Have you ever skied?"

"Nope."

"Me neither, but it looks like it would be fun."

"I heard that the Elves bought a ski resort in Colorado."

I wrinkled my nose at him. "Nah, Elves are too snooty and arrogant. I'll bet their customer service sucks. Maybe we could try it in Switzerland next winter."

"I thought Elves were never rude," Cass said.

"Oh, they'd be polite, while doing their damnedest to let you know you really were a lower form of life." I laughed. "Hell, some of them give me a hard time because I have green hair. And if anyone sneered at you because you're a halfling, I'd have to kill them, and I'd prefer to avoid that mess."

Bess called us for dinner, and as I reached for the remote to turn off the TV, I heard, "The Vampire Rights League plans a rally outside the United Nations building in New York tomorrow..."

I turned it off. Dinner smelled divine.

###

268

If you enjoyed **_Witches' Brew_**, I hope you will take a few moments to leave a brief review on the site where you purchased your copy. It helps to share your experience with other readers. Potential readers depend on comments from people like you to help guide their purchasing decisions. Thank you for your time!

Get updates on new book releases, promotions, contests and giveaways! Sign up for my newsletter.

Books by BR Kingsolver

The Dark Streets Series
Gods and Demons
Dragon's Egg
Witches' Brew

The Chameleon Assassin Series
Chameleon Assassin
Chameleon Uncovered
Chameleon's Challenge
Chameleon's Death Dance

The Telepathic Clans Saga
The Succubus Gift
Succubus Unleashed
Broken Dolls
Succubus Rising
Succubus Ascendant

Other books
I'll Sing for my Dinner
Trust

Short Stories in Anthologies
Here, Kitty Kitty
Bellator

BRKingsolver.com
Facebook
Twitter